Trace of a Ghost

Cherie Claire

For more information and to sign up for Cherie Claire's newsletter, visit http://www.cherieclaire.net.

ISBN: 0998197456
ISBN-13: 978-0998197456

DEDICATION

For Mom, who calls me her angel, but in reality, she's mine.

CHAPTER ONE

"Our feet are planted in the real world, but we dance with angels and ghosts."
—John Cameron Mitchell

We're late and we're hauling down the long hallway of the New Orleans Convention Center through the throngs of dark suits and briefcases, thanks to the national intellectual property law convention being in town.

"Wow, I think I see a pink shirt on that woman," I say to my traveling buddies. "She'll be black-balled by noon."

Carmine ignores my humor; he's not in a good mood. TB doesn't get it, stares off into the crowd searching out said infraction with a frown, a clueless state which unfortunately happens way too often with my ex-husband who's not really my ex.

"Wait." I pause and point. "Is that person wearing Mardi Gras beads? Call the cops."

Neither man stops walking at break-neck speed or looks around so I rush to catch up.

"Are you two still alive? And can we please slow down?"

I'm goofy today and I admit it. It's my first SCANC convention and I'm excited as hell. So far, I'm the only one.

Carmine doesn't diminish his sprint nor look my way. "You're the one who wanted to make the keynote address."

"True," I manage to utter through my accelerated heart rate. I'm starting to have trouble speaking through the exercise, these boys are going that fast. Okay, yes, I'm out of shape, but I'm a travel writer and currently working as a restaurant reviewer for SouthInYourMouth.com so I have an excuse.

"You must admit that attending a lecture titled 'Living the SCANCy Life' is pretty intriguing," I add.

Carmine and I are SCANCs, a stupid abbreviation for mediums who see specific types of hauntings due to trauma. It stands for Specific Communication with Apparitions, Non-Entities and the Comatose and I received my ghostly talent after Hurricane Katrina sent me to the roof of my home and my government left me there for two days. Ever since Aug. 29, 2005, I've seen ghosts who have died by water.

SCANCs are not new to speaking with the Other World. Usually, our types are psychic at birth but we repressed the talent due to society's acceptance of such gifts (note sarcasm). Trauma opens the door in a big way and our gift suddenly re-emerges, but we see ghosts only within a specific sense. For me, it's water. Mostly drownings but I've once helped a girl cross over who choked on Kool-Aid.

I'm new at this ghost hunting business, been at it for three years now, so even though Carmine calls this organization a group of mystic nerds who have nothing better to do than dream up ridiculous acronyms and get drunk — the convention theme this year is "Which Boos is Yous?" — I'm anxious to meet my fellow SCANCs.

We finally reach the far corner of the Convention Center, somewhere near the Texas border, and three men in *Ghostbusters* attire are seated at a table by the door. Carmine slams on the brakes and I plow into his back.

"Viola Valentine, Thibault Boudreaux," Carmine tells one of the men and I take the moment to resurrect my nose from the impact and peer around. Sure enough, these guys are really into their costumes, looking as if they walked off the movie set. The resemblance is uncanny and I wonder about the bucks that went into acquiring these outfits.

"Tie-bolt," the man announces, slurping something crimson out of a long tube that's attached to his backpack.

"TB," my ex-husband replies with an over-enthusiastic smile and I cringe.

I get it, I really do. Thibault, pronounced Tee-bow, isn't exactly a name you embrace, no matter that it followed generations of Cajuns going back as far as France. It's why his dad, Thibault Senior, was known as Bubba, and yes, that's how we get around difficult names in the South. The problem began when TB was born as Thibault Junior and everyone called him "Little Bubba," which in Cajun French turns into "Petite Bubba," shortened to "T-Bubba." My ex-husband thought to shorten it further because he thought it'd be funny.

It's not. And most often, as in the case of this Bill Murray wannabe, no one gets it.

"Viola Valentine?" I ask, stepping forward, hoping to move this conversation along.

"Ah yes," says a man closer in looks to Dan Aykroyd, sans the convenient tube sporting alcohol from the backpack. Instead, he cradles a plastic highball glass that announces, "Give the devil his due" on the side with little red horns tapped to the rim of the glass. He smiles when he notices me examining the creamy white drink with smoke rising from the top.

"My recipe," he says with pride. "Vodka, simple syrup, cream soda, and a secret ingredient. There are several competitors this year and this one's the winner."

"You get to vote on your favorite cocktail," Bill Murray adds, "but I recommend my 'Let's Get Sheet-faced.'" He nods to the tube resting on his shoulder.

Carmine huffs and whispers to me, "Told you so."

"How do you get the smoke to do that?" TB asks the first Ghostbuster.

"My special expertise, not to be known to the general public." Dan Aykroyd grins slyly and if he had a mustache I'd imagine he would twist the ends and say, "Broohawhaw."

Carmine rolls his eyes and it's then the three Ghostbusters look his way.

"This convention is for SCANCs only," backpack drinker says with equal smugness. "Do we need to explain what that is."

Carmine raises one eyebrow and I know what's coming so I hastily say, "He's with me, but he should be registered.

Carmine Kelsey."

There's a shift in the countenance of these three, as if the president suddenly walked into the room. They don't even look at the list of names, grab a packet and hand it to Carmine.

Carmine crosses his arms. "I don't need your stinkin' packet," he mimics in a bad Mexican accent like the characters from that movie I've never seen, and heads toward the door, TB and I hot on his heels.

"Was that humor I heard?" I ask.

Carmine pauses at the threshold and takes in the room full of costumed attendees, everything from Disney's *Hocus Pocus* and *Casper* to a man dressed as Bruce Willis from *The Sixth Sense* and a Jack Nicholson look-a-like carrying an ax and repeating "Here's Johnny!" to everyone who stops for a picture. Vendors line the circumference of the room hawking T-shirts and paranormal technology with open bars in between. I count at least seven portable bars with giant glass bowls next to the alcohol, no doubt for people to place votes, and all of them serving up a different cocktail. There's food in the center of the room, which makes my stomach growl, but no one's eating; they're all lined up for cocktails.

"Lushes," Carmine says with disgust.

TB and I, being New Orleans natives, look around the convention site and utter "Cool" simultaneously.

Carmine does that one eyebrow thing again. "I'm not holding back your hair when you vomit."

When a petite woman dressed as Demi Moore walks by carrying a piece of pottery — filled with a cocktail no less — and says "Ditto," Carmine loses it. He nods to a couple of normal-looking men at the food table, and waltzes off. Two feet away he halts and turns, looking straight at TB. "Keep an eye on her," he barks and disappears.

TB says nothing, watching Carmine walk off to greet his friends. After a few moments of waiting for my ex-husband to explain, I ask, "What the hell was that all about?"

Usually, my sweet but rather simple-minded man will turn

with a blank stare, utter "Huh?" and I'll have to explain myself but today TB ignores me while gazing around the room.

"I wonder where that smoke drink is."

I know I said I'm from New Orleans and we have no issues with drinking at any hour of the day but it's eleven a.m. and I'm not ready for "boos." I open my packet and realize that a SCANC convention only draws enough people to fill one small room of the Convention Center and two anterooms. I look to my right and find the latter immediately.

"I'm going to the keynote address."

TB looks disappointed since I'm almost positive he's spotted the smoky cocktail table while gazing at his own packet.

"You go get your drink and meet me there."

TB gazes at Carmine but our grumpy host is deep in conversation with those two men by the food table. I'm seriously stumped by what Carmine instructed TB but I don't feel like missing the first speech and I definitely don't need looking after.

"See you there," I say and hurry off. I don't even look around to see if my ex-husband has headed off for the devil drink. I know better.

The far anteroom boasts the keynote address with a giant sign but I pause at the first room I pass. For one, the topic has caught my eye — "Evolving your God-given SCANC talent." For another, the man at the door with eyes like the Caribbean Sea at sunset and a smile that promises heaven in a bedroom touches my arm and I swear I feel lightning bugs fluttering inside my chest. That is, if I knew what lightning bugs feel like. Did I mention I'm a journalist and we despise expressions not based on fact? I cringe thinking about the abuse I'm inflicting on the English language, even if it's only inside my head, and the man frowns.

"Something wrong?"

I straighten and smile at those gorgeous eyes, words now coming out like a twelve-year-old talking to her first beau.

"Not at all." Tee-hee. "I was just thinking about something." Tee-hee. "Conversations inside my head." Snort. Sheesh, did I just laugh like that?

Blue eyes offers his hand. "Dwayne Garrett."

I accept and shake, never taking my gaze off his intense stare, imagining myself lost in those blue depths.

Dwayne, on the other hand, reacts as if bugs have crawled up his skin.

"Wow."

I pull my hand back as if I did something wrong. "What is it?"

For a second, a shadow moves across his vision but Dwayne shakes it away and that charming smile returns. "Quite a handshake."

That bumbling child has thankfully left the building and hard-news Viola has returned. Learning the truth of something is more important than a good-looking man.

At least most of the time.

"It's just a hand attached to a body."

Okay, so maybe my teen years are still with me.

Dwayne leans in so close I can smell his delicious aftershave. I'm sure it's meant to disarm women with its intoxicating aroma and it's working on me. I feel a tingly sensation in places I shouldn't, especially since TB and I have gotten back together — sort of — since our separation following Hurricane Katrina.

"There's a lot of power behind that handshake," he whispers, "Unused power, I might add."

Forget lightning bugs. Goosebumps run up and down my arms and I swallow hard, wondering if it's the words he's spoken or that manly persona invading my space.

Dwayne moves back and the air turns cold. He hands me a flyer announcing the talk about to begin in the room behind us.

"Come hear my presentation. You're the perfect candidate."

"I'm heading to the keynote...." When I look down and

am reminded of the topic I realize this was no coincidence, as my Aunt Mimi would say.

"You're the presenter."

Dwayne hands a flyer to a person walking past, then grabs the door and pulls the door jamb up with his toe. "Yes, and we're starting now."

I'm hesitant because I don't want to miss the keynote address of my first SCANC convention. On the other hand, I want to learn how to evolve my ghost-seeing talent. There's a certain person on the Other Side that I'm desperate to reach, and she isn't related to water. I must admit, watching Blue Eyes speak for forty-five minutes wouldn't be a struggle either.

"Follow me," Dwayne orders and I do, the door closing behind me as I remember that I told TB where to find me — and it's not here. Oh well, I think, he'll figure it out, although I doubt that he will. Did I mention my husband can be a bit clueless?

I move to sit in the back row since the room is full of people but Dwayne grabs my shirtsleeve and pulls me to the front with him. Every seat is taken near the dais but Dwayne nods at one of the front row seaters and the young teen gets the message and nervously hurries away.

"I don't want to take someone's seat," I begin, but Dwayne lightly pushes me there and heads to the microphone, grabbing it and energetically welcoming the crowd who respond with loud applause. I sit down and gather my packet and purse in my lap, looking around to see what happened to the teen. He's standing at the side of the room, sending me a not-too-nice gaze, holding a finger to his ear as if he's listening to one of those cell phone earpieces.

"Sorry" I mouth.

"Never say sorry."

I look up to see Dwayne staring at me and my heart stills. Before I can ponder this too much, he continues speaking and I realize it's part of his spiel.

"We have a glorious gift, one we need to harness, not

hide," he continues. "Our evolving talents have been given to us by God or the universe or however you see the miracle of life and we must make the world a better place by utilizing those gifts. It's our duty."

The crowd responds with clapping and I look around to spot numerous happy faces, many of which are nodding their heads and a few offering verbal agreements. It's almost like attending a charismatic church service.

"And like everything in life, we limit ourselves, how we act, how we think, and how we expect life to be."

The woman next to me yells out, "Amen."

"We are the ones who can connect with the Other World. We are the ones who can bring those to their life's fulfillment, bathe them in the glorious light of God, and help them ascend to the love that awaits them in heaven."

More "Amens" rise from the crowd and one stands and loudly proclaims, "Yes, Jesus!"

I'm not opposed to religion, really I'm not, even though I was raised by two college professors who felt religion was a salve for the uneducated. I've attended Catholic services with TB's parents and friends and got a solid dose of the spirit from my Baptist Aunt Mimi in Alabama. But I consider myself a student of the spiritual universe and find too much of one side to a story rattles my journalistic brain. This gathering feels like a rural tent revival, reminding me of the time Aunt Mimi's church friends overstepped their boundaries when they heard I saw a ghost and prayed over me relentlessly. I was but a child at the time and it freaked me out. I'm a bit freaked right now, so I start looking for a way out.

I pull my packet and purse to my chest and look around, but there's no easy exit since I'm in the middle of the front row and Blue Eyes stands directly in front of me. In fact, he's staring at me again, no doubt thinking I'm about to flee.

"I met this young lady only a few moments ago," he says and everyone arounds me turns to stare as well.

When I glance back at Dwayne, his hand is over his heart

and he says, "I think I know what troubles you."

My first inclination is to turn cynic; it's my natural defense. I want to shout "Doubtful" but something about his gaze tells me he's genuine. He truly cares. Either that or I'm the most gullible person in the room.

"You've lost someone," Dwayne says, jumping off the dais and standing directly in front of me. "Someone very close, who left the world way too soon."

We've all experienced loss, especially for someone my age who just hit the thirty threshold, so for people faking mediumship this is the easiest route to gain someone's confidence. I say nothing, try to keep emotions at bay although the buzz that usually arrives before a ghost appears comes ringing in my ears. It's not the usual quiet hum, like bees circling a hive, but a sound more akin to an alarm. I still want to flee but how would that appear on my first hour at the SCANC convention?

Dwayne pauses and, because he's standing, I must tilt my head back to gaze into those cerulean eyes.

"She's right here," he says, tapping his hand over his heart.

I can't help myself. I laugh. It's what everyone's told me since Lillye died several years ago, leaving me heartbroken, scarred, and a shell of a human being. I know grief is a process, an emotion everyone deals with differently in their own time, and the pain of loss never fully disappears. I'm now a SCANC and watery ghosts appear to me everywhere I travel — and I travel quite a bit through the Deep South in my job as a travel writer. I didn't ask for this specific talent, and truth be told I could live without it, no problem at all. But the question remains, why was I bestowed a "gift" to see ghosts and not be able to reach my precious daughter?

Dwayne doesn't appear taken back by my reaction. Instead, his eyes reflect an understanding. He leans closer. "You can reach your 'precious daughter.' You just have to learn how."

Goosebumps race up my arms and my breath stills in my chest. I feel like a *thousand* lightning bugs are fighting underneath my skin. Dwayne senses my panic and lightly touches my upper arm and it's like an electric bolt descends from the roof, striking me at the top of my head and shocking my senses all the way to my toes. I gasp and the breath returns in a rush. My head feels light and I'm almost certain I'm seeing stars at the corner of my vision.

"Praise Jesus," says the lady to my right.

I turn in her direction because I'm desperate to know what's really going on here and I spot the teenager leaning against the wall, shaking his head. Thankfully Dwayne moves toward the center of the aisle and his gaze scans the crowds. As I'm searching for a discreet way to flee, Dwayne begins explaining how SCANCs can develop their specific gifts to see all who have departed.

I'm halfway off the seat when this comment stops me cold. I've heard rumors about SCANCs who have "evolved," although Carmine routinely labels them crazy and the process nonsense. When I viewed ghosts last summer at a lake in central Louisiana, ghosts who did *not* die by water, I was convinced my talent had developed and Lillye was in reach. I was mistaken — the incident had been the result of something supernatural, but that's another story — and even though I should have since made peace with the fact that I'll never see Lillye again, I can't give up the ghost, pun intended.

I need to reach my daughter, who left me so young. If I could just speak to her one last time.

"It's possible," Dwayne shouts out and turns my way, those blue eyes settling a gaze on me that reaches deep into my soul. "We can reach those who have left us but who are not in our," and he uses his fingers to denote parenthesis, "'specific communication.'"

Once again, I feel the man has listened in on my thoughts and the goosebumps go crazy.

"Isn't he amazing?" the woman to my right asks.

I honestly don't know what to think about this man, but I settle into my seat and listen while Dwayne explains his theories, mainly that the more we use our talents to allow ghosts stuck on this earthly plane to "Climb the ladder," or reach heaven or wherever it is the departed go into the white light of love, the more we will evolve. In other words, the more people I help ascend, the stronger the chance I will see Lillye on the Other Side.

Time flies by while Dwayne talks and most of us are enraptured by what he's saying. A man opens the back door and the light of the main room floods in, jolting us all.

"Time," the guy at the door announces.

Dwayne thanks everyone for coming, the room bursts into applause, and several people move to the dais. Within seconds, Dwayne is surrounded by people asking questions, shoving books into his hands for autographs — apparently, the guy wrote one — and a couple of women fawning. Dwayne ignores the attention and instead searches the crowd until he spots me. He offers a smile that sends sparkles down to my toes and I can't help but smile back. He mimics using a phone and typing on a keyboard as that grumpy teenager arrives at my side and hands me his card.

I accept the card and am about to ask Grumpy Teen questions when Carmine arrives and grabs my upper arm. Hard.

"What are you doing in here?"

"Nice to see you, too, Carmine." I pull my arm free. "And that hurt, by the way."

Carmine looks over at Dwayne and frowns. Dwayne sends back a stern gaze, then returns all smiles to his beloved fans.

This is weird.

"What's going on?" I ask.

Just then TB arrives, drink in hand. "Where have you been? You said you were going to the keynote address."

"You need to tell us where you are," Carmine says, but his gaze never leaves the dais.

"This is ridiculous," I say, accepting Dwayne's card from the teenager who's backing away from this mess. "It's not like I'm lost in the mall, moms."

I slip the card into my pocket and head for the door, my

body guards following behind. I can hear TB asking Carmine what's going on, what's wrong with her being here, that kind of thing, but Carmine says nothing. When we hit the lobby and the costumed SCANCs imbibing heaven knows what, I suddenly am ready to go. I've had enough of this SCANCness and I learned what I came here to find out.

"Let's go," I say.

"Great," Carmine answers and we all head for the Convention Center lobby.

"But you're not off the hook," I tell Carmine. "I want an explanation for that rude display."

I instinctively move to walk the long hallway back to the parking lot but TB stops me. "I'll go get the car. You all stay here."

"I can walk…," I return, but TB's already off in a trot.

Something's wrong here. I can feel it as sure as a ghost arriving. I give Carmine a look and he motions for us to sit down on the bench beside the door.

"It's a long story."

"It's a long hallway back to the car so spill."

After a few moments of silence, he exhales, loudly. "Dwayne Garrett's not to be trusted."

I wait for more information but none comes. "That's it?"

"I have my reasons."

I shake my head. "That's not good enough, Carmine."

He takes my hand and squeezes. Carmine's been my good friend, travel writing colleague, and SCANC mentor since this business of me seeing ghosts began. I love him dearly, treasure our friendship, and absorb his advice faithfully. So, if there's a reason he thinks I should avoid the charismatic, devil-eyed Dwayne Garrett, I'm apt to listen, but not without something to back it up.

"I don't want you to get your hopes up," he finally says, and something about this doesn't ring true, as if it's only half of the issue.

"I know you think I can't evolve enough to see others who have not died by water," I begin. "I know you think that because I'm desperate to see my child I will believe anything, and that's probably true. But all Dwayne was advocating was helping others to climb the ladder."

Carmine looks at me sternly. "He didn't ask to meet up with you or have you contact him in any way."

I think of the card in my pocket and wonder what that contact entails. Is Carmine worried that after first separating from my husband, — believing we had nothing in common — then tentatively resuming that relationship, that I might still be on the prowl for another man? Carmine loves TB, even though intellectually the two are miles apart. He once likened TB to a puppy, insinuating that puppies are loyal and protective offering unconditional love, which is TB to a — well, a T.

"Vi, get your intellectual stimulation elsewhere," he once told me. "Keep those who love you close at hand."

"Why are you so protective today? Why the big brother attitude?"

Carmine looks out the window at two lawyers waltzing by wearing those ridiculous Mardi Gras beads, carrying cocktails, and laughing. Still in those horrible all-black outfits, mind you.

"Why does everyone feel the need to get drunk in this town?" he asks instead.

"Because New Orleans is the 'City That Care Forgot,' unlike all those other uptight cities in America. You're avoiding the question."

Carmine keeps staring at the drunk lawyers, a scowl on his face, and I wonder if he's reliving how he became a SCANC all those years ago. Carmine was one year shy of graduating high school, one year away from escaping the torment of boys threatened by his feminine traits, even though Carmine isn't what I'd call openly gay. (In other words, he could pass if he wanted to and tried to do so in high school.) A group of boys from the wrestling team got drunk one night and discovered him walking home alone from the library. They beat him close to death and it took months of physical therapy for him to recover back to normal. He said it was a blessing, really, for he was home-schooled until graduation. Like me and my specific talent, Carmine sees apparitions who bat for the other team.

I must admit, I'm envious because gay ghosts remaining on this plane are few and far between so his life doesn't require the effort to constantly shut off ghouls begging for attention or the mysteries I feel compelled to solve when they present themselves. Carmine also encounters artists and writers, many of whom are famous and whom I'd love to meet.

I'm still curious about Dwayne and I'm about to ask for more information when TB drives up in my Toyota. We climb in, Carmine in back and me in front. I'm ready to begin my hundred questions when TB suggests picking up poboys at Parkway Tavern and heading back to the house, and Carmine eagerly accepts. A silence descends, as if both men are done with this conversation, so I keep quiet and stare out the window at the tourists enjoying the Warehouse District full of art galleries and overpriced restaurants.

We grab the poboys and drive up to the house TB and I shared for several years, five of those with Lillye. I hate coming here. One, for the memories of both watching our child sick with leukemia and two, for that horrid morning in 2005 when Katrina flood waters poured through and we axed our way to the attic.

Carmine and TB waltz through the door but I pause at the threshold and the memories slam into me so hard it knocks my breath away. TB notices, bless his heart, and he guides me to the renovated kitchen and dining area, both totally different from when we lived here.

"Do you like it?" he asks.

It's gorgeous, really: new tile, backsplash, granite countertops, and stainless steel appliances. I sound like those shows on HGTV, but I still remember those tiny feet running through the old kitchen while I cooked Lillye's favorite, seafood gumbo. I wonder where my gumbo pot is now. No doubt the flood waters ruined everything within the cabinets that are now long gone.

We sit and eat the poboys in silence. I still want to interrogate my two buds about their reactions at the conference, but the memories of Lillye have silenced my tongue. I stare at my delicious shrimp poboy — dressed, as we say in New Orleans, which means lettuce, tomatoes and, for me, extra pickles — but my appetite has disappeared as well.

Just then I feel a silky movement at my legs. I look down to find Stinky, the orange stray cat I feed in Lafayette who's become my pet. He's at TB's this week while I attend a press trip with Carmine in Mississippi.

"Hey, Pal." I reach down and scratch behind his ears, then between the shoulder blade, and finally the butt. His eyes glaze over in appreciation.

"He'll be fine while you're gone," TB says. "He loves it here."

Traitor, I think as I give him a look. The cat gives me one back.

Did I mention Stinky might be psychic?

They say owning a pet lowers your blood pressure and makes you a happier person. Just giving Stinky a massage has changed my outlook. I turn back to my favorite men and enjoy the poboy.

After lunch, we grab our bags and TB drives us to the airport for the flight to Florence, Alabama, the beginning of our trip down the Natchez Trace. The press trip is being sponsored by a Mississippi public relations firm — we're expected to write about the Mississippi portion of the Trace — but the Florence airport is closest to the trail's northern-most point of the Magnolia State. We're to spend the night in Florence, check out a few musical hot spots in Muscle Shoals, then head west and join the Trace near Tupelo. After that, it's several days exploring one of the oldest highways in America, ending at the historic city of Natchez.

I've been looking forward to this trip for months,

especially since Carmine and my old friend Winnie Calder will be joining me. Having like-minded friends on a press trip cranks it up a notch, and Winnie's from Mississippi so no doubt she'll offer lots of insider information.

We pull up to the curb and TB retrieves our luggage from the trunk. He pulls me into a tight embrace as if we're back to square one before the separation, but I'm not feeling it today. I don't know if it's the morning's event at the SCANC convention, the memories haunting me at the house or that I'm not completely sure we should be together. I hug him back but he senses my hesitation and frowns.

"Thanks for everything," I say, which sounds hollow, like a friend thanking another for a ride to the airport. To make up for the insensitivity, I rise on my toes and give him a kiss. It, too, comes off as platonic, however, and I know TB's disappointed.

Thankfully, Carmine holds out a hand. "See you in a week."

TB ignores the hand and gives Carmine a big hug, which surprises but delights my stalwart friend. They end up patting each other on the back like men do, then release. As Carmine and I head to the ticket counter, Carmine turns and yells to TB, "Good luck with the test."

"What test?" I ask as we head through the doors, but Carmine says nothing.

We get separated during security — Carmine is TSA pre-checked and I'm not — but I meet up with him at the gate. I want to again inquire why Carmine was so weird at the convention, what he has against Dwayne, and what test TB is taking but he remains sullen, checking his email by way of his laptop. I dig through my carryon to find my book, hoping a good romance novel will save me, but I'm ticked he's ignoring me again.

"She's important," a voice rings out.

My old friend the opera singer stands in the middle of the aisle while tourists rush past. She's soaking wet, as usual.

"Who's important?" I ask her, which causes Carmine to

look up.

"Who is what?"

Carmine knows that one of the first ghosts I spotted after Katrina was the woman hanging out in the Louis Armstrong Airport, singing *You Are My Sunshine* at the top of her lungs. The airport was used to house people after Katrina, plus served as a morgue for those who perished in the flood waters, so it's a wonder there aren't more of these watery ghosts here. Even though I've offered, the opera singer does not want to move on, prefers to linger on the earthly plane. Instead, she gives me advice when I travel through.

My initial thought when I met her was to convince her otherwise, one more person climbing the ladder. If that theory holds, as Dwayne attests, the action gets me closer to evolving and seeing Lillye. But, the opera singer shakes her head, as if she's reading my thoughts.

"Be careful," she says. "Not all is what it seems."

She starts to fade but I want to know more. "What is?"

"Ask Carmine," she utters before disappearing.

"He's ignoring me," I want to shout but she's gone. Carmine shuts his laptop and I know he's going to ask who I'm talking to, but I suddenly feel frustrated by the events of the day. What they don't tell you about seeing ghosts is that truths come at you in fragments, riddles, and images that hardly make sense. It's like a game they play. Today, all I've received are tidbits of information and the one person who made sense, a man offering to assist with my SCANCy abilities, is supposedly off limits.

I hear the gate agent call our zone so I bypass the steamy sex novel and rise. Carmine and I are not sitting together and his zone follows mine, but he grabs my hand.

"What's happening?"

"You tell me," I reply.

When Carmine remains silent, I shake my head and board the plane.

CHAPTER TWO

It's a quick flight to Florence, Alabama, and I'm barely to the juicy parts of my novel when the pilot announces our arrival. In all honesty, I was lucky to get past chapter three with my mind wandering so. I'm not one to focus anyway, but the events of the day have my thoughts in a buzz.

I exit the plane via a set of stairs and a cool breeze greets me. I pause and soak it in, so grateful for a taste of fall after a long hot and humid summer in South Louisiana. On the edge of the runway I spot trees turning autumnal colors and almost let out a squeal.

"You going?" the guy behind me says.

"Sorry." I speed up but turn and smile. "Just enjoying this touch of fall."

The man says nothing and moves past — obviously not from the swamps where fall arrives at Christmas when the bald cypress turn burnt orange — but I take my time. There's a skip in my step contemplating wearing sweaters for the next few days. I feel a tug at my side and find Carmine pulling my carry-on from my hand.

"We need to talk," he says.

I'm about to agree and insist on carrying my own bag since now he was two, but he struts ahead and suddenly we're hauling down the airport toward baggage claim.

"We do need to talk," I yell to his back. "First item on the agenda is where's the fire."

For the first time today, Carmine slows down, turns, and smiles. We're back on friendly terms and my heart lightens.

"Sorry," he says. "I'm a fast walker."

I catch up to his side. "I thought I was, too. You leave me in shame."

"Years of running to catch planes, I guess."

Carmine's been a travel writer for more than twenty years;

I started the winter after Katrina so two years now. It's what I've always wanted to do following journalism school but I never could get Southern Living or those other magazines with travel sections to hire me. I ended up covering cops and school board meetings in St. Bernard Parish for the New Orleans Post, the smaller city newspaper to the notable Times-Picayune, the latter of which won a Pulitzer for its Katrina coverage while we ceased publication.

I despised hard news reporting, wrote travel articles on the side, but when Katrina washed away my job — literally — it was time to follow my dream. I moved into a mother-in-law apartment in Lafayette, two hours west of New Orleans where we evacuated, and started over. I had lost everything in the storm and severed ties with the rest, TB included, so life was a clean slate. I hit the ground running and loved every minute of my new career — even the ghosts I found along the way. The recent recession grounded me for several months, time I spent reviewing hotels and solving ghost mysteries back home. I'm back in the saddle now and that makes me smile even more, although I must stop using all these metaphors and clichés!

This press trip is one of my favorites, a slower stroll down one of America's most historic highways. Usually, public relations companies or tourism boards invite us to visit a destination and fill our days with activities from early morning to late at night. It's fun stuff, mostly, and all of it comped, but it's still work. We meet and interview notables, visit attractions, take lots of photos, perform social media, and type up notes before bed. On the outside — mostly what my friends imagine I'm doing — I'm having a blast in a cool destination, living the life of luxury. The reality is I'm having a blast but it's still work.

When I received the invite to this trip, however, it was remarked on three separate occasions that we would enjoy the Natchez Trace *slowly*, as travelers had in years past. There would be time for hiking, picnics with scholars on ancient Native American mounds, and relaxing historic accommodations. After the summer I had, this was just what I needed. Having an autumnal nip in the air is *lagniappe*, as we say in Louisiana, a little something extra.

Shelby Constantine of the Zelda Walker Agency waves to us as we enter the baggage claim area. She's impeccably dressed like most PR professionals and carrying a sign that spells out our names. She recognizes Carmine instantly. Everyone knows Carmine.

"Hey, Babe," Carmine says as he plants a kiss on Shelby's cheek.

"Hey, yourself." Shelby holds out her hand and I shake it. "You must be Viola."

Behind her line of sight, Carmine cringes at her pronunciation. It's Vie-o-la, not Vee-o-la, like the instrument. I smile. I'm used to it.

"Y'all wait here and I'll bring the van around. But here are y'all's packets." Shelby hands us our press kits. "And wait until you see what's in store for you."

Shelby hurries off in her high heels that I would never wear on a press trip, considering the amount of walking we do, but then I'm not the most girly girl on the planet. I never leave home without my Converse, if that tells you anything. I glance down at the packet with a re-enactor on the cover, a man who looks like he stumbled out of bed in 1840s Kentucky, but the pause allows me to focus back on Carmine.

"You want to talk now?"

"We're staying at a Marriott tonight?" Carmine's busy looking at the itinerary.

"It's just for tonight. The Natchez Trace starts when we enter Mississippi."

Carmine shuts the folder and sighs. "I realize that but even if we're in Alabama, I was hoping for something more historic."

"You're avoiding the subject."

"What subject?"

I sigh and he grins, slips the folder into the outside pocket of his carry-on. "Okay, I was a bit annoyed this morning."

"A bit?"

Carmine gives me that sly smile with a tilt of his head. "Maybe slightly more than a bit?"

I hug the press kit to my chest. "What the hell was going on?"

"Who were you talking to at the airport?"

Now, it's my turn to smile slyly. "A woman who said you had all the answers. And you're still avoiding the question."

Carmine turns solemn and begins picking lint off his jacket. "The SCANC convention is a complicated thing."

"I thought it was just an excuse to party."

The grin emerges but he's still staring at imaginary jacket dirt. "That too."

A pause ensues, what my Aunt Mimi would call an angel passing over. Heavenly host or not, I'm getting frustrated as hell.

"Carmine!"

Finally, he sighs and looks up at me. "There are people there I don't trust."

"Obviously. You nearly killed Dwayne Garrett earlier with your stare."

The air between us sparkles, like electricity before a lightning strike. It reminds me of when Dwayne shook my hand and remarked that I had power behind my handshake. But he was smiling. Carmine's gazing at me like I'm the devil incarnate, clouds seemingly floating in those big brown eyes. It's a side I've never seen of Carmine before, a dark foreboding nature that's giving me the creeps big time. I back up, still gripping the press kit tightly against my chest.

Carmine takes a deep breath and his countenance shifts. He smiles and we're back to being buds, but I can't forget the darkness that emerged just now, or the feeling that he's keeping something from me, something scary.

"I'm sorry, Vi." He touches my arm and it's like nothing happened. "There's certain people in the world that rub me wrong."

I act like nothing's happened but that uneasiness remains. Something's way off here.

"How about a drink later?" Carmine offers. "There's a great bar at the top of the hotel, has a beautiful view of the river. Or we could go to the one off the lobby. That's actually my favorite."

"Have you been here before?"

Carmine laughs and starts relaying all the times he's visited Florence and Muscle Shoals, a couple of times for music pieces on the legends of rock 'n' roll who recorded hit after hit in this small Alabama town, another on the birthplace of two legends, W.C. Handy, who arguably fathered the blues, and Helen Keller, water pump included. The clouds have lifted and we're back to old times, me laughing at his stories and Carmine relating them in his typical dramatic fashion.

Before I know it, he takes my press kit and places it on my bag, then pulls me into a bear hug.

"I'm sorry, Vi."

All disagreements long forgotten, I hug him back.

He pulls away and looks at me like the big brother he imagines himself to be; he's twelve years older and the touch of gray at his temples gives that away. "Drinks later. I promise I'll explain."

I rise on my toes and kiss him on the cheek. "You better."

We hear a horn and see Shelby waving from the front of a blue rental van. We head out, and while I open the side door Carmine grabs my suitcase and heads to the rear. I jump into the van and land on the far seat, waiting for Carmine to take the one closest to the van's sliding door, when I realize there's someone in the front passenger seat. As soon as I rearrange my oversized purse with a host of travel gear, not to mention the press kit, and make myself comfortable in the seat, I look up to see who my traveling companion might be.

My breath stills and my chin drops against my better judgement. Shelby jumps into the front and pulls her seatbelt on, rattling on about getting us checked into our rooms in time for dinner, then Carmine does the same, pulling the side door closed. In a heartbeat, we're off. I'm still too stunned to utter a sound.

Carmine notices right away. "What is it?"

It's then that Dwayne Garrett leans around his seat and gives Carmine one of his dazzling, blue-eyed smiles. "Hey buddy. Small world."

Shelby begins telling us about the trip ahead, how we'll spend the day in Florence and Muscle Shoals, then make our way to the Mississippi border where we'll learn about the old road at the Natchez Trace Parkway Visitors Center in Tupelo. Dwayne pipes in enthusiastically, gushing about how excited he is to finally be visiting a bucket list item. He asks Shelby about the firm, where she's from (a little town outside Athens, Georgia), and if she's married, has kids, that sort of thing. Shelby responds like any woman in his presence, smiling like a schoolgirl and giggling like I did at the convention.

I glance over at Carmine and give him a questioning look, one that says, "Did you know he would be on this trip?" But the darkness has once again invaded Carmine's soul and he turns away, staring out the window as we drive across the Tennessee River into Florence.

Dwayne glances back at me, gives me a wink, but I feel like a child torn between divorced parents, not sure who to please. I take the opportunity to look out my own window into the peaceful waters below, and in that moment of aloofness, I swear I hear a woman singing.

We pull up to the Marriott, an imposing hotel on the banks of the river with a tower off to one side.

"Here we are," Shelby says and that sugary sweet Southern accent wakes me after festering in the darkness of the back seat with Carmine. The woman's singing has stopped, too, which makes me wonder if the radio had been on all this time.

I exit the left side of the van and head to the back to retrieve my luggage. When I come around, Carmine and Dwayne are deep in conversation, and it's anything but friendly. When they notice me, however, they act like nothing's wrong, Carmine heading into the hotel.

"We're old friends," Dwayne tells me with that million-dollar smile.

"Sure sounds like it." I'm journalism cynical, the kind who considers sarcasm a vital part of the English language.

Dwayne leans forward and there's this delicious whiff of after-shave that makes me weak in the knees. What is it about this man?

"Carmine and I have some history but we'll work it out. How about a drink later and I'll explain."

How about the two of you own up to whatever tiff you have going on here and leave the drinking for happier times, I want to say, but I smile. "Perhaps."

"They have a great bar off the lobby," Dwayne says as we walk into the hotel.

I can't help but laugh. "So, I've heard."

Before I can take in the magnificent ceiling that stretches up two floors or the enormous aquarium at the center of the lobby, one full of interesting fish, I hear a shriek and find my old travel writing friend Winnie Calder sitting in what is most likely the famous bar. She's holding a drink in her hand but that doesn't stop her from rushing over and hugging me tightly, drink held high with nary a drop spilled.

"It's about time you two bums got here."

I hug her back, so happy to see my crazy friend. Winnie owns a farm outside Oxford — Mississippi, not England — full of goats and weird plants she sells at the farmer's market. Travel writing is one of her many jobs; she helps her husband run the city planetarium, fills in for friends at their businesses, and has two boys and a girl. How she does it all is a mystery, but I do love hearing about it.

Winnie is also one of two — Carmine being the other — friends who know of my SCANCy abilities.

"Carmine," Winnie yells when she lets me go, but Carmine's busy being angry with Dwayne at the front desk.

Shelby looks at the two men and approaches us nervously.

One thing PR professionals fear on a press trip is discord among the journalists. That and rain.

"Are they okay?" she asks.

Winnie, too, looks over concerned, but before I'm able to calm everyone's nerves, Carmine grabs his room key and heads off to the elevators. Dwayne delivers a brilliant smile and Shelby's fears are relieved instantly.

"Sorry about that, Shelby." He touches her arm and she giggles. Honestly, she giggles like a schoolgirl. "Carmine and I have some history but we'll work it out, no worries."

Now's my chance to find out what this motivational speaking SCANC is doing on our press trip. "Dwayne, this is Winnie Calder. She'll be on our trip."

Dwayne grabs her free hand and delivers a kiss upon her knuckles. Blue eyes and charm notwithstanding, I want to groan at this ridiculous display. Maybe that's what pisses Carmine off so much. He hates fake people.

Winnie, thank goodness, does too. She gives him a mom look she probably bestows on her children when they claim they really did their homework and the teacher's lying. Dwayne realizes instantly he's getting nowhere with his charm but he continues to smile seductively, shrugging in the process.

Forgetting my manners but now hoping to get more information, I add, "Winnie, this is Dwayne Garrett. He's from…."

Dwayne sends me a gaze that sends shivers up my back.

"You cold?" Shelby asks.

This gives me a chance to escape.

"Yes, my sweater's in my bag." I turn to Winnie who's studying Dwayne intently. "Want to come up to the room with me?"

Winnie nods but she's still giving Dwayne the mother examination; nothing gets past this woman. Shelby hands me my room key and we make our goodbyes. Before we reach the elevator, I turn and Dwayne's studying me. The shivers start again. As soon as the elevator doors close, Winnie turns, hands on her hips.

"What the hell was that about?"

I decide to act cool since I want to know Winnie's first impression. "What do you mean?"

"There's something weird about that guy."

I let out the breath I didn't know I'd been holding. "Yeah, we need to talk."

Once we get inside my room, which has a lovely view of the Tennessee River, Winnie falls on to the bed and once again fails to spill her drink. The woman is next to goddess status, Mississippi accent and mannerisms included.

"And what the hell is going on with Carmine? He didn't even say hello, the brat."

I relay everything that had gone on that day, from the SCANC convention to his aloofness at the airport to Dwayne showing up.

"Who the hell is this guy?"

"I don't know." I pull out my laptop. "Let's find out."

We do a Google search but nothing comes up but a couple of recent articles he wrote for *Traveling Times* magazine, which is pretty impressive since their circulation reaches half a million. I check Facebook, LinkedIn and search through Yahoo as well. Nothing.

"Weird."

"Yeah." I close my laptop. "Maybe we take Carmine down to that favorite bar of his and make him spill."

"I'll hold his nose and you inflict the bourbon."

"Seriously, Winnie, I need to know."

Winnie downs her drink, including sucking the ice cube. "I know, Sweet Pea, just having some fun."

I sit down and sigh, realizing I'm tightly wound and need my own supply of Jack Daniel's.

Winnie looks at her watch and rises. "It's time for dinner. Get your sweater on and let's go."

I pull out my sweater, which unfortunately doesn't match my outfit. I give Winnie a questioning look. She shrugs and says, "Who cares?"

I do. I look in the mirror at my plaid blue shirt and jeans now covered by my LSU purple sweater. "Two minutes to change the shirt?" I plead to Winnie.

She grabs my sleeve and hauls us toward the door. "We're late as it is and I'm so hungry I could eat the north end of a south-bound goat."

I told you she was from Mississippi.

By the time we hit the elevator, Shelby is there on her cell phone. "I was just about to call y'all."

"Sorry," Winnie offers. "We had a hard time digging that LSU nonsense out of her bag."

I'm about to defend my alma mater but for once I wish I had Ole Miss colors. Red would match this outfit so much better. Still, I can't let Winnie have the last word. I lean close to her ear and utter, "Piss on Ole Miss."

She bristles but there's a smile there too. She changes the subject as she turns to Shelby. "So, who is this Dwayne Garrett."

Shelby is busy refreshing her lipstick, so she replies when we leave the elevator and start down a long hallway to the tower.

"He's freelance. Lives in Dallas. At least that's where his flight originated from."

Winnie gives me a look. That's where Carmine lives — or some tony suburb nearby.

"I think he's new to the business, only seen a couple of his articles."

Another look from Winnie. Explains the lack of Internet presence.

"But he's quite good."

I don't know if it's the way she says it but this time Winnie and I give each other a sly smile. We're not thinking about travel writing and it's everything we can do to stifle a laugh.

We hit what appears to be the tower and take another elevator up to the 360 Grille restaurant, sharing small talk and SEC banter along the way. Winnie, as usual, makes wise cracks but only I'm laughing. Guess only blue-eyed, charming men can make Shelby giggle.

The restaurant at the top of this tower is circular and apparently rotates so when we make our way to the table, our view is of the parking lot and the entrance to the hotel.

"No worries. You'll have a gorgeous view of the Tennessee River in good time."

I turn to find Mona Tillerson, director of the area Convention and Visitor's Bureau extending her hand — it's on her lanyard — and I accept it. She has a firm handshake and a nice smile, so I like her right away. She turns to introduce herself to Winnie, but Miss Ole Miss is busy checking out the seating arrangement. I look at the table and get her meaning instantly. How do we seat near Dwayne to find out more about the guy without ticking off Carmine?

Winnie sends me a look as if to say she's figured it out. She grabs a seat across from Dwayne and I ask Mona if I could sit near her and find out more about this enchanting region. It works out great because I'm now between Mona and Carmine, the latter of which I whisper to, "We have to talk. After dinner. Lobby bar."

Carmine says nothing, but he sends a worry glance toward Winnie, who's laughing at something Dwayne said. Winnie looks briefly back at us and winks, and Carmine's shoulders drop an inch while he lets out a breath.

"We're not that easily deceived," I tell him.

Carmine downs his glass of wine in one gulp and utters something. I can't make it out but it sounds something like, "He's the devil," and shivers run up my spine. Yes, again. I tend to absorb weird energy coming off people.

"There's a real nip in the air," Mona tells me as she sits down. "Isn't it lovely?"

I smile and nod. "Lovely indeed."

The rest of the evening revolves around Mona explaining how in 1959 Rick Hall created a recording studio with a white backup band called The Swampers and brought in artists, black and white, to produce some of the greatest rock hits the world has ever known. It was called the "Muscle Shoals

Sound" and when The Swampers began their own studio at 3614 Jackson Highway, more hits followed. We're talking Rolling Stones, Aretha Franklin, Bob Seger, Etta James and the Osmonds cutting hit albums here, not to mention Lynyrd Skynyrd, who included mentioning The Swampers on their hit song, *Sweet Home Alabama*. We're going to visit these places tomorrow, Mona promises, plus a special spot on the way out of town.

After viewing the Tennessee River twice and enjoying a wonderful meal, it's time to call it a night. Tours begin early in the morning, Mona tells us, with a trip across the river for an "Alabama-style breakfast."

"Fried elephant," I tease, but no one gets it so I add, "You know, Roll Tide?"

Guess it's not funny for Mona starts talking about W.C. Handy's birthplace as we head to the elevators. The pause gives me time to say hello to the rest of the gang who were busy talking to other CVB people at the other end of the table. There's my favorite couple, Stephanie and Joe Pennington, two hard-working newsletter publishers from Wisconsin, and a young girl named Pepper Snipe (not making this up) who just graduated Knoxville and is working as an intern for *America's Highways* magazine, a trade publication for motorcycle enthusiasts. She's dressed all in black with multiple piercings beneath a head of dirty blond dreadlocks.

"She's a first," Winnie whispers to me.

Kelly Talbot, editor of *Southern Gardens* and not one of my favorite people because she's drop dead gorgeous and a snob, is on the trip as well. We didn't leave on good terms on a press trip to Eureka Springs but that's another story. I'm not in the least bit surprised to find that she and Dwayne are now ogling each other. This could be good. I'll make amends with the woman and pick her brain for no doubt those two aren't going to the lobby bar now.

The rest of us are, however. The CVB people bid goodnight and head off to their cars while Shelby arranges a tab at The Swampers Bar so we can enjoy free drinks. The only people drinking, however, are the Penningtons, Carmine, — who should go to bed considering how much wine he's had with dinner — Winnie, and me and, because our trio is not alone, we small talk with Stephanie and Joe until Winnie loses patience and blurts out, "What do y'all know about that Dwayne guy?"

Carmine bristles, I hide my smile inside my bourbon, and the Penningtons shake their heads.

"No idea," Stephanie says. "I've been in the business a while and I've never heard of him."

"He's a sweet talker," Joe adds. "He was reeling in that gardens editor after hello."

Now, it's my turn to bristle. Miss Georgia (Kelly hails from outside Atlanta) nailed a cop I knew from New Orleans. I was married when the guy and I worked together in New Orleans but he was so hot it made me want to slap my mamma, as we say in Louisiana. He was my sexual fantasy and I ran into him at the Eureka Springs press trip and Miss No Hair Outta Place reeled him in. Not like I was going to sleep with the man but it chaffed my butt. Plus, she's a stuck-up prima donna.

"Dwayne's from Dallas," Carmine says solemnly and we all glance his way. "But I don't know where he lives anymore."

"Dallas." This gives me pause. "Shelby said he had flown in today from Dallas."

Carmine and I share a knowing glance. The man was in New Orleans this morning.

Winnie senses something between us. "What?"

Carmine and I say nothing.

Joe rises. "It's a big day tomorrow. Think I'm going to head up."

"Me too," Stephanie says and follows and we wait until they are in the lobby elevators before we begin.

"What?" Winnie says as soon as the elevator doors close.

"He was in New Orleans today," I explain. "At the SCANC convention."

"He's a SCANC?"

Carmine shakes his head but when he doesn't say anything, I place my bourbon on the table and lean close so he must look me in the eye. "What the hell is going on?"

"He's evil," Carmine whispers and those shivers return.

"I kinda got that," I answer, pulling my sweater about my chest, "but I could use more information."

Carmine downs his drink and tries to stand but he's unstable on his feet. "I'm going to bed."

Winnie and I both grab an arm and keep him in his chair.

"Not until you tell us what's going on," Winnie says.

Carmine looks at each of us and realizes he's trapped. He leans back in his chair and run fingers through his salt and pepper hair. "You won't believe me."

I laugh because Carmine's the one who first explained to me why I was seeing dripping wet ghosts everywhere.

"Try us," Winnie says.

Carmine leans forward and we huddle close. "Have an open mind."

"We're journalists," I say with a smile. "Don't we always?"

But Carmine's not in the mood for jesting. He drains whatever drops of bourbon are left in his drink, then takes a deep breath.

"What do y'all know about angels?"

This takes us back.

"I was waiting to hear that handsome Dwayne Garrett is a vampire," Winnie says, then looks at me and winks. "Or worse, an LSU graduate."

I send her a scowl but Carmine doesn't break a smile. He leans in closer and I can tell he's drunk.

"Fallen angels."

I've heard this story. Aunt Mimi married a Southern Baptist and they lived on a small farm in Alabama. I loved visiting but they made me attend their community church that preached a gospel a bit too scary for the child that I was. Damnation, hell and all that. My mom is a holiday Catholic so outside of Jesus suffering on the cross in front of us during

Mass, I didn't feel as intimidated. Now that I think about it, those depictions of Jesus were pretty frightening.

Did I tell you I'm ADHD? I shake my head to focus on what Carmine's saying. Only he's not saying anything.

"Angels are the messengers of God, is all I know," I say. "That and they look over us, or so religions tell us."

"Not all of them," Carmine says. "Lucifer, for instance, didn't share God's love with humankind and refused to love them as God did. He was kicked out of heaven for it. So were others that agreed with him."

"And sent to hell," Winnie adds.

Carmine smiles sadly. "If that's what you believe. Personally, I see heaven and hell as being right here on earth, in the choices we make."

"Lucifer," I add, remembering my Sunday School days, "only wanted to love God and not humans. I always thought that was strange that he became the devil in religion. More like a jealous lover."

"So, what does this have to do with Blue Eyes?" Winnie asks, smiling. "Are you saying he's Lucifer?"

Carmine rubs his hands across his face and looks at us both intently. "Remember, keep an open mind."

We don't say anything, wait for the big reveal. And even though Carmine's swaying with the effect of the alcohol, he's as serious as…well, you know who.

"If those stories are true," he begins with a strange smile, "our lovely colleague is of the latter. Or more like a descendant from the days when angels and humans copulated and produced offspring." He smiles weirdly again. "If you believe that stuff."

I'm dumbfounded, not sure how to respond. Winnie, on the other hand, is all curiosity.

"How do you know this?" she asks.

"Long story," Carmine says sadly. "One for another night because I think I need to go to bed."

Carmine rises and it's then we realize just how drunk he is. We help him to his room, unlock the door (it took him several minutes to find the key) and Winnie, bless her heart, undresses him to his underwear and leads him to bed.

"Will you be alright for tomorrow?" I ask.

He waves me off. "Call me about twenty minutes before."

I'm doubtful he's going to make it but then he's a press trip veteran and a cocktail aficionado; he writes for one of those suave male magazines. Winnie tucks Carmine in and we're about to head out when Carmine grabs my hand.

"He's the one who led the attack on me in high school. He's the one who made me a SCANC."

Before I can absorb this shocking piece of news, Winnie grabs my sleeve and pulls me toward the door.

"Get some sleep, Carmine."

I'm contemplating how this blue-eyed devil beat one of my best friends within inches of his life as we enter the hallway. Just before the door shuts behind us, I hear Carmine warn, "Stay away from him."

CHAPTER THREE

I'm from the Deep South and I've traveled extensively on its back roads so I can say with good certainty that nothing much shocks my sensibilities. The chocolate gravy — yes, chocolate — poured over my biscuit is a new one, however.

We're at the River Road Café in the rural area outside of Muscle Shoals, the morning sun rising over the fields across the street and slapping me right in the eyes. I'm almost envious of Carmine and his sunglasses. Almost. Because I know what pain lingers behind them.

"Are you actually going to eat that?" Stephanie asks me while Joe moves every which way to photograph the dang thing in this blinding morning light.

"Might as well," as I watch Joe in action. "I doubt we'll get a good picture out of this."

Joe, bless his heart, agreed to take some photos for me, since I've forgotten my camera back home. I pack my single lens Canon inside a thick camera bag and place that inside my suitcase but for some reason I arrived and it's not there. It's the one thing I always remember, too.

Joe looks at the gloppy mess in front of me. He shakes his head. "There's no way to make that look good in a photo."

Not one of us has the nerve to dig in.

"Oh, come on, y'all," Mona says at the head of the table. "Try it."

I fork a piece of my biscuit, dripping in chocolate gravy, and take a bite. To my surprise, it's pretty good. I look around and notice everyone's watching me do this so I give them a thumbs-up.

"See," Mona proudly says. "Told you it was good."

Winnie sends me a questioning look and I shrug.

We finish off breakfast and head to the van, ready for our magical musical tour. We start at FAME Studios, where almost fifty years ago Rick Hall started recording artists such as Wilson Pickett, the Osmonds and Dame Aretha. We're met by a local music historian who not only drops names like a Mardi Gras float rider spitting beads but tells us inside stories, too. Like the time Pickett arrived in Muscle Shoals during segregation and was greeted by Hall, who's white, at the airport, envisioning Hall the sheriff come to haul him off to jail. Or the time pre-pubescent Donny Osmond rode around town on his bicycle and Muscle Shoals girls chased after him.

The best story, though, is of the African American musicians meeting The Swampers back-up band for the first time, never imaging that these local boys were white. The fact that all these hits were made with an integrated sound in the 1960s makes it even better. That and Hall getting into a fight with Aretha's husband or telling Duane Allman he couldn't sing, to let his brother take the mic. Yeah, we heard those, too.

Pepper, who's dressed completely in black with several piercings on one ear and a drop of obsidian hanging from her neck, looks bored.

"Do you know these people?" I ask because she's likely under twenty-five.

She shrugs. "I've heard of Wilson Pickett. The Hypstrz did a cover of *The Midnight Hour.*"

We then head over to where The Swampers, originally known as the Muscle Shoals Rhythm Section, later formed their own studio at 3614 Jackson Highway, the exterior made famous on a Cher album. Two of The Swampers — Jimmy Johnson and David Hood — greet us at the door and show us around the studio that's in the process of being renovated. On the walls are signatures of the legends of rock 'n' roll, musicians such as Paul Simon, Bob Seger, Rod Stewart, and Joe Cocker. If these walls could talk, I think.

Johnson and Hood sit and take questions and we go to town. The studio produced about fifty albums a year, Hood says while he pulls out a massive list detailing all the hit records. The Stones wrote and recorded *Wild Horses* here, we're told, although Johnson said they weren't fans of the band until they played with them. R.B. Greaves recorded *Take a Letter, Maria* in one take. The stories fly at us fast and furious. Who knew this little northwestern town in Alabama had such a long, illustrious musical history.

"What is it about Muscle Shoals that inspired all this?" Joe asks.

Hood and Johnson laugh. "Might be the singing river," Hood says.

My head jolts up. "Excuse me."

"It's a local legend," Mona pipes in. "The Native Americans believed a woman lived in the Tennessee River and sang to them."

The idea that the river sang to *me* on my arrival floats through my mind, no pun intended, and I might deem the whole thing crazy if I hadn't met a mythological creature earlier this year in a small Louisiana town. As I'm contemplating this news, I find Dwayne studying me intently. Once again, I shiver, and the involuntary reaction my body keeps making is getting on my last nerve.

We do a drive-by of W.C. Handy's house and a couple of new studios in town because we're running out of time. For lunch, we stop at City Hardware, a sweet café in downtown Florence, none of us hungry but all of us eating. They feed you heartedly on these press trips but no matter how full we journalists may be, we never say no to a free meal.

After indulging in a cast iron skillet brownie, we embark on our trip to the Natchez Trace and say goodbye to Alabama and its vast musical past. I pause outside the van and take in Florence's cute downtown but mostly I look toward the river, hoping to hear that sweet woman's song that greeted me last night.

"Listening for something?"

I nearly jump at Dwayne's sexy voice to my rear.

"Didn't mean to scare you," he says.

I shrug. "Just taking in the town."

For some reason, I suspect he doesn't believe me. He gives me a curious stare, then that old charm emerges. "Sit next to me. We can discuss how to evolve your abilities."

Carmine has insisted time and again that SCANCs will only see the departed of their specialty. The key word here is ghosts. Whereas my Aunt Mimi never repressed her medium talents — thanks to a mother who encouraged her gifts as opposed to mine who told me I was crazy — she can speak to anyone on the Other Side willing to communicate. I, on the other hand, only see those who have died by water who are remaining on this plane.

Which means my precious angel, who died so young of leukemia, is off limits. I'm desperate to reach my beloved Lillye, and Carmine's insistence or not, I will do anything to fulfill that dream.

I decide to sit in the row in front of Dwayne. It gives me enough distance but I'll remain close enough to hear what he has to say. Carmine and Winnie are two rows ahead and I feel Winnie turning to watch me but I don't acknowledge her. Besides, I convince myself, my journalistic instincts are urging me to find out for myself.

Dwayne leans over the back of my seat. "Finally, I get you all to myself."

His breath is hot on my ear and it awakens parts of my body that shouldn't be aroused. My defenses warn me to be careful and I look over and see Southern Belle giving me the evil eye. I can't help myself; I return a coy smile.

"Tell me your theory," I say.

"It's not a theory. It works."

The idea of seeing and talking to Lillye beats out sex, so I shift in my seat. I'm all ears.

"The more you practice your craft," Dwayne tells me in a soft voice so no one can hear, "the more advanced you become."

He sends a glance toward Carmine. "I don't care what other people say. You don't have to spend your life only seeing apparitions of your specialty."

Hope fills my chest but his words remind me of something Carmine said the night before — or didn't say. "What's *your* specialty?"

Dwayne looks away and for a moment I suspect he's hiding something. "Everything," he finally says, that confident smile returning. "I've evolved."

I turn further in my seat so we're facing each other. "How?"

He leans across the back of my seat and I get a delicious whiff of that after-shave again. My head starts feeling light. He looks around to make sure no one is listening.

"The more you send people to the Other Side, the stronger you will become."

"Like how many?"

"How many have you accomplished so far?"

I make a mental count inside my head. "About six, I think."

"Try ten, or twelve. You'll feel a difference."

Too many to accomplish on this trip, I can't help but think. If he's blowing wind up my skirt, I won't know for sure until we've said our goodbyes.

"You don't believe me."

In truth, I was hoping for some grand secret that would change my life instantly. "I've been told time and again that SCANCs can't evolve. And I've known people who have had dozens of crossovers."

Dwayne sends a glance toward Carmine again and it's not a friendly one. "Maybe you're talking to the wrong people."

Once again, I feel like that child of divorce parents. I want to be loyal to Carmine but if I could talk to Lillye….

"What are you thinking?" Dwayne asks. "You know what I say makes sense, right?" I was actually reminded of something my sister Portia recently said. About my father coming back into our lives. My parents divorced a few years ago and it wasn't pleasant, then my father split at the worst time of my life. I told you I was ADHD.

"Tell me more," I instruct Dwayne and make myself

comfortable while he does the same.

"It's fairly simple. There's a light that appears when our work is done, when those trapped here become released."

I nod. I've seen *Ghost* and my experiences haven't been that different from Patrick Swayze's.

"It's a beautiful thing, being one with the light of God."

We're back to skirting religion and I shift in my seat, wondering if more of that charismatic talk is coming. Dwayne appears lost in thought, and I wonder if this idea of communing with heaven might have him soon conversing in tongues.

He looks back at me and his countenance shifts, as if he suddenly remembered he had an audience. He clears his throat. "Anyway, when that happens, you need to tap into that energy."

The ghosts I have helped climb the ladder didn't waste time moving on. "How do you do that?"

That devilish grin re-emerges. "Next time you get close, let me know. I'll show you."

This is a first, someone helping me cross over a wet ghost. Something about it feels impersonal, like he's invading a space between me and my client, but I nod anyway. If I get to that point on this trip, I'll think about it.

"We're here," Shelby announces and we look out the window to find rows of cotton growing alongside the rural road with a house off to the side. We saunter off the bus, approached by an excited Mona who's been following us in her car.

"Y'all are in for such a treat," she gushes.

We follow Mona and Shelby in their high heels down the gravel road and across a rural highway, the two women stumbling as they go.

"Someone needs to tell these PR people that it's okay to dress like the rest of us," I tell Winnie.

When she doesn't respond, I look up from digging through my purse for my notebook. "What?"

"Why were you talking to that man?"

I glance over at Dwayne who's now at Miss Georgia's side, no doubt saying something like, "Of course, last night meant something. I only sat next to that New Orleans girl with the crazy hair because I felt sorry for her."

"I was picking his brain." Not really a lie.

Winnie leans to whisper in my ear. "Carmine said to stay away from him."

"Yeah, he's a fallen angel. Did you remember how drunk Carmine was last night?"

Winnie straightens and doesn't say a word, so it's my turn to whisper in her ear. "There's bad blood between those two. Doesn't mean I can't talk to him."

We're almost across the street, following the PR heels up a small driveway. The house beyond is hidden by thick woods and a stone wall lines the property along the street in both directions. An elderly man with soft white hair and a gentle demeanor greets us at the entrance.

"This is Tom Hendrix," Mona says. "He's going to explain his unique and beautiful home."

I'm in the rear of the crowd — still trying to find that dang notebook — but as I approach I see Tom has arranged a group of chairs for us to sit on. On the side of the driveway he has items placed on a piece of the wall: a book, a binder, and a straw basket that looks native made. As I pass, I get a better look at this section of wall and find it's full of gorgeous stones, all of which call out to me.

I have this thing with rocks.

Tom begins talking so I quickly take a seat but my eyes are locked on a brilliant piece of quartz. Smooth and round, it's perched high on a larger stone like resting on an altar. The fall sunlight hits it from behind and it glows. Around this quartz rests fossils, green aventurine that my Aunt Mimi calls the heart chakra stone, chert, amethyst, and black tourmaline, the latter a protection stone Mimi always carries with her.

I told you I love rocks. I reach into my pocket and wrap my fingers around a piece of Angelite, enjoying the smoothness of the stone and feeling a calmness rise inside me. I purchased this lovely blue rock on my first press trip, when I saw a young girl clear as day hurt and bruised inside a cave. And yes, she was dead. Long dead. The cave owner gave me this stone, one associated with the spirit world, hence the name.

Angels, I think. As I turn to look for Carmine, I realize he's at my side, an arm stretched behind me on the back of my chair. He gives me a friendly smile and a warmness spreads through me. I need to listen to my friend, I think, but something about this place ignites a powerful yearning and that rises in my blood, too.

Tom relates how his grandmother told him tales as a boy. She had mentioned an ancestor, Mary Hipp, who was a Yuchi Indian, a woman who loved her home. She believed, like many others of the area, that the river sang to her.

Tom looks at me and smiles and I shiver. Carmine brings his arm to my shoulder and gives me a warm squeeze but I'm not cold. I'm thinking about that mythical lady in the water.

As it turned out, Hipp and her teenage sister were relocated to Oklahoma during the Trail of Tears, Tom explains. Both were given silver tags with numbers on them and Hipp's was fifty-nine.

"But the waters didn't sing in Oklahoma," Tom explains. "And Hipp dreamt of her mother calling her home."

Tom's ancestor left her sister, who had adjusted to Oklahoma life, and walked back to Alabama. It took her five years, hiding off the road to keep from getting caught. When she returned to Florence, she met a white farmer who married her and, had it not been for Tom's grandmother still owning that silver button that read fifty-nine, the story might have been lost.

Tom researched what he could, then visited the Yuchi tribe in Oklahoma who welcomed him in. He longed to pay tribute to this remarkable woman, so he built a stone wall on one side of his property in honor of Hipp's journey to Oklahoma and one stretching to the other side for her long walk home. A tribal elder advised him to lay one stone for every step she took.

Tom offers us his binder of photos and stories written of his feat, a wall now consisting of twenty-three million pounds of stones he laid down over thirty-something years. "Tom's Wall," as the locals call it, is the longest un-mortared wall and the largest memorial to a Native American woman in the United States. More than one hundred indigenous tribes and visitors worldwide have come to both admire his handiwork and leave gifts, including the stones I can't stop watching and that exquisite basket made from a tribe in Louisiana.

"We have a visitor from Louisiana," Shelby inserts, and looks my way.

Tom gives me a gentle smile and then encourages us to wander the multi-acre property and enjoy his wall. We're free to act like journalists but his only requirement is that we refrain from shooting photos in the prayer circle, a sacred space off to our right.

I can't wait to explore this wonderland but as I head off to the left where the woods are thicker, I let my hand brush those crystals beckoning me. There's a vibration pulsating from the earth and those stones and I let their hum calm my soul.

One might think Tom's Wall a fascinating undertaking but one that's quickly enjoyed. But the wall goes on forever, and I'm only walking the first phase of Mary Hipp's journey as I venture off to one side. Along the way are stone benches to rest upon and indentions in the wall where people have left items: a meteorite, shells from the Gulf Coast, a leather pouch with tokens, beaded necklaces, crystals and little notes I want to read but wouldn't dream of doing.

The other journalists are chatting away as they explore the wall but talking seems sacrilegious in this sacred space. Joe is busy taking photos while Stephanie gives direction, Winnie and Kelly talk gardening, and the PR women chat back at the entrance. I wonder where Dwayne has gone and turn to search for him but he's nowhere to be found.

"Amazing, isn't it?" Carmine sneaks up from behind.

I don't know what's come over me but I'm so glad to see my old friend, especially since he's talking, that I deliver a bear hug, resting my chin on his shoulder and sighing.

"What's this all about?" But he doesn't release me. I sense he needed the hug as much as I did.

It's then that I spot the photo on a deep indention in the wall. Two to be exact, both sporting images of the same woman dressed in a tight corseted outfit, full skirt with enhancements underneath. I'd say a hoop skirt but I've never been good with historic detail. The smaller photo curls at the edges and the photo is faded but the woman holds a child in her arms, smiling like only a new mother would smile. Her happiness pours off the page. The other resembles cardboard, those old photos people had professionally done with the photographer's name listed at the bottom. There's a man in this one, a dapper fellow seated with his hat resting on his lap, an arm about the object. The same woman stands at his rear, a hand on the back of his chair. I've seen these photos before, and usually the woman has a hand on the man's shoulder in reverence. Something about this woman's aloofness is significant, I think. That and the fact that she's not smiling. Her grief emanates through this picture as well.

"Why grief?"

Carmine pulls back and follows my line of sight. "What are you looking at?"

I step closer and now I'm sure this woman was miserable at the time of that photograph. The child isn't there so I'm assuming....

I close my eyes, blocking out the debilitating pain that arrives without warning. It's been years since Lillye's death but the knife cuts as sharp as the day she passed. I feel Carmine's arms about me and know I don't have to explain.

When the pain finally relinquishes the fist at my heart, I look up at Carmine. "He said I could evolve. After ten or twelve crossovers. Please tell me you at least have an open mind about that."

Carmine's eyes tell me differently. He smiles sadly and

shakes his head. "He's lying, Vi. You can't trust that man."

"I have to see her," I whisper because the tears are so close. "I need to talk to her."

He's about to place his hand over his heart but I don't want to be told she's always with me there. I want to touch my baby, smell her hair, hear her laugh. I pull away but Carmine grabs my hand.

"We have to talk. But not now. Not here."

I give him that and nod.

Carmine leans over and kisses me on the forehead. "And I'm always here for you. Always."

I smile. "I know."

Carmine nods toward the two photos on the wall. "I think she wants to go home with you." And with those final words, he heads off down the wall.

I move closer to get a better look at my sad woman in black. Her eyes entreat me, call to me. She reminds me of Mary Hipp, someone far from home who needs to return.

And that's when the humming begins. It always happens when a ghost is about to appear, murmuring like a creek gently rolling through the woods. I look around but no one's there. I'm only surrounded by nature's bounty, endless trees in all direction, and Tom's lovely stone wall.

I shouldn't do it, considering that someone left these photos as some sort of token gift; I would never consider such a thing otherwise. But this woman needs me. I can feel it. I take the two pictures and slip them in my sweater pocket. In return, because I feel it's appropriate, I place my Angelite in its place.

After more exploration, I head back to the entrance and those pretty crystals. They sit on top of the piece of wall outside the prayer circle, and even though that humming has returned when I hover my hand over the stones, the circle beckons me. The center stone bench lies empty, the ground around it covered in fall leaves. There's serenity about this place I don't think I'll ever find in church, maybe because my cathedral has always been the rocks and trees.

I glance around and no one's here, which is preferable since I'd rather do this in solitude. I sit on the bench and close my eyes, beg God or the universe or Mother Nature to let me have a glimpse of my child. To send me a sign. Let me know she's okay wherever she is.

I hear nothing but the breeze at the top of the woods, something soft and meditative. I squeeze my eyes shut and think again, but all I get is the sound of a far-away lawn mower.

I feel my heart rate rising and I squirm. I run a hand through my hair, even though I know movement works against prayer and meditation, something I have never been good at, whether because of my ADHD or my lack of faith, I'm not sure.

I take a deep breath and try to relax. I feel like crying. It's not going to happen, I think, feeling like my chest will break from the pain. A rebel tear slips free and I try to breathe, try to release the pain gripping my heart.

And that's when I feel them. Two hands. One on each shoulder.

I open my eyes and of course no one's there. But I know it's Grandma Willow and Mamaw, my parents' mothers, their touch telling me Lillye's with them and all is well. Suddenly, I do know through no effort of my mind that everyone lost to me does exist close to my heart, that those who have perished live in a blessed existence. At least those who are not bound to this earthly plane.

The wind ruffles my hair and I pull my sweater closer. My grandparents have gone. They were here for only a moment and this time the tears are ones of thankfulness. It wasn't what I was looking for, but somehow it's what I needed.

I slip my hand inside the sweater pocket and touch the photo that lies inside. I pull out the small photo, the one weather would have destroyed almost instantly, I say to myself to justify what I've done. The woman in black stares back at me with such happiness, a feeling that resonates to my soul. It's what I experienced years ago at Lillye's birth.

I run a finger over the lovely woman's face and that humming returns. In an instant, I'm standing in the parlor of someone's home.

"Cora," a woman dressed in a calico skirt and white blouse calls out, "please change your mind. I worry for you."

On the other side of the room a woman wearing a similar costume but with a riding shawl — my thoughts seem to reflect the language of the day, weird! — smiles at her friend and places a hat on her head. "Mary, I'll be fine."

"We're talking Mississippi."

Cora laughs and takes her friend's hand. "You make it sound like the ends of the earth."

"It is as far as I'm concerned. I wish you would stay in Kentucky."

Cora's smile fades. "I know, sweet Mary, but I'm weary of being a burden on you and your family."

Mary starts to retort but Cora squeezes her hand. "You'll be married soon. I can't stay forever."

"But Mississippi, Cora? You don't know a soul there. And you have to travel that horrid Natchez Trace."

Cora glances out of the front parlor window at the man waiting beside a horse and wagon filled with Cora's things and a tarp stretched above.

"I have Reynald. My uncle trusted him when he traveled to and from the South so I know he will see me there safe."

Mary also turns to look at Reynald, who's cleaning mud from his boots. Their gazes cause him to look up and there's nothing friendly about his demeanor. He tips his hat in their direction but it fails to relieve Mary's nervousness.

"You can stay here," Mary says. "I'll talk to Phillip. He'll understand, let you have the back bedroom, I'm sure."

Cora tightens her hat straps at her neck. "I inherited property, Mary. It'll give me independence I've never had, insurance for my old age." She leans forward and takes both of Mary's hands. "It's my chance at life."

Mary pulls Cora into an embrace and Cora grabs her hat to keep it from falling off and the awkwardness of it all makes them both laugh.

When they pull away, however, both have tears in their eyes.

"Write often," Mary pleads.

"Of course."

"Don't do anything rash."

"When do I ever?"

Apparently, quite a bit for they laugh once more.

Mary turns solemn. "Sell the place and come home if you need to."

I can tell by Cora's reaction that she hopes this scenario never happens. Whatever lies on the other end of the Natchez Trace is her chance at adventure and freedom. She nods, but her mind's too busy thinking of the happy possibilities.

Cora picks up her satchel and joins Reynald on the wagon seat. Mary stands at the door, a handkerchief to her mouth to hold back tears while Cora waves and smiles.

"Watch out for highwaymen," Mary says as Reynald rolls his eyes and kicks the horse into action.

"Write to me in Natchez," Cora calls out as the wagon turns the street corner and slowly moves out of view.

"Miss Valentine?"

At first I think it's Mary calling my name but that would be absurd. When my name is called again, I open my eyes to see Shelby peering into the prayer circle.

"I didn't want to disturb you."

I look around and see none of the other journalists. Surely, I can't be the only one left behind.

"Where is everyone?"

"On the bus. Waiting for you."

There's a slight tone in that last remark and it makes me feel guilty. How long have I been sitting here? I jump up and hurry toward the van, now parked right in front of Tom's driveway. Tom's there, too, seeing us off.

"Thank you for everything," I say to Tom, but it seems so insignificant for what I've experienced here, so I give him a big hug. We Southerners tend to do that so he's not surprised and hugs me back.

I smile at this kind man who built an homage to his

ancestor the size of several football fields and jump on the van. Within seconds, we're heading toward Mississippi to travel the Natchez Trace.

"Where'd you go?" Winnie asks as I sit in the aisle behind her. Carmine's off to the right working on his laptop.

I pull out my photos of Cora and gaze into her face, one so full of hope and another of despair. I wonder what happened once Cora left Kentucky and the warm embrace of her friend Mary. On the back of one photo is written, "Briarwood, Natchez," so I know she made it safely to Mississippi. And why am I seeing this woman's story through a photo? Did she die by water? Or am I evolving like Dwayne insists is possible?

Shelby begins explaining the history of the Natchez Trace and the sites we are about to see that day. We turn on to the historic highway and I gaze out the window and see the dramatic entrance announcing our arrival, a National Parks sign featuring a man on horseback. Whatever is happening through my SCANC abilities, one thing's for sure. Cora and I are taking the same trip.

CHAPTER FOUR

I study Cora's photo. I'm still amazed at the revelation. She's not an apparition in the traditional sense; she came to me in a vision. This happens occasionally when I'm haunted by folks. Sometimes ghosts appear in front of me speechless, and sometimes, such as the wet opera singer at the airport, they talk and impart messages. There are instances when I see their stories in dreams or visions. It's my preferable way of communicating, as you can imagine, since it's like watching a movie as opposed to having someone appear and scare the hairs off the back of your neck.

"Who's that?" Winnie asks when she turns to talk to me.

"Her name's Cora." I glance down into those sad eyes, so hopeful in my vision. "I think."

"You think?"

At this, Carmine turns and notices the photo. "She stole it from Tom's Wall."

I check to make sure no one's heard and grateful that Shelby did not. "You told me to, you devil." Just for fun, I add, "Oh wait, that label belongs to someone else."

Carmine gives me the evil eye. "He's not good enough for that title."

"Maybe he is." Winnie nods her head in Dwayne's direction and he's at the back of the van charming Miss Georgia again.

I can't help it. This smarts. In all truthfulness, I'm not going to cheat on TB for this guy, — or any guy for that matter — but this is the second time that perfect specimen of a woman has nailed a good-looking man in my presence, both of which I had elicit thoughts about so in a way I'm feeling jealous.

I touch my wild curls that love to explode when the humidity levels get high. Breakfast was early and I didn't have time to tame them so they are a little wilder than usual. "Do I look okay?" I ask Winnie.

She rolls her eyes. She doesn't suffer from self-deprecation. "Who's Cora?"

I show her the two photos.

"You stole these from that nice man?"

I lean in as much to whisper my answer as to signal for her to be quiet. "Carmine made me."

Carmine laughs and places a hand at his chest.

Winnie studies the two photos, then turns them over. "'Briarwood, Natchez.'"

"Must be the property she inherits," I explain, sharing what came to me in the prayer circle, basically Cora leaving Kentucky.

"Weird." Winnie hands them back. "Did you really take these from the wall?"

"That's what you came away with just now?" The woman never fails to amaze me.

Finally, Carmine comes to the rescue. "It asked to go home with her."

Winnie gives us both that mom stare. "Y'all and that woo-woo stuff."

Now, it's time for Carmine to roll his eyes. "Woo-Woo? I thought you understood."

"Yeah, yeah. Y'all are SCANCs."

"SCANC or no SCANC, I had a vision of her in the prayer circle." I look at Carmine. "Do ghosts haunt photos?"

"They can." He studies the photos. "I had a friend who used to buy old photographs in antique stores and try to find their owners. He's had a couple of weird experiences."

This perks Winnie up, mainly because she loves antique stores. As in *loves* antiques stores. "Like what?"

"Weird dreams, mainly."

This perks *me* up, because one, I was hoping to have a fun trip and not have this involve a research experiment. And two, on the flip side, if I solve this mystery, I might evolve like Dwayne promised.

"Does this mean *I'll* have weird dreams?"

Carmine shrugs. "Maybe. What happened in the vision? Exactly."

I explain to them both about Cora saying goodbye to a friend named Mary, how she joined some creepy looking guy on a buggy ride down the Natchez Trace, heading to Natchez. And something about an uncle.

"One thing's for sure," Winnie says, "she ends up at Briarwood, whatever that is."

Carmine opens his laptop and starts a search while Shelby announces that we're coming up to Buzzard Roost Spring. We're entering the Natchez Trace at this point, although still in Alabama, and within minutes come to the historic site. Carmine abandons the search and we all look out the van's window to a historical marker.

"That's it?" asks Joe.

Shelby laughs. "You have to use your imagination for this one. It used to be a place for visitors traveling along the Trace to rest. There's a spring nearby and this was where Chickasaw leader Levi Colbert ran a plantation and grist mill."

"A Chickasaw leader named Levi Colbert?" Sue asks.

"He was the son of an early Scottish settler and he married into the tribe," Shelby explains. "He helped the tribe fight off a Muskogee invasion and became one of their leaders. His brother, George Colbert, ran the ferry a few miles north of here. It's a quick drive between the two but on horseback, back in the day, more like two hours."

"A plantation? That sounds Anglo to me," Joe inserts.

Shelby shrugs. "All kinds of people owned slaves. Even Native Americans."

"Or Scottish Native Americans."

For the first time since we started this trip, Pepper pipes up. "Are there deer?"

Dwayne laughs and Pepper blushes, looking down at her lap. Shelby comes to her rescue. "There's all kinds of wildlife on the Trace. Keep your eyes open."

Pepper smiles tentatively and pulls one of her dreadlocks

behind an ear. It's then I notice she has at least four piercings and a pentagram tattoo on her neck that's been hidden so far by hair. When she notices me staring, she quickly pulls the hair down. I want to assure her I'm not judgmental but Shelby's calling for us to disembark.

We exit the van and walk down an incline next to woods and rock outcroppings, the path ending at a peaceful spring that chills the air around us. I pull my sweater close and that buzzing returns. I wonder if Cora stayed the night here as she traveled the four hundred and forty-four miles from Nashville to Natchez along the Trace. Depending on where she started in Kentucky, the trip must have taken weeks. I long to find a quiet spot and close my eyes, see if Cora comes through, but Shelby calls us back to the van. Next up is Bear Creek, where a Trace historian will meet us for lunch.

I haven't been on the Trace for long but I'm already loving the rolling hills, the thick woods, and the lack of traffic. The speed limit is only fifty miles per hour and we've passed several bicyclists and hikers before pulling over to the Bear Creek turnoff. Sure enough, there's a man waiting and John Henderson greets us all coming off the van.

"Welcome to Mississippi," he says in a soft southern accent.

"We're still in Alabama," Shelby whispers in his ear but the elderly man ignores her, instead beginning his speech about Bear Creek Mound, the oldest prehistoric spot on the Trace that's just up the road and one we'll visit after our box lunch by this creek. We settle on to picnic tables situated over soft grass and beneath trees swaying in the fall breeze, while Shelby calls out our choices for lunch, something we decided upon when we filled out applications for the press trip.

"Vegetarian?" Dwayne admonishes me as he walks past.

"Seriously?" Carmine asks when he sits down across from me.

"Why does everyone have a problem with vegetarianism?" I unwrap my sandwich of cucumbers, lettuce, tomatoes, and hummus.

"I'm not making fun of you," Carmine says. "Just surprised considering you're from the South and you write about food."

When you're a travel and food writer, you must eat just about everything — or at least try it. Ditto for being a Southerner; I had an uncle who loved to barbecue road kill. But if I didn't reign in things somewhere, I'd be as big as a house, so I take advantage wherever I can.

"Because I eat like a pig on these trips, I try to do something healthy every chance I get," I tell Carmine.

"So, you'll be enjoying the barbecue at dinner?"

I bite into a raw carrot and laugh. "Probably."

I'm so glad that Carmine and I are back to old terms that I fail to apprehend the buzzing when it first starts. While Mr. Henderson talks about the prehistoric history of the area the noise gets louder and louder. I'm starting to feel lightheaded and the food I've already eaten sits unsettled in my stomach.

"Excuse me," I say as quietly as possible and rise. I need something else to drink beside the water I picked up, something carbonated and awful like a Diet Coke. "Drink," I say to Shelby as I walk past, heading to the van and the cooler that's lying inside.

"Forget something?"

I'm surprised to find Dwayne lingering in the back of the van, appearing as if he's talking to someone on his cell phone. How he left the group and got here that fast baffles me.

I say nothing, grab my Diet Coke and am about to head out when he rises and reaches my side in two quick strides.

"Cell phone reception here sucks."

I smile because my cell phone is several years old, one of the first flip phones people thought were so cool. I bought it in my newspaper days, when we had money, but now I'm embarrassed to pull it out since I live on a freelance writer's income and can't afford anything else. Dwayne, of course, is sporting the latest smart phone, whatever that is.

"Are you as bored with this talk as I am?"

It's then I realize his arm stretches in front of me, blocking the exit from the van.

"Actually, I need to hear what he has to say. I just came for a drink."

Dwayne doesn't move, stares intently, those gorgeous blue eyes turning cold. I don't know what he's thinking but suddenly I'm very uncomfortable.

I nod to the door. "Do you mind?"

Dwayne reacts as if he's awaken from a trance and removes his arm. That charming smile returns. "Sorry, yeah. But sit next to me at dinner."

"Won't Miss Georgia be upset about that?" I can't help myself.

"Who?"

I give him a look Winnie gave only a few minutes before.

Dwayne laughs. "She's a big girl."

Not exactly what I expected to hear and the whole thing's still making me uneasy so I head out the door.

"I heard there's a good ghost story at Tishomingo," he says to my back. "Something involving water."

I pause on the bottom step. "At the state park where we're staying tonight?"

He passes me leaving the van, that heady aftershave teasing me as he does. "Yep. Sit with me at dinner."

Dwayne heads off towards the others, this time apparently getting cell phone service for I hear him talking loudly to someone, which disturbs Mr. Henderson and his discussion of a cave nearby. Shelby sends us both a frustrated look. I mouth "Sorry" even though I had nothing to do with it.

Everyone's attention returns to their lunch and the historian and that buzzing now is more than I can bear. I head over to the creek bank and sit down, slurping my Diet Coke in the hope that it quells my queasy stomach. Or at least makes me burp.

I close my eyes and take deep breaths, praying that this isn't some awful stomach bug. Nothing worse than puking your guts out on the road, especially on a press trip. I did that once on a back roads culinary tour through Alabama and the memory of the awful trip and the cracklings I revisited makes me want to vomit now. Maybe that's why I'm not a fan of meat.

Of course, we did visit Tuscaloosa and that awful school. Roll Tide will make any LSU grad want to puke.

I chuckle at the thought — I can always make myself laugh — but that buzzing won't leave me alone. I lean back into the grass and rub the back of my neck, hoping to relieve the pressure building in my head. I think about what Dwayne said back in the van, about the water ghost near the state park. How did he know there was a ghost there? How did he know I saw ghosts who have died by water?

I begin to contemplate whether the SCANC convention people share information about our individual talents when the noise stops. Suddenly. In its place I can hear the creek bubbling by but I'm not myself. I'm not in 2008. I look down to where my feet should be and see a dark skirt reaching my ankles, which are covered by heavy boots with buttons instead of laces.

Someone calls Cora's name and she stands, leaving me behind. Were we one and the same for that moment, I wonder, and how is that possible? I'm quickly rising to a sitting position and watching Cora walk up the hill to what looks like a log-hewn house with a chimney in its center, a long open porch off the back. Reynald is there, talking with a group of men and spitting tobacco off into the grass.

Cora appears to be happy, taking in the pristine woods, creek, and spring with a smile, a kick in her step. Still, she's a bit apprehensive about Reynald. I feel this more than view this and again wonder how I'm able to get inside her head. It's also in the way he looks at her, that creepy smile and something he's saying to the other men under his breath, which makes them all laugh as they take in Cora head to foot.

"Go to that woman," I say in my head to Cora, and sure enough, she moves toward the only woman in this crowd. The lady, dressed in rugged attire for a frontier outpost, wraps a shawl around Cora and leads her off to the side of the building and away from the men.

"Good call."

I turn and find a young African American boy watching me. Did he just talk to me?

I wake with a start and Bear Creek is rolling along like it did before this vision. I sit up and knock my Coke over and let out a strong "Damn" which makes my friends at the picnic table look over once again, Shelby included.

"Sorry," I say.

Shelby frowns but Dwayne is having a good laugh at it all.

I rejoin the lunch party but everyone's finished and we all head toward the bus. I bring along the leftover lunch which is soggy due to the hummus. As I pass Shelby counting out her wards, I apologize again.

"I wasn't feeling well," I mutter and I'm not sure she buys it.

I fall into my aisle seat and munch on the raw carrots and broccoli which sits at the bottom of my stomach as hard as the Diet Coke.

"What was that all about?" Winnie asks.

"Sick to my stomach."

"Too much vegetarianism," Carmine says with a smug smile and I poke him in the shoulder.

I missed the explanation of the Bear Creek Mounds so when we exit at the site I pause and read the historical signs while the rest of the group heads to the earthen hill with a wide flat top created by early Americans as a temple. According to the markers, migratory hunters first utilized the area for its abundant game and vegetation, dating back around eight thousand years. It later became a Native American hub of sophisticated hunting and agriculture.

"You are standing next to thousands of years of American history," I hear Mr. Henderson say.

"And it's in Mississippi," Shelby adds.

Standing apart from the others, I find peace in the breeze that teases my hair and the afternoon sun warming my face in spurts as the leaves wave in its path. I imagine the village that once existed here, its people experiencing this lovely spot as I am doing right now. There's an absence of buzz but I know that Cora has been here, too. She stood at this very spot, viewing with awe the creation built centuries before. I sense her wonderment, even though Reynald urged them on, uncaring to the significance of this scared spot.

How I know this is beyond me.

We get back on the van and stop less than a mile up the road to quickly look at a cave that's deemed dangerous with a spring that's undrinkable.

"Then what's the use of going there," Miss Georgia says as she files her nails.

Miss Georgia and Dwayne remain on the van, Dwayne insisting he needed to use his cell phone to call some important editor in New York. Shelby's not too happy about that but she herds the rest of us off to hear Mr. Henderson talk at great length about the Trace. He recalls its history, from the Native Americans who might have used this cave, to highwaymen who preyed on American colonists and settlers before and after statehood. Like most historians, he drones on too long and we're all getting those mid-afternoon sleepies. Shelby gets the message, bless her heart, and touches Henderson's arm, and mentions something about staying on schedule.

When we get back on the van, Dwayne and Miss Georgia are sitting in the back aisle, giggling. Joe huffs as he sits in the aisle behind me and we share a look. We've been on enough press trips to know what happens when two journalists find each other attractive and take the opportunity to enjoy themselves. It's totally unprofessional but I'm convinced these two don't care.

We head out, pulling into Tishomingo State Park, which straddles both sides of the Trace and named for Chickasaw Chief Tishomingo. I perk up immediately for there are woods, interesting rock formations, wildflowers, and stone bridges over fern-filled creeks. The park exists in the foothills of the Appalachian Mountains so there's elevation here, something I don't get back home in flat, swampy Louisiana.

"You'll each get a cabin," Shelby announces, "although don't expect the Ritz. These are rustic but very comfortable."

"I hope the beds are adequate," Kelly says. "I have a bad back."

Winnie leans over and whispers, "I doubt it will be the bed that hurts her back," and I struggle not to laugh.

"There's plenty of opportunities to enjoy the park before dinner," Shelby says. "There are hiking trails and disc golf, volley ball courts — lots more."

"And deer?" Pepper asks quietly, afraid, no doubt, of scorn from the rest of us.

"Yes, lots of wildlife here," Shelby says with a kind smile, making me like her all the more. "Especially around dusk."

"The wildlife will most likely be in her cabin," Winnie says with a grin, nodding toward Kelly.

"Just make sure you are in the lodge for six p.m.," Shelby announces. "For dinner."

"Where's the lodge and will someone pick us up?" our Prima Donna asks.

At this point, I stop listening. Journalists can be so needy and Kelly Talbot lets forth a stream of questions all demanding Shelby's attention. I look out the van window and enjoy the scenery as we make our way to the cabins, all located next to Bear Creek. As we pull closer, I spot a pickup truck that looks like TB's. On closer inspection, it has a Louisiana license plate and a similar dent in the right fender.

"That's odd," I say.

"This is where we pick up our new fellow traveler," Shelby announces and looks at me. "Viola's husband will be joining us to Natchez."

Before I can digest this piece of information or say "Boo," the driver opens the van door and TB struts inside.

"Hey baby," he says.

CHAPTER FIVE

"I don't know why you're angry."

TB throws his suitcase on the bed and it causes the bedspread to pull toward the middle, upsetting any chance I would have for a photo. If I had my camera, that is. Regardless, TB follows my line of sight and realizes what he has done. It's always an unspoken rule when we travel together. Don't mess up the hotel room until I've taken my photos!

"Sorry."

I shake my head and throw *my* suitcase on the bed. Might as well. "What are you doing here?"

"Shelly said I could come."

"Shelby."

"Whatever. She said it was fine."

I run a nervous hand through my hair. Press trips are for working travel writers — not a vacation, not for husbands or wives, not to be taken lightly. Public relations firms, city convention and business bureaus, and tourism agencies pay for everything and they don't want to spend money on people who won't give them results. I stand by the rules religiously because this is my dream job and it took me years to get here. When I got pregnant close to graduating LSU, TB and I married and immediately got jobs, he as a carpenter working construction for his dad's company and me covering cops and school board meetings in St. Bernard Parish. I always wrote travel on the side, whenever we managed to go anywhere, but it was hit and miss at best. Now that I'm living the dream as a freelancer, I'm not doing anything to ruin my chances at getting invited on press trips.

TB senses my agitation and puts up two palms. "Look, Vi, I know what you're thinking but I was invited."

"Invited?"

"She was real nice about it, said she would make it a surprise."

I huff. "Surprise all right."

At this TB straightens to his full six-foot height, more man at this point than boy, which has been happening a lot more lately. Usually my husband, who's adorable and sweet mind you, routinely acts inappropriately, says the wrong things, stares at me like a puppy dog. Loyal to a T but aggravating as hell. But, lately….

"You don't want me here, is that it?"

"I didn't say that."

He grabs his coat and pulls the suitcase off the bed. "You didn't have to."

I catch up with him at the door, touch his forearm, and squeeze. "Please, wait."

He pauses, but doesn't drop the suitcase. I watch the torment behind those gentle blue eyes, witness the tension in that adorable face framed by a head of blond curls. He's really the greatest guy, was the best father any child could hope for. We just married too young, and later, when Lillye left us and Katrina washed away everything else, I wanted more. What I want now, I'm not sure, but I am glad he's here.

"Please," I add.

TB turns toward me, serious as a heart attack, which isn't like him. "I love you, Vi. You must know that."

This takes me back. "Of course."

"But I don't know how long I can wait until you love me the same way."

This is so unlike TB. I used the puppy dog analogy for a reason. He's always unconditional love and attention. In all fairness, he has every right to stand up for himself, to make me accountable. Ever since Katrina, when I demanded a divorce and moved to Lafayette and started my new career, TB's been trying to get us back together. I changed course and dropped the separation papers when I realized I could keep his health insurance if we stayed married — how considerate is that? I cringe, thinking of my insensitivity.

"It's that bad, isn't it?" he asks sarcastically, when he notices my reaction. He opens the door and is about to head out but I'm there first, quickly slamming it shut.

"I was thinking about how you're right. I'm stringing you along and that's not fair."

This isn't what *he's* expecting. TB drops the suitcase but he's still looking at me hesitantly. Once again, I'm tongue-tied. I know what he wants me to say, gush my love and fall into his arms and we'll be the happy couple for life. I'm just not there yet. If I'll ever be. I'm a journalist who reads voraciously and he builds houses, watches LSU football. Are we truly a match? Can we sustain a life together for the rest of our lives?

TB smiles sadly, because he senses my conflict. "Right."

My hand's still on the door and I'm not letting go. "I do love you." That much is true.

TB looks down at his feet and smiles grimly. "You're just not *in love* with me, is that it?"

"Yes," I think, but then, "No!" I'm so conflicted.

Instead, I slip between him and the door and run my hands up the front of his flannel shirt. That strong chest and shoulders from years of working construction incites parts of my body — he can arouse me like no other man. As for being good in bed, the man should win an Oscar. I look up into those baby blues and sigh.

"You really are the most adorable man and I'm the most insufferable person."

TB looks away but he's wrapping those enormous hands around me and I revel in that protective embrace, glad he's relenting.

"I'm sorry for being non-committal." I'm reminded that TB never finished LSU and doesn't own the best vocabulary so I add, "for always being on the fence about our marriage."

TB sighs. "It's okay, Vi. I know you wanted to start over after...." He's thinking about Lillye and my heart stills waiting for her name to be spoken; we hardly discuss her because it hurts too much. "...after Katrina."

I relax because we're not traveling down that enormously painful road and that he gets it, that following my dream and leaving everything behind needed to happen for me. I rise on my toes and kiss him and he returns the affection, then we break apart, smile at each other and wrap ourselves into a bear hug, that warmness of his touch emanating through me. It's always been like that, no matter the lack of intelligent conversation or familiar interests, we meld well together.

If only love could be about…well, love.

I feel TB tense again and pull back.

"What is it?" I ask.

"What the hell is he doing here?"

I look out the window and spot Dwayne waltzing past the front window of the cabin. He gives us a nod but doesn't add his usual charming smile. For a second, and I'm not sure why, I think to pull out of TB's embrace. But that's ridiculous, I think. I'm not attracted to this man. I do relax from TB's hug but it's more to think.

"Dwayne Garrett," I tell TB. "He's one of the journalists."

"The guy from the SCANC convention?"

"Yeah, and I need to tell you what Carmine said about him. It's a weird story and I still haven't gotten the whole tale from Carmine."

TB pulls me close, continuing to stare out the window as Dwayne stops to talk to Shelby, who's carrying two baskets. She hands him one and I notice how her body language changes, her head tilts, one hand straightens her blouse, even her foot starts twirling in the dirt. Weird, how this man affects people.

"Something's not right about him," TB says, which is unusual for my husband, who tends to like everyone. I hate to use another dog analogy but TB's like those overly friendly pups who love the world and lick you to death so if they growl at something, you know it's bad.

"Again, you should hear Carmine. He likens the man to the devil."

TB looks down at me and the gaze from those puppy dog

eyes turns serious. "Devil?"

The word gives me the shivers but I shake off the feeling. "You know, Carmine. He's always dramatic. But here's the rub. Carmine said that man was one of the teenagers who beat him up in high school."

TB looks out the window at Dwayne, who's now heading toward his own cabin. Dwayne turns at one point and winks at me, which sends a shiver down my back. TB, on the other hand, doesn't move a muscle, tightens his hold around my shoulders.

Shelby suddenly appears on our porch and we both jump.

"Sorry," she says through the window and holds up a basket. "I brought you refreshments."

TB and I both exhale the breath we didn't know we'd been holding and open the door and Shelby saunters in. She holds up the basket, which has a variety of goodies in it, namely cheese, crackers, some chocolate, a bottle of wine, and two glasses.

"You're not supposed to drink in state parks so keep this quiet," she says with a smile.

TB accepts the basket but he glances over at me, waiting for approval. He's worried to accept too much from this trip, which might cause problems for me.

"Thanks Shelby. That's so sweet of you," I say.

She motions to the basket, sporting that same smile she wore on the van when TB arrived. "There's two glasses."

TB's still acting nervous, like a kid found in an area of the playground that's off-limits.

"Shelby," I begin, "would it be okay if TB joins us to Natchez. He's so helpful with my research and he can stay in my accommodations. We'll be happy to pay for the meals."

Shelby waves a hand at the both of us. "Are you kidding? I invited him here."

TB sends me a "Told you so" look.

"When Carmine told me y'all never have a chance to be together because one of you is fixing up the house in New Orleans and the other is living in a potting shed in Lafayette,

I just had to make this work."

I cringe, because I don't live in a potting shed. It's a mother-in-law unit behind a larger house in the Saint Streets District of Lafayette, a city two hours west of New Orleans. We evacuated there after being pulled from our roof and I discovered this apartment on a whim. When I inquired about moving in, the owner, Reece Cormier, began crying. Yes, crying. He nodded, handed me the keys, insisted I live there rent free, and thus began my travel writing career because for the first time I had nothing to stop me and could afford to work freelance. I also had nothing to sit on but that happened, too. The word got out that a Katrina refugee — I hated that title — was living within the historic district and things began appearing every night at my doorstep. I would wake up and head out to retrieve my newspaper and there would be a table and two chairs, a bureau, a tea pot, a bicycle.

My ADHD brain suddenly comes back to the conversation. "Wait, did you say Carmine told you?"

Shelby smiles proudly. "Your husband called when we were having breakfast, said you forgot your camera and that he would drive up to deliver it since he's off work for a few days."

I look over at TB. It's one of those times when he would appear sheepish and shrug but he sends me a glance that says, "You need to trust me sometimes."

"Carmine overheard me talking to him on my cell phone and mentioned your situation," Shelby continues. "I was more than happy to get you two together."

TB wraps an arm about my shoulders and again, this assertiveness is so unlike him. I have to admit, it's pretty damn sexy.

"We cannot thank you enough," he says.

Shelby waves us off. "No worries. We had several cancellations so this worked out perfectly."

"Are you sure we can't pay for the meals?" I ask.

Shelby's eyes tear up and I know what's coming. Katrina pity. I've seen it time and again and honestly, after three years, it's become annoying, but also gratifying to know America still cares.

"No worries about anything," Shelby says, waving those manicured nails. "Just have fun."

"Thank you," TB says.

She waves again, the KP emotions still present, and heads off. As we watch her through the window, we see Shelby wiping her eyes.

"Amazing how people react to something they didn't experience," TB says.

"I guess that's it. In a way, they did experience it."

"Just not on their roofs."

I look up at him thinking he's joking; that's his usual MO. TB's hardly found without a grin and a funny anecdote. But TB's not smiling. Trauma runs deep, and that bitch of a storm laid a good one on us. Unless, he's still smarting about my capriciousness.

"Are you okay?" I ask him.

He looks at me as if he's come out of a trance. He shakes off whatever he was contemplating and smiles. "Sure. Just been a busy week."

Something's off here. I feel it and this sensation is starting to be a regular occurrence on this trip. Before I'm able to inquire further, TB's off to unpack his suitcase, talking about his latest house job that's been put on hold until December, enough time to follow us to Natchez and then drive me back to New Orleans. I open the wine and pour us two glasses, then suddenly remember something.

"Who's taking care of Stinky?"

TB doesn't turn around but I can sense his smirk. "Check out the bathroom."

He couldn't have possibly brought my cat on this trip, I think, but when I open the door my tabby cat is spread out inside the cool porcelain bathtub. He looks up at me and winks, then closes his eyes and resumes sleeping.

"There's something not normal about this cat."

I feel TB's hand on mine pulling me back into the

bedroom.

"Let's let the baby sleep and enjoy that wine," he says seductively. "And maybe something else."

I really am glad he's here, I think, as we start something else, forgoing that wine and the rest of the world with its fallen angels, antebellum Kentucky girls, and the Katrina mess we left behind.

By the time Carmine and Winnie knock on our doors, we've messed up the bed right and good. Thankfully, our friends can't see us through the front window since a large fireplace and half of a wall exists between the sitting area and the bedroom.

I slip off the bed, grab the clothes TB ripped off me earlier, and head to the bathroom while TB pulls on his jeans and calls out to our friends that he's coming. I know damn well Winnie and Carmine will not let us live this down. As I throw on my clothes in the bathroom, Stinky has awakened and is rubbing against my bare legs.

"Hey bud." I've missed this cat so much that I pause in my dressing and pick him up — which he hates and I don't care — and deliver a couple of annoying hugs. He's fighting it but he's also purring so I know he's secretly happy. Must be a cat rule that you can't enjoy too much affection from your owners.

Truth be told, no one owns this cat. He owns us. He's got TB and me wrapped around his paws.

"Are you hiding in there?" I hear Winnie shout.

I put Stinky down and pull on my shirt, then my cardigan sweater since it's starting to get nippy at night. Stinky's still making love to my ankles and when I look down I notice he's unusually happy.

"You love Mississippi?" I ask, and within a heartbeat he glances up at me as if I've lost my mind, then shoots out the bathroom.

"Oh my goodness," I hear Winnie say. "There's a cat in here."

"You brought Stinky?" Carmine exclaims.

I run fingers through my hair and emerge from the bathroom as if I've showered and changed for the evening activities. Which is crazy since my hair is now kinkier than usual and I'm wearing the same clothes. Not to mention that my friends aren't stupid.

"Having fun?" Winnie asks seriously, and I pinch her upper arm.

"I know you two had some exercise but anyone up for a hike?" Carmine asks.

There are thirteen miles of nature trails within the park and we decide on a less vigorous one that's short and sweet since dinner at the lodge begins in forty-five minutes. The Saddleback Ridge is advertised as having large outcropping of rocks, so I vote for it right away. Apparently, the Chickasaw used this trail to visit an area called the Freedom Hills and we've been told there are small caves along the way. So far, we've discovered two and when we've found a nice spot with a rock overhang, we all decide to pause and enjoy the wooded view.

"This ends at the dam," Winnie says, reading the brochure. "Well, damn."

"Puny," Carmine says. "We should head back soon. It's getting dark."

Winnie pulls a flask from her jacket pocket. "Apple Jack first?"

"You brought apple cider?" TB asks. "I love apple cider."

Winnie laughs and TB glances at us to find out what's funny. "What did I say?"

I take the flask from her hands and knock back a sip, wincing as I do. "It's moonshine, sweetheart. With some apple flavoring."

We pass around what tastes akin to rubbing alcohol that's been sitting in an apple barrel, talking and laughing like old times. When the shadows lengthen and we realize we've been gone longer than we should, we hightail it back to the lodge, following the markings on the trees, giggling all the way.

The van is parked outside our cabins, no doubt for Miss Georgia's bad back, and Winnie takes the opportunity to run inside and refill her flask. "Just in case," she says, and I know what she means. In case John Henderson or an equally dull speaker wants to fill our evening with boring tales. Native American stories and ghosts would be more apropos in this natural setting with autumn leaves covering the ground and a campfire crackling while we warm by the blaze.

I get my fire wish as we enter the Loochapola Lodge, an old Civilian Conversation Corps structure from the 1930s. During the height of the Depression, the government hired men to build parks, bridges, and other structures across the country through the CCC. The men learned a trade, helped build infrastructure, and were required to send half of their earnings back home to family. This lodge owns that Depression-era feel, consisting of Mississippi wood and sandstone and in the center, a stone fireplace.

"Now, we're talking," I say as I head for the warmth of the flames.

As I'm warming my buns by the fire and the rest of the group heads for the buffet spread on a long table, Dwayne sneaks up from behind.

"Want to learn about evolution?" he asks. "I'm going to check out that ghost story after dinner."

That warm feeling I've been enjoying from afternoon lovemaking and a moonshine-instilled walk through the wood evaporates. The hairs on the back of my neck stand at attention.

Dwayne leans a shoulder on the side of the fireplace. "It's up to you, of course. If you want to see your daughter again."

I know I should be wary of this man — lord knows I've heard enough warnings from Carmine — but his promises cause my rational mind to disappear. I must know what he's on about.

"What are you going to do?"

"Meet me at my cabin ten minutes after this dinner is over and I'll show you."

I try to laugh this off like it's no big deal but my heart's beating so hard I swear I can hear it. "I'm not going to waltz off into the woods with you."

Dwayne shrugs and that masculine charm is absent. "I'm not going to seduce you, Viola. You're married. My only wish for you is to send another soul into heaven and tune your gift so that you can see any spirit, including your daughter."

There's a buzz happening, but it's a distant one, different from the usual spirit messages. I look over and find my buddies huddled around the open bar and I wish I had not left their company.

Dwayne leans forward and moves to leave. "No biggie. Come if you want."

The words pour out of my mouth without thinking. It's as if my desire to see Lillye bypasses all logical thought. "I'll be there."

Dwayne pats me on the shoulder. "Good girl." And then he's gone.

I swallow hard. What have I done? According to Carmine, Dwayne's the last person I should be alone with in the wild of Mississippi but I can't help myself. I want to know what he knows, want to see for myself if evolution is possible. After all, what harm could he possibly do? He's a journalist like me, he's not going to murder me in the woods.

Still, as I join the others for barbecue ribs, fried chicken, and banana pudding with vanilla wafers on the side — it's the South, after all — I wonder what the hell I've gotten myself into.

After two hours of food and alcohol and another historian discussing how the park named for the leader of the Chickasaw nation contains archaeological excavations that have unearthed Paleo Indians dating back to 7000 B.C., there's nothing but glazed eyes and longings for bed. We climb into the van, all of us suddenly quiet in need of sleep. As Shelby drops us off at each cabin, I tell TB I need to ask Dwayne a question and head over to his cabin. I feel TB's gaze on my back the whole way there but when I reach Dwayne's door and turn to look back, he's gone inside.

Dwayne opens the door and smiles. "Good girl."

We silently walk into the woods toward Bear Creek, following a trail and those tree markers until we reach the creek's edge. Dwayne follows the creek for a while until up ahead I hear what sounds like a small waterfall. In the distance, an owl calls out and another responds on the other side of the woods. There's no moon so walking is difficult, but the darkness feels refreshing after living in a city. I've never been afraid in nature, feel the earth blanket me like a mother's arms.

"You still with me?" Dwayne asks from up ahead and it breaks the peacefulness I'm experiencing. Suddenly, I'm wary of this man and what we're about to do, whatever that is.

"How far are we going?" I ask. "I'm not up for a marathon hike."

Dwayne suddenly stops. "Here."

I look around and see the sparkle of water tumbling over rocks, hear bullfrogs on a placid stretch of water downstream, but nothing else. "I don't get it."

Dwayne takes my shoulders and turns me toward the water. At first, there's nothing but darkness with a slight reflection of stars. Then I spot her. A girl of about ten stands knee-deep in the creek, glowing transparent, and staring at us with wonderment.

"She drowned here," Dwayne whispers in my ear. "They never found her and she needs peace."

I want to ask how he knows this but I'm too focused on the child. "What do you need?" I ask her.

"My mother," she whispers back.

"Where is your mother?"

She points in the direction of the Trace highway, but that can't be. There's no housing on the Natchez Trace.

"Does she live in a nearby town?" I ask.

"Tishomingo," she utters.

"That's where we are."

Dwayne leans down and whispers in my ear, "There's a town called Tishomingo near here."

Again, I'm wondering how he knows all this, but I ask the child if the town is where her family resides. She nods, so I ask, "Do you want me to tell your family where you are?"

The girl's face lights up and she nods, but there's desperation in her gaze. "I want to go home."

I smile warmly, trying to ease her worries to get more information. "I know, sweetheart. Tell me your mom's name and I'll let her know where you are and you can go home. You do know where home is now, don't you sweetie?" She nods and points upwards and I relax. I'd hate to have this sweet thing believe she's still alive and capable of walking in her house, saying "Hey mom, do I have a story to tell you."

I swallow and hope for the best. "If I promise to tell your family, will you move on?"

She nods and relays information on her family, where they live on Jackson Street in Tishomingo, what their names are. I make a mental note and assure her I will do everything possible. Natalie Stephens — that's her name — smiles broadly and begins to climb the ladder as the warm white light appears and surrounds her. Like the other ghosts I have helped ascend, she closes her eyes and appears serene, as if her mother is present and wrapping her in kisses and hugs.

"Quick," Dwayne says, pushing me forward into the water. "Place your hands into the light."

I'm stunned that he jolted me so and even more so that I'm suddenly half immersed into the frigid water of Bear Creek, but I reach up, palm first, to feel the outer limits of what we call the God Light when ghosts transcend this plane for another.

"Move closer," Dwayne urges, but the light feels electric, reminding me of the static I felt when I first shook Dwayne's hand. It's an out-of-this-world sensation and I don't have time to contemplate its implications so even though Dwayne's practically yelling at me from the shore to immerse myself in its glow, I hesitate and within seconds Natalie has disappeared and with her, the God Light.

I watch the waters turn from iridescent to darkness and push my way back to shore through the cold waters. As I climb the bank I can tell Dwayne's disappointed, even though I can't make out his face.

"That light, it's what evolves us," he says, as if I'm a petulant child. "You should have embraced it."

By now my teeth are chattering I'm so cold and all I want to do is go back to the cabin, look up Natalie's family, and call them first thing in the morning so that Natalie rests on the Other Side.

"Next time," I mutter, and move to head back towards camp. "Just what was supposed to happen, anyway?"

"The more you come in contact with the Supreme Being's essence, the more spiritual you will become." He sighs like he's disappointed in me, reminding me of when my father, the math professor, tried teaching me algebra to no avail. That memory rises and pisses me off, that yet another man thinks I'm incapable of learning something. Makes me think of TB and how people treat him when he says something stupid.

TB. What am I doing out here in the middle of the woods, letting a strange man that Carmine despises make me feel inferior? Why am I letting him deal with a ghost that should have been my responsibility and mine alone?

"I'm going back," I say through my chattering teeth and head down the path. "I need to find out about her parents."

"Wait," Dwayne calls out.

I turn hesitantly and see that he's holding a flask in his hands, one that resembles Winnie's.

"I'll take care of Natalie's family. You get back to the cabin and warm up. At least drink something before you go."

I take a good look at the flask, wondering how it's possible they both own the same kind.

"It's Winnie's. She left it in the van. Alcohol's not my thing but I believe it will take the chill off."

I accept the flask and take a sip. Sure enough, it's her

Apple Jack. I take a longer sip, then another, and the warmth of the moonshine settles throughout my body.

"Take it with you," he says. "Get it back to her in the morning."

I nod and head off down the trail, watching for those tree markers, Dwayne following behind.

The next thing I know I'm being woken by TB, the morning light filtering through the windows. I'm still dressed in my nighttime clothes, everything below the knee still wet.

I lean up on my elbows and gaze around, my head suddenly feeling like it's about to blow.

"Had a good time?" TB asks, obviously pissed as hell.

"What happened?" I ask, trying desperately to figure out how I went from walking the creek's edge to waking up the next morning without remembering anything.

"You spent the night with Dwayne," is all my husband will say, as he grabs his suitcase and heads for his pickup.

CHAPTER SIX

My head's about to explode when I rise from the bed, but I must stop TB. Something's wrong and the dream I'm waking from has my heart beating rapidly. For a moment, I can't tell what's real and what's a dream state.

TB calls out to Stinky and the cat lets out a howl.

"Stinky, let's go."

Any other time I might look at this scenario and wonder why my husband's calling my cat like a dog, but the panic rising inside me insists I stop TB from walking out the door. I rise and sidestep my cat who's still bellowing and make it to the living area. I slip between TB and the door and grab the front of his shirt.

"Don't leave," I plead. "Tell me what's going on."

TB pulls back and my husband's sweet eyes are as cold as steel. "What's going on?" he asks exasperated.

I'm trying desperately to think, but I can't for the life of me know why I'm still in my clothes, my jeans remain wet, and TB thinks I slept with Dwayne.

I shake my head. "I can't remember."

TB stands there, suitcase in hand, saying nothing, which unnerves me to no end. He's usually so protective, so concerned. I don't know why he's not inquiring what happened as opposed to rendering me guilty on sight.

"Why are you so mad at me?" I ask, and his eyes enlarge as if I've asked the most ridiculous thing.

"Why? Maybe because you waltzed in an hour after we got back from dinner and passed out on the bed, drunk."

"Drunk?"

I rub my forehead, which is pounding but I don't feel hung over. I feel…strange.

TB attempts to move around me and grab the doorknob. "No worries, Vi. I'm going home."

I lean backwards and block his exit. I shiver hard, like a skunk crawling over my grave, as my Aunt Mimi loves to say, because I'm scared shitless. I can't remember how I got home last night and the dream I had before wakening mirrored what I hope hasn't happened to me.

"Please don't leave me," I whisper, close to tears.

Against his better judgment, TB drops his suitcase but he's still pissed. Underneath that anger, however, I find an ounce of caring.

"What happened, Vi?"

I bite my lower lip to keep the tears at bay. "I don't know."

Stinky arrives and rubs up against my shin and his purring relaxes me a bit. I pick him up and hold him tight and my heart rate seems to decelerate.

TB, on the other hand, isn't relenting. "What don't you know?"

I fall into the nearby chair, Stinky still in my arms. "How I got home last night."

"You don't know how you got back from Dwayne's cabin?"

I shake my head. "I didn't go to his cabin. We went to the creek to find a girl who drowned there. Dwayne wanted me to help her cross over so he could show me how a SCANC evolves."

TB pulls his hands through his hair. "Oh God, Vi. Not that again. Carmine told you…."

"I know what Carmine said!" I'm yelling now and Stinky leaps from my lap and hightails it to the bedroom.

TB finally gets my panic and slips into the opposite chair. "Then what happened?"

"It was strange, TB." I vividly remember that weird electric feeling when I touched the light. "I promised the girl I would tell her parents so they can be at peace and she started to cross over. Then, Dwayne pushed me into the creek so that I would touch the light, said I would evolve by tapping into it. But it was horrible, TB. I can't explain it but it felt unnatural, wrong."

Suddenly, the tears begin to fall. Thinking back on the experience, plus the horrors of the dream I just had, is all too much. I feel shaken to the bone.

"Did you come home, then?"

I try to recall what happened after Natalie vanished. I became cold, so very cold. There was Winnie's flask with Apple Jack to warm me up.

"He gave me Apple Jack."

TB picked up the flask that was sitting on a nearby table. "Yeah, you spilled it everywhere. That's why it smells like a distillery in here."

I take the flask and shake it, but there's nothing inside. Did Dwayne change out the alcohol, drug me with something else? When would he have had time to do that, I rationalize, and besides, it tasted like Winnie's moonshine. But to get that drunk on two sips? I'm an LSU grad, would never get drunk on so little, especially so inebriated that I can't remember a thing past walking up the trail and spotting one of those markers by the creekside.

Then there was the dream, of Reynald offering Cora whiskey to take the chill off a rainy night by the side of the Trace. They were huddled beneath the wagon, rain pouring down the sides, with Reynald way too close for polite company. Cora hesitantly drank his whiskey because she was cold, so very cold. When she woke the next morning, her skirt was above her knees and her undergarments tangled. She hadn't been raped by the man, she was sure about that, but she was fairly confident she had been violated in some way. For the life of her, she couldn't remember much more than the last sips of whiskey.

I've read about women being given date drugs and waking up not knowing what had happened, that maybe, just maybe something awful had.

"Vi," TB says, looking me over closely, "you're scaring me."

"Could what have happened to Cora have happened to

me?"

"Who's Cora?"

I look him straight in the eyes, hoping something might float to the surface and allow me to remember what occurred after seeing that tree marker by the creek. "TB, I can't remember. I only took two sips."

He's out of his chair in an instant, barging through the front door and heading towards Dwayne's cabin. Dwayne is lounging on his front porch with a cup of coffee and a cigarette so TB finds him instantly.

"What the hell did you do to my wife, you son of a bitch?"

I'm hot on his heels because as scared as I am that something might be amiss, I don't want TB to hurt Dwayne, or worse, get himself hurt.

Dwayne throws the rest of his coffee to the ground, but leaves the cigarette hanging from his lips. "What climbed up your ass?"

"What did you do to her?" TB yells.

Dwayne looks offended but in a cocky way. "I didn't do anything to her."

I catch up to them and grab TB's elbow. "TB, let's go."

TB pulls free. "Not until he gives us some answers."

At this, Dwayne throws the cigarette away and finally looks at me. "What's the problem, SCANC girl?"

I'm still shaking inside, fearful of the unknown, but I find my voice. "I woke up not remembering anything. I only had two sips of that moonshine."

Dwayne looks like he's about to laugh, but reins it in. "Moonshine is some powerful stuff."

TB moves forward and I'm convinced he's about to plant a fist in this jerk's face, so I stand between the two men, facing Dwayne.

"What happened after the creek?" I ask him.

He climbs down the steps so he's on our level. "You had a crossover, Vi. You tried to access the light. You got cold, which is normal considering you were standing in a creek, and I gave you something to warm you up."

"That's it?" TB demands.

"And then she walked home to your loving arms."

TB moves forward again, but I hold him back. "Then how come I can't remember the walk home?"

"Likely from the experience, coupled with the alcohol. That happens when you engage in the light." Dwayne frowns. "What did you think happened?"

I'm too embarrassed by the whole incident to admit that I worried he took advantage so I grab TB's sleeve and pull him toward our cabin.

"We leave in fifteen minutes," I hear Dwayne calling from behind. "You might want to shower and get out of those things."

I look down at my clothes which are exactly as they were the night before. If Dwayne had violated my person, it's doubtful he would have been able to dress me back up in the same way, wet jeans included.

"That's it?" TB asks, as I continue to pull his sleeve toward our cabin.

I'm too embarrassed to admit that I might have made a grave error, and something deep inside thinks there's more to this scenario than Dwayne's letting on. I don't want to go into it now since the van is leaving shortly, so I simply answer, "That's it" and head for the showers. But I check my body for anything suspicious when I do.

After I dress and emerge from the bathroom, I find TB in deep conversation with Carmine. When Carmine spots me, his face turns as red as a Bama fraternity man at a football game.

"You did what?" Carmine spits out at me.

My head's still splitting so I'm not in a mood to be lectured. "Let's talk about it later, okay?"

Carmine shakes his head and I realize he's furious with me. "You bet we're going to talk later."

I can't help myself. I bite back. "Well, that'll be a first. Not like you've been forthcoming with all this great information."

Carmine stares at me for a moment – no doubt not used

to me talking back — then leaves for the van. "We leave in five minutes," he tells TB.

I don't wait for TB's disapproval; he adores Carmine. I throw my clothes into the suitcase and head for TB's pickup truck, careful at the door to not let Stinky out. TB follows but leaves the door wide open. Before I can admonish him, he calls to the cat and Stinky trots out, then jumps into the cab of the pickup when TB opens the door.

"What the…?"

But I don't have time to ponder all this. Within a heartbeat, we're off and running, following the van to our next stop, breakfast at the Parkway Visitor's Center outside Tupelo. TB's unusually silent so I pick up Stinky and offer my signature cat massage. He purrs loudly, cuddles closer, and I feel myself relaxing.

"Who's Cora?" TB asks.

The horrid dream comes back in a rush, poor Cora wakening to find herself in disarray with a massive headache and no answers to what happened the night before. Her distrust of Reynald has evolved into fear and she wishes she had never started on this fateful journey through Mississippi.

"I found two photographs of this woman and I've been dreaming of her ever since."

"What woman?"

I lean over to my purse, careful not to disturb Stinky, and pull out the two photos.

"Those look antebellum," he says. "What's on the back? Anything?"

"It says 'Briarwood, Natchez.' In my dreams, a friend calls her Cora, but that's all I know."

"I'll do some research."

When I first started travel writing, my husband had offered to help me solve a century-old mystery involving female students at a Eureka Springs college. The school became the Crescent Hotel, claimed to be the most haunted hotel in America. I'm here to attest to that fact, although I helped one of their apparitions cross to the other side.

TB was instrumental in solving that mystery, much to my surprise, and has been helpful with my research ever since. Too bad he left college and went into carpentry because he'd make an excellent researcher or police detective.

We pull into the parking lot of the Visitor's Center and are greeted by several national park rangers.

"What about Stinky?" I ask.

"He'll be fine." TB closes the door behind him with a crack in the window. The weather's balmy and partly cloudy so heat isn't an issue and TB has placed lots of food and water on the cab floor. When I look back, Stinky's stretched out on TB's flannel shirt on the car seat, happily cleaning his face.

We all get an introduction to two park rangers by the front door, then are brought inside where coffee and a large array of pastries await us.

"Finally," Pepper says, heading straight for the bear claws.

"Youth," Joe whispers to me with a smile.

I want to laugh but the smell of it makes that headache return. When Dwayne walks by and his aftershave hits my nostrils, I head straight for the bathroom and revisit that nasty Apple Jack. I sit on the cold tile, head in hands, and wait for my stomach to calm down. I hear the door open and know it's Winnie coming to check up on me.

"I'm fine, Mom."

The door to my stall opens and it's Carmine. He sits next to me on the floor, — bless his heart, he has this thing about getting dirty — his back propping the door open. He rubs his hands over his knees.

"I'm sorry, Vi. I should have told you."

"That he's Lucifer and he's come to take my soul."

I'm joking but Carmine's not laughing.

"You're serious about him being a fallen angel?"

"He's a descendant, not an angel."

"Whatever. You really believe that stuff?"

Carmine finally looks up. "Have you ever wondered why there are psychic people in the world, wondered why us and not everyone else?"

Not really, I think, but I nod anyway.

"Most people in the Etherworld think it's one of two things, and one is that we're descendants of angels who long ago had relationships with women before God put an end to it."

Definitely not what I expected. "Are you kidding me? Etherworld? Angels?"

When our eyes meet, I know he's serious. He takes my hand in his. "That's a subject for another day. What you need to know right now is that when people cross over, their souls go with them into the light. You can't touch it, Vi. It's dangerous."

I completely agree but I need more information. "Why is it dangerous?"

"Because it's not meant for you." He squeezes my hand. "*Their* soul is rising, not yours. Do you understand?"

Hardly. "So, you're saying if I put myself into that light, my soul will ascend with theirs?"

Carmine's gaze turns deadly serious. "Likely, yes."

"So, why would Dwayne want me to do that, think that I will evolve by touching the light?"

"Why indeed?"

I'm so confused, and just as I'm about to inquire more, Winnie sticks her head in. "Am I interrupting something?"

Carmine rises, then gives me a hand to get me on my feet.

"We'll talk later," he says.

"You keep saying that."

I'm suddenly hungry and in need of a cool drink to get the vomit taste out of my mouth. Bless them both for they link elbows in mine on either side and we laugh as we trot to the pastry table. When we get to the food, however, neither one lets go. I look up at Carmine who's sending Dwayne the evil eye, as if he's sending a mental message to him to leave me alone.

Dwayne, on the other hand, ignores Carmine and sends me a wink and I can feel Carmine's muscles tense throughout his body. For the first time, I wonder if Dwayne is using me to get back at Carmine and some high school feud that still simmers.

"I'm cool, guys," I tell my buds and they release me. I grab a croissant and a coffee with lots of cream and follow the others into the auditorium for a film. Without realizing it, TB's been at my back the whole time. I feel like the president with a security entourage. All they need are earpieces and guns.

We make ourselves comfortable and watch a film that teaches us about Natchez Trace history, dating back thousands of years to Paleo Native Americans, then how "Kantucks" would move their crops down the Ohio and Mississippi rivers to sell at New Orleans, taking the Trace back home. Naturally, other travelers used the road through Chickasaw and Choctaw lands, and remnants of their presence are located at many sites that we will see, Shelby announces from the side.

The Trace was also plagued by highwaymen, robbers, and murderers, and the dream about Cora comes back in a flash. Is that why she looks so pained in the photograph, I wonder? But then, she was happy with child at some point. My head's buzzing and I can't shake that mysterious feeling, wondering if a piece of my soul was left behind at Tishomingo State Park.

After the film, we're left to browse the center, which has a nice collection of Native American and colonial artifacts. For the first time since we started this trip Goth Girl lights up.

"I know this," Pepper says pointing to a selection of herbs on display titled *Native American Medicine*. "Yellowroot is great for when you have an upset stomach. And this," she points to a piece of bark, "is dogwood, awesome for headaches. I use it for my migraines."

I'm impressed because my Aunt Mimi taught me the same thing, walked me through the back woods of Alabama and explained how to use herbs in the wild as medicine.

"Shouldn't simply be called 'Native American Medicine,'"

Pepper continues with a frown. "We should still be using these. We're so cut off from our Mother."

I'm sorry I wrote off this Millennial for I find we have something in common.

"I grow all kinds of herbs in my apartment back home," I tell her. "I also use them for gris-gris bags."

Pepper's face turned on when she spotted the herbs, like someone flipped a switch, but now it's a ninety-watt bulb. I explain how Native Americans, voodoo priestesses, and African Americans routinely carried herbs with them as medicine and for protection. Some herbs were believed to assist with intentions. If you want to win at gambling, carry a Lucky Hand root in your pocket. If you want to attract love, herbs in a red bag do the trick.

"Also helps if you put a lock of their hair inside," I add with a smile.

"Watch out for her," Carmine warns Pepper with a laugh. "She'll put some mojo on you."

Pepper surprises us all and pulls a gris-gris bag from her purse. Naturally, it's black.

We have a good laugh at this — and for the record black doesn't denote evil, it's a powerful protective color. I look across the room and notice Dwayne staring intently at Pepper and her bag and remember he's a man of God. Some religions look down on relishing natural items, call them pagan when really it's about honoring our Mother, as Pepper likes to say. I doubt God thinks delicious smelling herbs culled from the earth he created dilutes our faith.

I head over to the food table for more coffee. I smell Dwayne's aftershave so I know he's behind me.

"Nothing happened, SCANC girl," he whispers in my ear. "I'm not that kind of guy."

I turn but he's looking off toward TB, who's watching us both carefully.

"Carmine and I have some history." He pours himself another coffee and nonchalantly rubs up against my side which — against my rational mind that has rendered him non-guilty — causes me to stiffen. "So, don't believe everything he says."

"And I'm supposed to believe you? A man who lets a woman stumble off in the darkness because what she has done has messed with her head."

He smirks. "I didn't make you drink that moonshine."

I grab his arm, a bit too hard, which isn't what he's expecting. "It wasn't the damn moonshine and you know it."

Dwayne removes my hand and his gaze turns cold. "If you'd have done it correctly, you'd be seeing Lillye right now."

"Don't you dare say her name."

"Come with me again and do it right and I'll prove it."

I'm about to retort that I will never do anything with this man but he grabs his coffee and walks away. And, I must admit, against my better judgment, I'm still curious.

The rest of the group climbs into the van and TB and I follow behind in the pickup, with Stinky happy in my lap. It's going to be a day of the dead — we visit an old Confederate graveyard next to a piece of the original Trace, then drive through the Tupelo National Battlefield. I'm not a fan of Civil War history so I only half listen while a local historian drones on about the "War Between the States." Yes, he refers to it that way, which makes me want to yell, "Time to move on!" TB, on the other hand, loves every minute.

"I so want to do that," he whispers to me and nods toward a man dressed as a Union soldier. I roll my eyes.

Finally, we head into Tupelo to enjoy lunch at Johnnie's, the oldest restaurant in town and supposedly once visited by the King. When TB realizes that Tupelo was Elvis's birthplace and we might be sitting where Elvis once placed his gyrating hips, my husband's about to hyperventilate.

"You're an Elvis fan?" Joe asks.

"Anything from the seventies," I answer, because TB has spotted the Elvis booth and hightails it across the room to take a million photos.

Pepper, on the other hand, looks around clueless. "I thought Michael Jackson was the King," she says.

Johnnies, and Tupelo for that matter, is famous for their doughburgers, a combination of ground beef and flour mixed into the patty that's later fried on a grill and served with mustard, pickles, and onions on a bun. We all order one, along with milkshakes, and squeeze into the booths; Johnnies' isn't that big.

"I thought you were a vegetarian," Dwayne says, watching me eat the burger.

"Can't miss the King's favorite meal," I answer with a smile, and Carmine gives me a stare. I guess I'm not allowed to get back on good terms with the devil.

After lunch, we head over to Elvis' birthplace and the look on Pepper's face has us all laughing.

"What?" she asks.

"You look lost," Stephanie says.

She shrugs. "My mom listened to this music but I don't see what the big deal is."

At this point, Joe is about to hyperventilate. Stephanie grabs his arm and pulls him off to the Presley homestead before he launches into how important Elvis was to rock 'n' roll.

"He was a big deal," I say instead to Pepper.

She shrugs again and heads to the gift shop.

After we walk through the shotgun house where Elvis lived as a child, we move to the church that offers a surround-video giving visitors a chance to witness what a country church service was like. Dwayne's now charming Shelby and her high heels are popping beneath her on the church's wooden floor. Her nervous tapping is almost drowning out the movie and I long to put a hand on her knee and make her stop. Miss Georgia sends them both evil glances.

We head back toward the Trace but not without a stop at the hardware store where Elvis bought his first guitar. There's an Elvis competition in town and several of the Elvis tribute artists — they don't like to be called impersonators — are visiting and gaping over one of the store's original guitars, just like the one Elvis purchased so long ago. Joe and TB look like kids on the eve of Christmas and ask one of the artists to sing an Elvis song and the whole lot of them grab guitars and start singing together.

I've never been a big Elvis fan but a dozen Elvi singing a rendition of *Loving You* has goosebumps racing up my arms. Shelby grabs my sleeve and pulls me toward the back. I want to resist but she's up to something. Sure enough, we climb the back stairs to the second story that overlooks the hardware store and I'm able to not only hear these men singing harmony Elvis-style, but take some excellent photos as well. As I capture some video on my camera I glance down at my husband, whose eyes are glistening.

It's late afternoon when we get back on the van and we're all getting those afternoon sleepies again, which is why when we approach the Black Belt overlook on the Trace we all opt to simply look out the window at the hills of rich soil which gives the area its name. We do the same for the Chickasaw Council House, which is now an archaeological site, and the spot where Spanish explorer Hernando de Soto spent the winter in the mid-1500s.

I find it fascinating, really, but that burger and milk shake followed by singing Elvi have done a number on my eyelids. I want only to arrive at our next accommodation and take a snooze. We all listen patiently at Shelby's description of the historic sites but Pepper gets right to the point.

"Where are we staying tonight?"

Shelby stops explaining about the Native American mounds found in the area. "Oh, yes, right. We'll be at the Davis Lake Recreation Area."

"Another cabin?" Pepper asks.

"You're actually in for a fun night," Shelby says. "We have something special planned."

TB grins at me and I can tell he's having the best day. But he and Pepper appear to be the only ones. Miss Georgia rolls her eyes, Carmine and Winnie say nothing, and Stephanie and Joe seem unfazed. Dwayne, if I'm gauging him correctly — it's quiet in the back — has dozed off beneath a World Series cap. Shelby's smile fades and she turns to the driver.

"Maybe we should head for the campground, Charlie."

"Campground?" Kelly asks. "Seriously?"

Shelby deflates even more and before I can come to her rescue Dwayne bounds up to the front of the van and puts an arm around her shoulders. "Whatever you have in store for us has to be awesome because everything has been superb so far."

His charm does the trick even if Carmine is now the one rolling his eyes.

We pull into the campground located on Davis Lake and find several Airstream trailers parked alongside. TB perks up instantly.

"We're staying in those?"

Shelby's slowing coming back. "Yes, we are," she says with a smile although I can tell she's guarded.

"Cool," says TB.

He moves to leave and I snag an elbow. "Don't forget. Charlie has to take you back to the battlefield parking lot to get the pickup."

We all get dropped off at our individual trailers but TB, much to his chagrin, stays on the van.

"I'll warm it up for you," I promise him.

I head into my personal Airstream, leaving the door open to catch the cool afternoon breeze, and feel as excited as TB for I've always wondered what was inside these Space Age motor homes. Mine appears to be the oldest of the group, with an inside that's been updated but sporting the original seventies style.

"Wait until TB gets a hold of this," I say to myself.

"Except that there are two twin beds."

I turn and find Dwayne standing on my threshold. The first thing that runs through my mind is he's blocking my escape, but I smile and exhale the breath I've been holding,

91

reminding myself that this man is a fellow travel writer, and despite what Carmine thinks, I doubt I'm in danger.

"Well, we'll figure something out," I say, but it comes out sketchy and I know Dwayne senses I'm nervous.

He leans an arm on the doorframe making his shirt stretch across his chest and I realize this man works out regularly. My breath catches once more.

"What do you want, Dwayne."

He relaxes, looks around my trailer. "Nothing, I just feel we might have gotten off on the wrong path."

"What makes you say that?"

He smiles and I relax a little. Nothing like having people appreciate good sarcasm.

"I wanted to make sure you still don't think I was inappropriate last night."

I'm way past that fear but now that he's mentioning it, that horrid dream comes back in a flash. That and another thought that's been roaming around my brain all day.

"So, if SCANCs touch the light, it can make them woozy?"

"Sometimes."

"And you knew this."

He starts to say something, but thinks better of it.

"On top of that knowledge, you gave me moonshine," I add.

He huffs, looks down at his feet and shakes his head. "I was just coming over here to make amends."

He moves to leave and he's halfway down the steps when I blurt out, "You have no idea what it feels like for a woman to not know what she did the night before. What happened to her."

He pauses, nodding his head, but I can't see his face. He doesn't turn, simply says, "Noted," and walks away. But before he hits the parking lot and I can close the door, he turns, those icy blue eyes turning serious.

"I tell you what, why not come watch me do it?"

I swallow. "Watch you cross someone over?"

"I'll show you how it's done right, what my reaction is, and you can make up your own mind if I'm legitimate or not."

I think back on Carmine's warnings, both in his hotel room and sitting next to me in the bathroom stall. There's history between those two and I'm not one to take a person's word over actual experience. And yet, there's something seriously off about this man. Maybe he really is a fallen angel, I think. Truth be told, that scenario only makes me want to see him in action.

"I'll think about it."

"Don't think too long," he answers. "There's only so many opportunities."

"Yeah, about that...," I start but Dwayne's heading off to his trailer.

"French Camp," he calls out without turning around, disappearing into an Airstream that's much more modern than mine.

I'm beat, as much from all the food and tourist sites as from the ebb and flow of fear with Dwayne's visit. I lock my trailer door and text TB to knock loudly when he returns, then lay down for a nap. Almost instantly, Cora's there to greet me.

I'm sitting in the wagon seat next to Reynald who's once again too close, his thigh rubbing up against mine as the wagon jerks and rolls through the dips in the highway. Each time his leg touches mine, my heart lurches. I turn my head to avoid his gaze, that creepy smile.

But wait, I think, it's not me. And yet, it is. I extend my arm and gaze at my hands, both covered in leather gloves with mother-of-pearl buttons. Before me, my lap lies covered in calico material all the way to my boots.

CHAPTER SEVEN

"What's with you?" Reynald says, and suddenly I'm on the outside looking in on the scene, watching the two of them approach an area where a wagon has stopped and several women are milling about.

"Let's stop here," Cora says.

"We'll stop later."

The fear builds in Cora's chest. I feel it as if I'm still inside her body. She's longing for company, anything to be away from this man who may have done her harm.

"It's getting dark. I want to stop here."

Reynald's resolve is firm. "Not a good place," and it's then that Cora hears fear in his voice.

She jumps off the wagon, even though the horses are still in motion, and heads for two women sitting by a campfire and another cleaning clothes along the side.

"Greetings, sister," the blond at the campfire says.

"Greetings," Cora answers.

Reynald calls from the road, stern and demanding, but Cora ignores him, twisting her hands in front of her. The blond rises and takes one of her hands.

"Are you in trouble, dear?"

Tears fall instantly and Cora can only nod.

"Are you afraid of that man?" the blond asks.

Reynald calls her name again, this time louder, and Cora nods.

"I'm not going to stay here," Reynald announces, then releases a string of obscenities.

The older woman lingering by the fire rises and turns to Reynald, who immediately quiets.

"We don't appreciate that kind of language," she yells back. "You're welcome to park the wagon nearby and leave us be but we will not tolerate ugliness. Now, move on and we'll see you in the morning."

Reynald grumbles beneath his breath and drives the wagon a few hundred yards up the Trace, then parks beside the stream. He's far enough away that the horses can be heard but too far to be seen.

"Thank you," Cora whispers.

"What's your name, dear?" the older woman asks.

"Cora Schumacher, ma'am."

"I'm Nancy," the blonde says. "And this is Melinda Jackson, who prefers to be called Mel. My sister, Teresa, is cleaning out back."

"Nice to meet y'all," Cora says.

"Do you want to tell us what's going on?" Mel asks.

Cora explains how she inherited property from her uncle who lived outside Natchez and how she hired his driver to bring her south to claim it.

"He was kind and polite at first," Cora says. "Then he took to drink and has become belligerent. I'm worried he may have done inappropriate things in my sleep and I fear he may do worse."

Nancy takes hold of Cora's hands and squeezes. "You're safe now, sister."

"But I have to find a new driver."

Mel gives Cora a motherly smile. "First of all, there aren't many out here to hire, and second, do you have money to hire someone?"

Cora looks down at her feet. "I sold everything I owned in Kentucky and gave it to Reynald for the journey."

The two women look at each other, Mel shaking her head and saying, "We don't have room."

"She can walk behind," Nancy says.

"I have my own wagon," Cora inserts. "My driver doesn't own any of it."

Teresa appears, wiping her wet hands on her apron. "Well, then, I guess we have a new member to our party."

Cora falls to the ground and begins to cry. "Thank you."

Mel sits beside her and holds her close. "Don't worry, sweetheart. The worst is over now."

Cora peers over Mel's shoulder. "What about him?"

"He won't hurt us," Nancy says confidently. "He's scared of us."

After all that Cora has witnessed in the past week — Reynald killing several animals, his drunken escapades at Buzzard Roost, and the fight he had with one of its visitors — she doubts he fears anything.

"This is Witch Dance," Nancy explains. "Men don't venture here."

Cora wipes the tears away with the edge of her sleeve. "Witch Dance?"

Teresa sits at the campfire and makes herself comfortable. "The Trace is dangerous, more so for women. In fact, it's doubtful you'll see women traveling here unless absolutely necessary."

"When they do," Nancy inserts, "they try to appear in ways to keep men at bay."

"How do they do that?" Cora asks.

Teresa smiles knowingly. "By acting like witches, of course."

Nancy sits on a log next to Cora, her legs folded beneath her for comfort as opposed to propriety. "Men have us at a disadvantage, Cora. They are stronger than we are and hold the power."

"But they are secretly afraid of us," Mel adds.

Cora straightens. It's obvious she's enjoying this new knowledge. "Why would they be afraid?"

"Because we're smarter," Nancy says with a broad smile. "And we're powerful in numbers."

Teresa laughs. "And there's that witch thing."

Mel leans in close. "They're afraid we will put a spell on them and they will lose their power, not be able to tame us. So, the more we let them believe that, the more power we have over them."

Nancy rises and walks past the edge of the campfire to a stretch of grass where a ring of dead foliage exists. "When women camp here, they pour a circle of salt around their camp. Men believe them to be witches and don't come near."

Ingenious, I feel Cora think, and know that for the first time that day she smiles.

"And," Nancy adds, "it kills the grass and leaves behind circles so men don't dare enter this area. They believe witches have danced here and caused the grass to die."

Cora laughs and it feels good to hear her spirits soar. The women talk among themselves and she relaxes, leans into the fire for warmth, and the three travelers spoon her out a plate of beans and fatback.

Then, like thunder roaring from out of the blue, Cora stops eating, turns and looks straight into my eyes.

"Do you hear that?" she asks.

There's knocking somewhere, as if evil is demanding entrance to this

peaceful commune.
"Vi," she shouts. "Wake up!"

I gasp and sit up in bed, shocked that a ghost arriving in a vision spoke to me. I've conversed with them while awake but dreams and visions had always been me watching from the side. I pull my fingers through my curls and try to make sense of it all, failing to contemplate that the loud banging was someone knocking at my door.

"Miss Valentine."

I instantly think of TB but in my fog, realize that it's Pepper's voice. I open the door to find my Goth friend on the outside steps, looking as startled as I feel.

"Help me," she says, tears falling down her cheeks.

I grab her shoulders and look her over but she seems unhurt. "What's the matter? What happened?"

She wipes the tears with her sleeve, much like Cora had done in my dream, but she's wearing black leather and it doesn't satisfy. I grab my purse and pull out tissue — I'm from South Louisiana, which is notorious for sinus issues and I wouldn't be caught dead without them — and Pepper blows her nose good and hard.

"What is it?" I ask and step back as if to invite her inside.

She shakes her head. "It's at my trailer."

We walk the lakeside road that connects the campsites until we reach the last trailer. Pepper hangs back, her arms tight about her, and those tears falling once more. I don't know what she wants me to see but I follow her line of sight and head to the side of the trailer where a picnic table and fire grill are located. As I turn the corner, I spot the horror. A fox has been killed and left at the trailer's back door, its entails pulled from its body and spread about, its eyes enlarged as if it died in immense pain.

I cover my mouth and fight back the urge to gag. I sense Pepper behind me and when I turn to comfort her once more, she's pointing to the side of her trailer. There, in the fox's blood, are the words, "Death to pagans."

97

"Holy shit."

I hear footsteps running and suddenly TB is there, glancing around the horrific scene. "What in the hell happened?"

Neither Pepper nor I can speak; we're still too traumatized by the scene. TB pulls out his cell phone and makes a call. I hear him talking to Shelby, his voice elevated in fear, but all I can think of is who would be this disturbed to do such an inhumane act.

I grab Pepper and move her to the other side of the trailer, hold her close to try to calm her shaking. I hear a trailer door open and close a couple hundred feet away, see Shelby rushing to our side.

"Brace yourself," I warn her as she moves to where TB is standing.

I hear Shelby's startled reaction and TB calling the cops, but I can't move. Pepper keeps shaking so I suggest we head back to my trailer and wait until the police arrive. We're not there five minutes when TB comes in and looks us over.

"When did this happen?" he asks Pepper.

"I'm not sure," she answers. "I came in and put my suitcase down, checked out the trailer. I'm pretty sure when I arrived I looked out the back window and nothing was there because I remember hoping to see some wildlife on the lake." The tears come back in a rush. "I never thought...."

I squeeze her again, and glance up at TB. I think of the conversation Pepper and I had at the Visitor's Center and Pepper showing off her gris-gris bag.

"Could someone have done this in the time it took you to get the pickup?" I ask.

TB sits down next to us on the seat. "If they had already found and killed that fox, maybe. But, how likely is that?"

Pepper groans and TB, bless his heart, rubs her shoulder. There's a knock on the door and it's Carmine with the rest of the group in tow, all except Dwayne.

"The police are here and they want to speak with Pepper," he says.

Pepper leaves our arms and heads to her trailer with Joe and Stephanie on either side. The rest of us settle into my trailer while I pull out some water bottles conveniently left in our fridge, by Shelby no doubt.

"Forget that," Winnie says. "She put a bottle of wine in the cabinet."

I pull out the cabernet and wine glasses and we all down the first glass almost instantly.

"Who do you think did such a despicable thing?" Winnie asks.

I pour them another round. "I can't help thinking someone did this who knows her. 'Death to Pagans?'"

"You think?" Carmine says inside his glass.

"You're not assuming Dwayne did this," I say.

Carmine places his glass on the table and sighs. "Oh, of course not. The man who nearly killed me, who took you out in the woods last night and messed with your head. He couldn't have possibly done this."

"He did what?" Winnie asks, looking at me.

"It's a long story," I answer, adding, "and will likely be much longer once Carmine decides to explain."

He downs his glass. "Not the time."

"And when is the time, Carmine?"

"What the hell is going on?" Winnie asks.

"Vi doesn't know how to take simple directions," Carmine says.

I shake my head in disbelief. "Yeah, I'm supposed to hear that this man is a 'fallen angel'" — I mimic parenthesis with my fingers — "and take your word for it."

I've gone too far and I know it. I trust Carmine, and even though the angel thing is a bit far-fetched to believe, if he knows it to be true I should accept it, or at least open my mind to the possibility. But I can't help myself. I'm a journalist for a reason. I mean, really. Fallen angel?

TB moves forward on the table and puts his hands up. "Okay, let's all take a breath and refocus."

We exhale, almost in unison, some of us gulping down

more wine. We're quiet for what seems like an eternity until TB says, "Fallen angel?"

It's the respite we needed and we don't know if it's the words he used or that he waited so long for my statement to process — I did say TB wasn't the quickest — but Carmine, Winnie and I begin to laugh and it's hard to stop.

"What?" TB asks, which makes us all laugh harder.

And that's how Sergeant William McGee finds us when he shows up for our statement.

"Am I interrupting something?" he asks when I open the door.

"No, officer." Oh lord, am I slurring my words? "We were trying to make sense of it all and got into a nervous laugh."

He doesn't say a word or react, walks into the trailer and looks around.

"Do you know who did this?" TB asks.

He picks up the empty wine bottle and shakes it. "If I did, I wouldn't be here."

We all look at each other, like puppies caught peeing on the floor. Finally, Winnie clears her throat and straightens. "Sergeant, we are old friends but as far as I know, none of us have been on a trip with Pepper Snipe before. She's quiet, she keeps to herself, she's been no trouble."

"She's dressed like a punk and there's writing on her trailer that seems to match," he answers. "How do you explain that?"

I look at Carmine, waiting for him to pipe in about Dwayne, but he remains silent.

"Have you spoken with the whole group?" I ask.

The cop flips open his book. "The Penningtons, Pepper, Shelby Constantine who's running the show and the driver, who showed up a few moments after he dropped off a man by the name of TB."

He looks puzzled so TB raises his hand. "That's me."

"Oh, and a man named Garrett."

This has us all ears. "Dwayne Garrett?" Carmine asks.

"Yes, he's been really helpful."

"Dwayne Garrett?" I ask again.

The cop's eyes narrow. "Why?"

"No reason," I begin, "except that…."

Now, how do I explain this, I think. We're all quiet while McGee looks from one to another.

"He's a little odd, that's all," Winnie finally pipes in.

"How so?" McGee asks and we're on the spot once more.

Before we're able to come up with an answer, there's a knock on the door and it's Shelby. McGee takes our names, — even though I'm sure Shelby gave them to him — asks where we were when the incident happened, excuses himself and leaves, and we can hear them discussing the incident outside.

Finally, Carmine finds his voice. "We can't explain this."

"Explain what?" TB asks.

I exhale the breath I've been holding. "Carmine thinks Dwayne's evil."

Carmine rises abruptly. "We need to figure out where Pepper's going to stay tonight. She can't sleep in that trailer."

Winnie also rises. "She can stay with me. They gave me a huge trailer for some reason. I have plenty of room."

They both head out the door and I hear them talking with Shelby and McGee, then the voices die out.

"What was that all about?" TB asks.

It's then that I remember Stinky, who we left in the pickup for a few hours while we visited Tupelo. "Where's Stinky?" I ask.

TB on the other hand, doesn't appear in the least bit concerned. "He's on the bed."

I glance toward the bedroom, the one with the twin beds, and there's my orange cat lounging on one like he owns the place.

"How? When?"

TB shrugs. "I let him in."

"You let him in?" I exclaim, but TB's halfway down the hall, pausing to pet Stinky's orange and yellow head. I can hear the purring from where I sit.

"That cat's not normal."

TB leans down and rubs his chin on top of Stinky's head and the cat eats it up. "Why be normal, hey Stink."

We decide to stay put until we hear from the others, unpacking a few things and noshing on the cheese and crackers Shelby left behind. The wine's done for but we find a couple of Mountain Dews and sip on those until Shelby arrives.

"Obviously, plans have changed," she says, looking as ragged as we feel. "But y'all have to eat. We had planned to head over to Witch Dance and do another barbecue...."

I shake my head. "Where?"

"It's a spot on the Trace not far from here where these unusual circles used to appear and people believed it was caused by witches dancing there."

Oh. My. God.

TB looks at me funny, sensing I'm having one of my ghost experiences. If he only knew.

"But we have to scrap that for tonight," Shelby says. "I'm taking orders for this lovely café in Tupelo. Charlie has offered to drive there and deliver our meals to us."

"That's sweet, but not necessary. We've been eating what you left us."

"I insist," Shelby says, and it's then I witness what this horrific act has done to her, a woman whose life is planned to the exact minute. "It's the least I can do."

TB and I check out the menu and order some wraps and salads. I have no appetite considering what I saw this afternoon but I want to appease Shelby and allow her to feel that she's taking good care of us. She moves to get more orders and we deflate at the kitchen table, TB with his laptop and me now petting Stinky since he's jumped into my lap.

"Briarwood Plantation," TB says, looking at something on his screen.

It makes me remember the dream and how Cora turned and called me to action. I can't help but wonder if it's my mind playing tricks on me, but how do I explain Witch

Dance?

I suddenly remember something, a piece of the puzzle that's important. "Her name's Cora Schumacher."

"The woman in the photo?"

"Yeah."

"Those two photos you found somewhere."

"Yeah."

He turns the laptop around and he's settled on a website by a Civil War scholar discussing early Mississippi planters and their secretive fight against slavery. Briarwood Plantation is mentioned. I lean forward and read the introduction.

"Briarwood was once the antebellum home of Wendell Meyers of Kentucky, who helped move slaves through the Underground Railroad."

There's no picture of this Wendell Meyers, nor Cora. "Maybe this was the uncle, the one Cora inherited the plantation from."

TB moves the laptop back so it's facing him. "I don't see anything about a Cora here."

Needless to say, I'm disappointed. But TB's fingers are busy typing up a storm and after a few minutes his eyes light up.

"There's a Cora Schumacher from Paducah, Kentucky, in the 1840 census."

"Where did you find that?"

He shows me the Ancestry.com website. "I'm working on my family genealogy."

"Since when?"

TB pulls the laptop back around, frowning. "Since a while. I don't tell you everything."

"Apparently."

"There's a Schumacher in Natchez around the same time. Born in Germany like Cora's parents so they could be related. His name's Walter."

I look at what he's pulled up and agree. "But where's Cora?"

He checks out the 1850 census and finds Cora's parents

deceased. She's living with Mary Bradford and her parents in a country town outside Paducah.

"That works," I tell him. "I saw this Mary in the first dream I had about Cora."

"Walter's still alive for the 1850 census," TB finds. "But I have a death certificate for him in 1858 in Natchez."

"That must be when Cora travels the Trace."

The food arrives and we dive in, amazed that we were hungrier than we thought. All the while, TB keeps ploughing through the Internet, trying to find pieces of our illusive Cora who danced with witches on the Natchez Trace.

We awaken the next morning to rain pelting the tin roof and the darkness of the morning mirrors my mood, for I've spent the night in and out of sleep with disturbing dreams. The fox visited, naturally, but alive until a shadowy figure arrived with an ax. I won't go into details with what happened next but I awoke with a start and had a devil of a time getting back to sleep. The next dream had Carmine hiding behind a tree in the woods watching the whole scenario, but when the shadowy figure arrived this time, Carmine burst forth in a stream of white light so intense, I failed to see what happened next. I heard the word *aggelos* and I woke up.

When I fell asleep once more, Cora sits by a pond's edge, a water source more accustomed to languishing softly but it's spring and the water reaches high up the banks. She's facing away from me, singing a hymn. Then a shadow appears between us, the outline of a person approaching her from behind. The person lifts something above Cora's head, ready to strike.

That revelation woke me as well. The rest of the night contained snippets of images: Dwayne in the woods pushing me toward the light, Pepper's black gris-gris bag, the laughter of the women at Witch Dance, and Cora turning to gaze into my eyes.

The last image stays with me all morning.

Shelby knocks on our door around seven and informs us

that plans have changed, that breakfast scheduled for the group shelter overlooking the lake has been scrapped due to the rain. She stands on our threshold, yellow raincoat dripping wet, appearing lost as to what to do next, no doubt rattled from the evening's horror.

"Charlie's gone," she also tells us. "He freaked out over what happened and left us.

"But don't worry," she quickly adds. "We have a new driver on his way."

She appears ready to cry, and before I can say something astute, TB pops in. "I have my pickup. Let me drive into town and get breakfast for everyone. One less thing to worry about."

The change in Shelby is startling and I want to kiss my husband for his kindness. Before either one of us can utter a word, TB grabs his keys and wallet and heads out the door.

"Should we ask everyone what they want?" she calls after him.

I touch her elbow. "Let him do it. Once we open that can, it'll take three times as long."

Shelby pulls the hoodie of her raincoat over her head. "I'll inform the others."

Before she heads off to the next trailer, she pauses at the door, looking at the floor of our aluminum home. "Who's that?"

I don't have to look to know she's wondering where the cat came from. Pets are not allowed on press trips, nor in many accommodations.

I decide to come clean. "Stinky's with us. TB couldn't leave him at home and he's so easy to travel with."

Shelby teeters on the threshold for a moment, but only a moment. "I didn't see anything," she says and heads off into the rain.

I look back at my cat. "You're safe for now."

Stinky winks at me and turns his attention to the bathing of a paw.

I take the opportunity to look through the Internet as TB

had done the night before. I open his laptop to quickly find the Briarwood site and instead spot a folder titled "LSU." I'm not one to infiltrate people's private computers but curiosity gets the better of me and I open the folder. There, inside, are documents such as "Astronomy worksheet," "English term paper," and "Library Science application." Opening the term paper document finds a work in progress, a piece comparing and contrasting *Cold Mountain* by Charles Frazier with *The Red Badge of Courage*. Everything is dated within the last few months. Also in the folder are tuition bills and student fees and an application for sporting events.

"I'll be damned," I say to Stinky. "Daddy's gone back to school."

I can't help it. I feel betrayed. Why didn't he tell me? Obviously, Carmine knows because he mentioned a test back at the New Orleans airport. So, why not let me know? I would be thrilled, so very proud that my husband, who dropped out of college when I became pregnant with Lillye and immediately went to work, would take night classes to finish his degree. In Baton Rouge, no less, a city seventy miles from New Orleans.

Stinky gives me a funny look and I feel like the cat's admonishing my feelings. In truth, I'd always assumed TB never liked college, saw it as a chance to party and attend free LSU sporting events. He never seemed upset about leaving to join his father in the family's construction business, happily took the job and moved into the rental house his parents gifted us after we married. Even after his parents retired and moved to Florida, leaving the company in the hands of TB's uncle, he never mentioned doing anything else.

Maybe I've been wrong, I think.

By the time TB returns, I've showered and dressed, packed both of our suitcases ready to head out. TB's soaked and is carrying two coffees, a bakery box, and a paper bag.

"The only thing left are two glazed donuts," he informs me, placing it all on the table. "And I think the coffee's cold."

"No worries. We have a microwave."

Underneath that LSU cap I expect to see a sly smile when he raises the white paper bag and tells me, "But I saved two chocolate croissants for us." Instead, TB looks tired.

I'm reminded of his secret, that he's been attending classes for months without telling me. He grabs the coffee to heat them up but steals a glance at his laptop, which I've left slightly ajar.

"Yes, I know," I want to say, but I leave it unspoken.

"I passed Shelby on the way," he says. "We leave in ten."

We eat our chocolate croissants, commenting how coffee outside of South Louisiana is more akin to brown water than java, then grab raincoats to head out. This time, TB doesn't call Stinky like a dog but pulls him underneath his raincoat.

"I'm going to ride in the van," I tell him.

He looks disappointed. "Why?"

"I need to hear what they say about the sites we're going to see."

Not really true since I bought a book on the Trace at the Visitor's Center. Something about seeing that LSU folder makes me desire distance. At least for a while.

"You want to be with Dwayne, is that it?"

My head pops up. "Why would you say that?"

"Never mind." He pulls his hood up over his head, grabs his suitcase with his free hand, and heads out.

I do the same, but join the rest at the van, still reeling over that last comment. When I climb the van's stairs I find Pepper seated next to Dwayne, the two deep in conversation and Pepper smiling as if nothing happened. In fact, she's thrilled to be the center of Mr. Blue Eye's attention.

I fall into the aisle behind Winnie and Carmine and sense they are as taken aback at the friendship as I am. I'm about to ask them what happened when Shelby bounds on board, her PR smile fading as soon as she spots the duo.

"It appears Dwayne spent the night with our tour guide," Winnie whispers. "And now he's on to someone else."

I glance over at Kelly and almost see the steam pouring out of her ears.

"Wow," is all I can manage.

Our first stop — you guessed it — is Witch Dance. Shelby relates the story of witches dancing here and how grass withered and died beneath their feet. I can't help but smile thinking of the real women who created those circles and why.

"Since the rain has stopped a bit, does anyone want to get out and see if they can find a witch circle?"

Pepper agrees, but no one else takes the bait. I decide to go with her. Once we get off the van, however, the ground is so wet that we immediately get our shoes covered in mud.

"Oh well," Pepper says, but I grab her elbow before we return.

"What did Dwayne say to you?"

She seems surprised at the question. "He's been amazing. So supportive. He helped the park people clean up the patio and bury that poor creature."

We jump back on and head toward the Bynum Mounds, a series of burial mounds dating back to between 100 B.C. and 100 A.D. that are located right off the Trace. This time, we all disembark for the sun now peaks through the clouds and there's a nice gravel path to the two mounds left for public viewing. Everyone takes turns shooting photos, then moves to a different area of the former village site for more shots and to read the historical markers. While TB's busy reading about the village, I head to Carmine's side by the larger mound.

"I see TB's gone back to college."

Carmine looks up from his note taking. "He told you?"

"No, you just did."

He closes his reporter notebook and sighs.

"Why did he tell you and not me?"

Carmine looks to make sure TB is out of ear shot. "Because his parents and his uncle think it's a waste of money, that a general ed degree won't matter since he already makes good money in construction."

"A college degree is priceless."

"I agree, but they don't." I'm still confused. "But why not tell me?"

Carmine sighs. "Because he believes you're smarter than him and he thinks that's the reason you don't want to stay married."

I glance over at my husband who's scratching his head gazing at a photo of archaeologists.

"Thank you for not arguing with me on that," Carmine adds.

I feel terrible but what he says is true. It's not that I feel superior but after Lillye died, TB retreated into zombieland, watching endless hours of sports and mindless TV shows. He'd never read much after college, but we had Lillye for conversation. After she died, before Katrina separated us, we had nothing to talk about.

Shelby calls us to the van and I decide to ride with TB to the next stop.

"I don't get the dates," he says on the way to the pickup. "It says Indians were here between one hundred something and one hundred something."

It's always been like this, TB not quite getting what most people understand. He's routinely been the brunt of jokes, and I've watched my share of people giggling at his inane remarks over the years. My heart feels heavy knowing that he considers me part of that group.

"It means they lived here one hundred years before Christ and one hundred years after his death," I explain. I see the wheels turning inside his head, so I add, "That's about two thousand years ago."

The lightbulb goes on and he smiles, but the guilt still presses hard on my heart. How could I have been so insensitive to one of the sweetest men on the planet?

"By the way," TB says opening my door to the pickup, "I called Briarwood."

I jump in and settle next to Stinky. "What did they say?"

He enters the car and starts it up. "Not much. They said Wendell Meyers had been married to a woman named Cora.

She was his first wife."

"That's great. Why did you say not much?"

TB backs up and begins following the van back to the Trace. "Because she died young. After going crazy and being put into an insane asylum."

The buzzing returns, hard and furious, and my head begins to pound.

"That's not right."

TB looks at me, recognizing the now familiar haze that arrives when I'm channeling a ghost. "Vi, are you okay?"

I shake my head. "No. Because Cora Schumacher wasn't crazy. She was murdered."

CHAPTER EIGHT

We're paused at the entrance to the Trace, waiting for a line of cyclists to pass. TB continues to study me hard.

"What aren't you telling *me*?"

I smirk. "What aren't *you* telling me?"

The van pulls out so TB's attention shifts. I wish I hadn't said anything because even though I'm hurt that TB chose not to tell me he has gone back to LSU, I'm guilt-ridden that I may be the cause.

"Never mind," I say beneath my breath.

We're silent for a long time and our cat, who's enjoying the hum and warmth of the floorboards, looks from one of us to the other. Finally, TB speaks.

"We should call around and find that plantation. Maybe the owner can shed some light on Cora."

"I'm seeing her clear as day so she had to have drowned," I say, and then a lightbulb goes off in my head. "Unless...."

"Unless what?"

Unless I'm evolving like Dwayne insists.

"Is it because he's so good looking? Or is it because he's gotten inside your head?"

This stops me cold. "Who?"

"Who indeed?"

I shake my head because I'm fairly confident Carmine's at the base of this conversation.

"If you're talking about Dwayne, neither is correct, but I don't see the harm in listening to his theories about SCANC evolution."

TB glares at me. "You were the woman yesterday morning who was scared she had been violated in some way."

"I wasn't violated."

"Vi!"

We're pulling into another historical site and once TB

111

parks and pulls up the brake he turns in his seat and looks me dead in the eyes.

"I know you want to see Lillye. So, do I." His voice catches and he looks away. "But you don't have to follow some lunatic who may do you harm."

TB rubs his eyes and grimaces and I haven't seen him this upset discussing Lillye in quite some time. Again, guilt assails me. I rarely speak of my daughter, especially to the one person who understands. It's been too painful. My mother, friends, and TB have insisted I seek professional help. I visited a doctor for a while, but nothing assuages my pain. TB, on the other hand, grieved and talked incessantly to everyone. Have I assumed, again incorrectly, that because he verbalizes his heartache he's worked through the grief?

"We all miss Lillye," he quietly says. "But retreating from the world and jumping into dumb and dangerous situations doesn't make the heartache go away."

"I know that, TB...."

"And Dwayne Garrett is a dumb and dangerous situation."

"Perhaps."

He stares at me now. "If you don't face this, Vi, you're going to move away from what your heart and soul was put here to do and end up in places where there's more pain."

Whoa, what? This is totally new coming from my husband. I touch his elbow and find his muscles taut as ropes.

"I won't do anything stupid," I finally say, "but I have to explore the possibilities."

TB shakes his head and turns off the engine. He looks at me, more serious than I've seen him in years. "She's right here, Vi. If you stopped chasing rainbows long enough, you'd know that."

And with that last comment, he jumps out the truck. I follow, realizing we have paused at a stretch of the old Trace, a ten-foot-wide original roadbed where evidence of wagon ruts and footsteps remain. The historical marker encourages visitors to notice the giant trees growing on either side.

"These trees are mute testimony to the endless struggle between man to alter and change, and nature to reclaim, restore, and heal," I read.

"Fat chance," I hear Dwayne say at my side. "Humans will always try to destroy God's creation unless we stop them first."

"Fellow environmentalist, I see."

Dwayne looks at me as if he's now acknowledged my existence and there's no love in that gaze. It's unnerving, but after a moment he shakes it off and that old charming smile returns.

The rest of the day is much the same. We visit a former trading post that housed passenger pigeons and a creek that served as the boundary between tribes. As we head south, Shelby informs us, we're entering what used to be Choctaw land.

TB and I rarely speak, and for the first time since we started this road trip, Pepper can't stop. According to Winnie, Dwayne poured his magnetic attention on the Goth Girl who "ate it up with a spoon."

"A spoon?" I ask.

"Shut up." Winnie pulls our her camera and shoots a lovely section of woods, then turns back. "I don't know what they have been talking about back there in the van but it was animated and full of feminine giggles."

"From Pepper?"

"Yeah, go figure. They act like...."

"Like what?"

Winnie shakes her head. "Like something happened the night before."

The thought that sweet, young Pepper would fall for that man makes me cringe. I lean into Winnie so no one can hear. "Do you believe Carmine and all that stuff about angels?"

Winnie gives up the photo and shrugs. "I don't know, Vi. Call it mother's intuition or plain ole mistrust of sweet-talking men but I trust Carmine over that devilish man any day."

"Devil?" I ask with a laugh.

But she's not laughing.

Further down the Trace we stop at the Jeff Busby picnic and primitive camping area, named for the U.S. Congressman from Mississippi who authorized the survey of the old road that four years later became part of the National Park System.

"Thanks to Thomas Jefferson Busby, we're here today," Shelby says proudly.

We're once again growing weary of the historical explanations so thankfully it's time for lunch. Shelby's new driver — a bearded man ironically named Jeff — leaves at the picnic spot and drives into Starkville to pick up platters of food from a popular spot called Remy's.

"You'll love this place," Shelby says to TB and me. "They have Cajun food."

I fight back the urge to groan. I adore Louisiana cuisine, but rarely eat it once I cross the Louisiana state border. Mississippi and other parts of the South sometimes do gumbo well but for the most part, the attempt at Creole and Cajun cuisine lacks authenticity. Besides, I don't want to eat my food somewhere else. I want native dishes.

But Remy's stands up to my discernable palate. We enjoy roast beef sandwiches the restaurant calls poboys like in New Orleans, Cuban paninis, platters of red beans and rice, jambalaya and sides. I'm really digging the potato salad, cole slaw, and curly fries.

"Back to being a vegetarian?"

Dwayne slips in next to me with his ham sandwich.

"I eat everything, but I try to limit the meat."

"Health reasons or humane reasons?"

I have a mouthful of pasta salad but I utter, "Both."

"Then you must have been really disturbed by what happened last night."

My fork is halfway to my mouth when the image of that fox returns. I place the fork down and push my plate away.

"Sorry, didn't mean to upset your lunch."

Dwayne continues eating and I decide to pick his brain. "What did you mean about French Camp? We're staying there tonight."

He takes a drink from his coffee and I sense a smile behind the rim. "Ready for another lesson, SCANC girl?"

"Don't call me that." I look around to see if anyone has heard but the others are either too far away or deep in conversation.

Dwayne laughs. "You're a closet SCANC?"

I send him the evil eye and he raises a palm. "I won't say a word."

"And just what is *your* specialty, Dwayne?"

He smiles. "Meet me tonight and I'll show you."

I'm about to inquire more but he's wiping his mouth with his napkin and rising. "Time for a hike," he says. "And God knows, I need to walk off this meal."

Shelby waltzes by with a plate full of cookies, cupcakes, and slices of red velvet cake. I was planning on indulging, but Dwayne's last comment makes me shoo her away. Besides, he's heading toward the Little Mountain Trail, Pepper and Joe in tow, so I follow. When Kelly realizes her male squeeze has two women accompanying him, she decides to go as well.

The rain disappeared mid-morning and what followed is next to perfection. There's enough chill in the air to keep us comfortable on our trek through a hardwood forest that's been releasing its leaves for weeks, leaving us a soft path to tread. I breathe in the peacefulness of the woods, glad for the quiet of nature, and the thoughts plaguing me these past two days. I look around but it's only we five and wonder where TB has gone.

Joe and Dwayne discuss photography while Pepper and Kelly follow close behind, each one trying to slip next to Dwayne. I half expect them to start fighting over who will be the one to carry his coattails. I'm glad, for hanging back by myself allows me to savor the smells of the rich earth and decaying leaves, touch the sandstone and shale that runs in patches by the trail.

It's a good walk to the highest point on the parkway, peaking at six hundred feet at the overlook. There's an exhibit shelter there, explaining much of what we've been enjoying. We pause to savor the view as a chilly breeze blows, causing us all to pull whatever jackets or sweaters we're wearing tight across our chests.

It's there the two women begin fighting.

It started with Pepper mentioning that leather isn't as warm as other materials and Dwayne wrapping an arm about her shoulders. Kelly bristled, crossing her arms defiantly about her, and mentioning something beneath her breath.

"What did you say?" Dwayne asks. He's not pleased.

Kelly doesn't go down easily, however. "I said, 'Is she next?'"

The two begin arguing so Joe starts backing up, thinking, no doubt, to escape this *ménage a trois*. Pepper tries to make peace but Kelly won't have any of it, turns on her as well as Dwayne.

At this point, the buzzing begins. The signal that I'm tapping into something supernatural usually appears soft, like a faraway alarm or a hive of bees. Today, it's louder, sounded more like the airport alarms when you walk through forgetting you're wearing a metal belt buckle.

The sound makes me wince and my head pound. I find a boulder and sit down, absorbing deep breaths to relieve the pressure building there. I look out at the overlook and wonder what the hell I'm supposed to be receiving from what Carmine calls the Etherworld.

And then, oh so brief and faint as if in a fog, I imagine I hear Lillye's voice.

One word.

"Mom."

"Lillye?" I breathe.

Then everything goes black.

There's a hand on my shoulder, and the autumn breeze causes the wide hoop skirt to sway, bouncing against my ankles. Since heading south with the Witch Dance clan, I've loosened the aggravating corset but it still pinches my side from walking incessantly. Nancy squeezes my left shoulder and Mel appears on the other side. I look at one and then the other, grateful they're here as I enter my new home.

The house stands neglected, a few shutters askew, the porch beams in need of paint, and the front yard overgrown with chickens and a goat milling about. But, for the most part, Briarwood's in good shape. We walk through the front door, checking out the parlor with its few furnishings, the sparse dining area, and then the kitchen, the most important room of the estate, at least to a woman. I'm thrilled to have a home of my own, a source for my independence, even if there's hardly a chair to sit on.

There's wood in the stove and coffee brewing, which takes us aback.

"Someone's been here or squatting," Nancy says.

We head to the back porch and look around. It's then we spot several slave cabins and my heart sinks.

"Slaves?"

Young Negro boys play in the mud around the cabins, some chasing each other with sticks. An older Negro woman sits on the porch of one cabin, mending a shirt but eyeing us suspiciously. In the distant fields, I see people working.

I swallow hard, my abolitionist mind trying to make sense of it all. Uncle Walter never mentioned slaves, always insisted the practice was an abomination to God.

"I think you have bigger things to worry about," Teresa says.

I turn and see writing on the back porch wall, words written in what appears to be blood. On the porch floor is a headless chicken.

The words read, "Deth to Wiches."

I awake with a start, TB looking down at me.

"Vi? Are you all right?"

I sit up, wondering what happened. Had I dozed off or fainted?

I rub my forehead which is still pounding. "I was Cora."

"What?" TB glances over my shoulder as if he's needed elsewhere. It's then that I hear the commotion in the background.

"What happened?"

TB looks me over once more to make sure I'm okay.

"Kelly's been hurt. If you're fine...."

I wave him off. "Yes, go. I'm right behind you."

I get up slowly to not upset the throbbing pain in my temple. The buzzing has ceased and the pain's slowly subsiding, but the dream's still fresh in my mind. I was Cora, in every sense of the word. I felt her, saw through her eyes, witnessed her inheritance for the first time, including the slave cabins and that horrible message in blood.

Once I'm feeling myself, I head toward the overlook shelter where our group has gathered. The van pulls up and Shelby bolts from inside, followed by an ambulance from Starkville. I head to the gathering as fast as my pounding head will take me and grab Winnie's sleeve.

"What happened?"

"It's about time you showed up," Dwayne announces loudly and everyone turns to look at me.

I glance around the circle at everyone's questioning eyes until finally settling on Kelly, who's lying on the ground with Dwayne's jacket draped over one leg. She's not making a sound, her hand covering her eyes. TB's bent down by her head, talking softly to her, and Carmine's grasping her wrist on the other side, looking as if he's taking her pulse.

"What happened?" I repeat to Winnie.

"She fell off the side of the overlook, tumbled down that rocky cliff over there and it looks like she broke her leg."

The paramedics push everyone aside and take both TB and Carmine's places, checking Kelly's vitals and removing the jacket to reveal what is most certainly a broken leg. The shin bone hasn't punctured the skin — thank goodness — but it's close and the bump the break has produced makes my lunch want to return. Poor Kelly groans in pain when they examine her leg and I look away.

"Where were you?" Dwayne insists, causing everyone to glance at me once more.

"I was...." I point to the side of the shelter where I sat down in the grass but his tone and the resulting accusing looks has unnerved me. "Why? What has any of this to do with me?"

"You've been gone a while," Pepper says.

"So?"

I can't explain the sudden appearance of ghosts or why I was sleeping in the grass, but why would any of that matter to poor Kelly's broken leg? I look at Winnie for support.

"I just got here," she says with a shrug.

I glance at Joe, but he's avoiding my eyes. Stephanie is watching me carefully and Dwayne stares, arms crossed.

"I don't understand," I say. "What does Kelly's falling have to do with me."

"What indeed?" Dwayne asks and I see TB moving forward with the same expression he had the morning before at Tishomingo State Park. Carmine holds him back, but he's as upset with Dwayne as my husband.

"What the hell are you saying?" TB practically yells.

Dwayne steps so close to my face I almost gag on that aftershave. "I'm not inferring anything. Miss Valentine disappeared and Kelly suddenly fell over the cliff. I find that coincidence disturbing."

I back up and hit the pole of the shelter, suddenly feeling like the witches of Salem three centuries before.

"What is going on here?" I ask in desperation.

"What happened, my dear," Stephanie says quietly, "is that Kelly claims she was pushed."

I'm aghast, first that someone would push Miss Georgia over the edge of Mississippi's Little Mountain, which might have done more damage to the prima donna than a broken leg, and second, that they would assume it was me. Even if I don't like the woman.

"Why on earth would you think I did that?"

Dwayne steps forward once more, now right in my face.

"Because, Viola," he says, drawing my name out in three syllables. "She said it was a woman of your height, with curly brown hair!"

I'm sitting at the dining table of the Burford Cabin of the

French Camp Academy Bed and Breakfast. Normally I would be loving this 1800s former dog trot home that the owners moved here and enhanced, loving those hand-hewn logs making up the walls, or enjoying the fall weather on the cabin's porch, but Sergeant McGee has me hostage. I stare at the chocolate-covered strawberries and muscadine juice the owners have left for us, but I don't dare touch a bite.

"May I offer you something, Sergeant?" I ask him. "They do this for us when we're on these press trips. Leave out goodies so we never go hungry."

If I wasn't so nervous I'd laugh, because it's the truth. Tourism folks feed you until you pop. I usually go home and diet for a month.

"I'm fine, Miss Valentine," McGee says. "Or is it Boudreaux?"

"Valentine," TB and I say in unison. I never gave up my name when I married Thibaut Boudreaux because my mother's one of the foremost Shakespearean professors in the country — she'll say the world — and I have a twin named Sebastian, like the characters in Shakespeare's play, *Twelfth Night*. Viola Valentine flows off the tongue much sweeter than Viola Boudreaux, especially for a writer.

TB insisted he didn't mind but for all I know he may harbor that resentment as well. I glance at my husband sitting backwards in his chair, wishing we had had a moment alone so I could have explained where I'd been. At Briarwood in the 1800s.

"Where were you today, Miss Valentine?" McGee asks.

TB shifts in his seat so I correct him, "It's Mrs. Valentine."

"Okay, where were you?"

I explain how we hiked up the trail to the overlook, me trailing behind the rest.

"Why weren't you with the others?"

Because I didn't want to be near those two women fighting for Dwayne's attention.

Instead, I say, "Because it was nice and peaceful and the

others were deep in conversation. I live in a city surrounded by swamps. I wanted to enjoy the woods."

He writes something in his notebook. "And when you reached the overlook?"

I exhale. Loudly. "For the life of me I can't imagine how Kelly thinks I pushed her off a cliff."

Now, it's McGee's turn to exhale. "Just answer the question please."

How do I answer this, I wonder? Tell him I'm a medium and I needed to visit a woman by taking over her body?

"I get these headaches," I start. "They come out of nowhere."

"Like migraines?"

"Sort of." I grab the stem of the wine glass in front of me and turn it round and around. "More like sinus pressure. Maybe from the altitude?"

"Six hundred feet?" McGee looks at me funny.

I shrug. "Where I come from, New Orleans is below sea level."

He contemplates this and I think I see some form of emotion appear on that face but I'm likely imagining it.

"Then what happened?"

"I sat down," I tell him. "I laid down on the grass and closed my eyes, hoping that would help."

He writes this down. "For how long?"

Ghost visions sometimes seem like minutes but when I wake up hours have passed. It goes the other way too, dreams that never seem to end and I've only been out for minutes.

"I don't know," I tell him. "I must have fallen asleep."

He looks at me sternly and I know what he's thinking, how convenient.

"I wasn't anywhere near her," I insist.

McGee turns to TB and asks about his whereabouts, where he found me, what I was doing. TB explained how he had hung back at the picnic area, helping Shelby clean up but then felt a need to follow our group up the path.

"Felt a need?" McGee asks.

121

"You know, felt like going on a hike. After that big lunch and all."

There's something strange about TB's statement; he's not telling the truth. TB's one of those innocent souls who loves unconditionally and that means he has no talent to lie. None. McGee, thankfully, doesn't notice.

"When I got to the overlook," TB continues, "Kelly was on the ground with the broken leg, Joe said she had fallen over the side, and I didn't see Vi. When I walked around the side of that information building, Vi was on the grass sleeping."

"And that's all you have to report?" He looks at us both.

We glance at each other, wondering what else could be said.

"Yes," I answer.

"And yesterday?"

"Yesterday?"

"Were you sleeping, too, when that animal was killed?"

I sigh and rub my eyes, reminded that I was visiting Cora before Pepper came knocking at my door. "Yes, I was napping then, too."

"You take a lot of naps, Mrs. Valentine."

I'm getting tired of this inquisition, and my aggravation leaks out. "I told you, I've been having these headaches."

"What do you think she did?" TB asks. "Got off the van, ran into the woods, found a fox, killed it, dismembered it, and put blood on the walls of Pepper's cabin, all before I returned with the truck?"

McGee smiles grimly and closes his notebook. "They're both strange circumstances."

"I'll say," I say. Wow, I sound like Foghorn Leghorn. I demand myself to focus and get out of the Saturday cartoons.

"What did the others say?" TB asks. "Surely, they were there when Kelly fell."

"Or was pushed," I add, then wished I hadn't.

McGee finally relaxes, leans back in his chair, and much to our surprise starts scratching Stinky behind an ear. Naturally, our cat eats this up and McGee softens. "Mr. Garrett had a lot to say about the pushing."

TB and I exchange looks and McGee doesn't miss anything. "What?"

Now, how do I explain this?

"What?" McGee demands.

I exhale. "One of the people on our trip, Carmine Kelsey, knows Dwayne from high school, said he and some other jocks beat him mercilessly when he was about seventeen. He almost died." It's none of McGee's business but it might help the case, so I add, "Carmine's gay."

"Carmine doesn't like the guy, for good reason," TB adds. "Neither do I."

No one could deny my husband's truthfulness now.

"And you, Mrs. Valentine? Do you like this man?"

TB studies me hard, those normally sweet eyes staring at me accusingly. I send him a questioning glance because I can't understand why he's looking at me like that.

"No," I answer. "I don't trust him."

McGee drops his chair back on the floor and Stinky flees. "Anything else?"

"Yes," and both men look my way. "Kelly, Pepper, and Dwayne got into an argument, before I left for the shelter. Joe Pennington was there. He might be able to tell you more."

"You didn't see this altercation I assume," McGee asks with a sly smile.

"In the beginning. Dwayne showed Pepper attention and Kelly was furious. The first night, Dwayne was with Kelly. According to Pepper this morning, he was with her last night."

TB appears confused and sends me a questioning look. I send one back. His mind is traveling places I'm not following.

McGee stands, slips the notebook in his back pocket. "I'll look into it. But if Mr. Garrett's telling the truth, about you conveniently being absent when bad things keep happening, you can expect to see me again."

I'm appalled and am about to say as much, but McGee continues. "If he's lying, then I would watch your back."

His comment makes me change direction. "Why?"

"Because he's been saying lots of things about you, Mrs. Valentine. And none of them good."

CHAPTER NINE

After McGee leaves the cabin and we watch him head to the main house, where four members of our group are located, we breathe easier.

"Why did you lie?" TB finally asks.

"Why did you?" I retort, although I quickly add, "I wasn't lying."

He exhibits that same serious expression he gave McGee. "What are you talking about?"

"'I felt the need to go on a hike?'"

TB shakes his head and heads to the table where he pours himself a drink of the muscadine. "You're not the only one with intuition."

This stops me cold, never considered TB to come running because he felt the need, but I'm starting to think I don't know my husband very well.

"Why do you think I was lying?" I ask.

TB takes a sip of the juice and grimaces.

"It's not wine," I say. "This is run by a Christian academy."

TB swallows the juice anyway, then takes a deep breath and exhales, his shoulders dropping a good inch on the way out. "I saw Dwayne coming back from your trailer when I was delivering donuts."

Suddenly, I'm so very tired. I slip into the chair and pour my own glass of way-too-sweet grape nectar. "Dwayne Garrett's getting on my last nerve."

TB sits down across from me. "What was he doing there?"

I shake my head, anything to get the craziness of the past few days to make sense. "TB, when you were gone, I showered, changed, and packed both our bags. They were sitting at the front door of the trailer when you came back with the donuts. I cleaned the dishes from the night before, dried them, and put them away, in case you didn't notice. When did you think I had time to make love with Dwayne Garrett?"

TB drops his head in thought. "He was coming out of our trailer. Passed me on the way with a wink and said I had some amazing wife in there."

Now, I'm scared. Maybe Carmine's right, that this man has supernatural powers that I can't begin to understand. Maybe he really is Lucifer in travel writer clothes.

"He wasn't there, TB. No one was in that trailer but me until you arrived. No one."

We sit in silence for what seems like forever, TB studying me from behind his glass, me grinding my teeth thinking about what my husband thought he saw and the man who planted that brain seed. When we hear a door open and close and see McGee heading to his car through the front cabin window, it spurs me to action.

"Time for Carmine to do some explaining," I announce, and pull my jacket from the back of the chair.

TB starts to follow but I put an end to that immediately. "I'm doing this alone," I say sternly.

"Why?"

"Why?" I feel the heat rising in my chest. "Because you thought I cheated on you this morning. And I'm not sure I can forgive you for that."

With that final statement, I slam the door in my wake and head to the Carriage House. I find Jeff, our driver, talking up a storm while Carmine is pulling on his own jacket, something tweed with leather on the elbows that looks like it came out of Harrods of London. Knowing Carmine, that's exactly where it came from.

"Where are you going?" I ask Carmine.

"Where do you think?"

I look over at Jeff who's endlessly discussing "bagging a deer" in the wilds of Mississippi and doesn't understand why Charlie freaked out like he did.

"I mean, if you're from these parts, you've bound to see a

dead animal once in a while," Jeff says, adding with a laugh, "and hell, there's enough road kill to thicken up your skin."

I immediately surmise he's one of those people who turn on like there's a button you push and keep talking no matter who's listening, caring or talking back. I long to describe what this particular dead animal looked like but I do what I usually do in these circumstances, politely listen, smile, then find a way to escape. Carmine's heading out the door so I follow and say something insipid like, "That's so interesting, gotta go."

"Wow, he's a talker," I say once we clear the accommodations. "I hope he doesn't do that all the way down the Trace."

Like he did at the SCANC convention, Carmine's trotting off to the parking lot like a sprint pony and suddenly reins in at my last comment. I'm an inch away of slamming into that tweed.

"What do you want, Vi?"

Why is the world suddenly aggravated with me? "What did I do to you?"

Carmine crosses his arms across his jacket, which looks pretty spiffy on him, I might add. I'm longing to touch it and ask where he acquired this beauty; it looks that good.

"I'm heading to the Starkville police station, thanks to you."

My attention's back. "What? Why?"

"Sergeant McGee has to get back and he needs my statement."

I look over Carmine's Tallyho shoulder and McGee's leaning against his patrol car, cell phone in hand, eyeing me suspiciously.

"I might have mentioned to the good sergeant that Dwayne beat you up in high school."

"Yeah," Carmine says, eyes narrowed. He's not pleased. "There's that."

He turns to go but I catch that leathered elbow. "Why's that a big secret?"

He's got that look that TB had earlier, like he's holding something back. "It's my secret, Vi. My secret to tell."

Did I mention how tired I am? Exhausted from the visions, Dwayne's weirdness and deceit, being accused of everything from sleeping with the devil to pushing a prima donna off a cliff. Most of all, I'm weary of my good friend slammed shut like a clam.

I release my fingers on his tweed. "Fine. Go. I'm done with you and all your secrets, all your warnings of evil but 'Let's not discuss it now, Vi.' All your talk of angels but you can't give me rational reasons why I should avoid Dwayne except some crazy idea about souls. And now, when I'm being accused of attempted murder, you can't be bothered? Screw you, Carmine."

It's my turn to cross my arms about my chest but Carmine's face doesn't change emotions. At all. He stares at me for a moment, once again warns me to "Stay away from Dwayne," and then walks to McGee and his waiting patrol car. I stand there, in the middle of the parking lot surrounded by woods and buildings from the 1800s, a wonderful scent of wood burning filling the air, all of which would normally thrill me to no end, but I feel as frustrated as the day I first starting seeing my watery ghosts. And now that the one person who can mentor me in my "gift" has been hauled off to jail — well, not jail exactly — I don't know where to turn.

I decide to visit the Etherworld.

I stomp back in my cabin and TB's sitting at the table drinking that overly sweet grape juice. I think to warn him that he might go into a diabetic coma but I'm too mad to care.

"Vi," he calls out but I ignore him, grab my purse, and bound up the stairs to the cabin's loft and lay down on one of the twin beds.

"Vi, let's talk," is the last thing I hear as I pull out Cora's photos and close my eyes. That sad look she exhibits blurs as the vision comes through, much like the lights fading in a movie theater as the screen comes alive with the picture.

I'm outside the action this time, an observer. We're at Briarwood and the witch clan is still hanging around. Everyone is seated in the parlor while an African American kitchen maid serves them coffee and dollar biscuits with muscadine jam. Cora takes a sip of her coffee and grimaces.

"Is this normal?" Cora asks Nancy. "The coffee's mighty strong."

Nancy laughs. "It has chicory in it, pretty popular around these parts. It's an acquired taste."

The maid turns her attention to Cora. "May I get you something else, ma'am?"

Cora's uncomfortable with someone pampering her, not something she's used to having lived on the kindness of others. She can't even look this maid in the eye.

"No, thank you, Menasha," she says. "I don't want to bother."

"It's no bother," Menasha assures her, but when Cora fails to answer, Menasha shakes her head and heads off to the kitchen.

Nancy takes Cora's hand. "Honey, she's not your maid as you like to call her, she's your property, whether you like it or not. She's here to serve you."

"Tell her what you want," Mel adds. "There's no need for thank you's."

Cora shakes her head. "I was brought up to be polite and polite I will be."

"I agree with Cora," Teresa says while enjoying a biscuit. "No reason to be rude."

"That's all fine and dandy, honey, but you do have to act the boss," Nancy adds. "You're not doing them any favors by acting as meek as a mouse."

Cora shifts in her seat and it's clear bossing people around was not what she had in mind when she dreamed of financial independence. I also sense that Menasha and the other slaves scare her. I wonder if they are the first black people — or Negroes as everyone keeps saying — she has met.

"When we leave," Nancy adds, "you will have to run this place."

Poor Cora. Her eyes enlarge and she starts to shake. "Can't y'all stay longer? Do you have to move on to New Orleans?"

"Yes, honey," Mel says. *"Our family and friends are expecting us."*

Cora takes a deep breath and looks away, holding back tears. Nancy takes her hand and squeezes. *"We'll stay until the overseer arrives from town. After that, you will have to decide whether you want to stay here and make a go of things or sell the property."*

Tears course down Cora's cheeks and she doesn't bother wiping them away. *"I'll sell. I can't abide owning people. Although I don't know how and I dread having to travel the Trace back to Kentucky."*

The three women exchange glances.

"You'll have to wait until spring, dear," Mel finally says. *"With winter coming, it's best to stay put."*

More tears fall, because waiting months means bossing these people around in the meantime.

"My best friend is marrying next month," Cora whispers. *"I should have stayed in Kentucky."*

Menasha returns to the parlor, this time bringing Cora a cup of tea.

"Why thank you, Menasha," Teresa says, sending Cora a wink. *"While you're here, may we ask for your input."*

Menasha is taken aback; I doubt she has ever been part of a conversation in this male-dominated household, although as kitchen slave she likely runs the place.

"Yes, ma'am," she says.

"Your mistress, Miss Cora Schumacher, has never run a household," Teresa explains. *"She was orphaned young and went to live with friends of the family, who took care of her."*

"Yes, ma'am," Menasha says although she doesn't look at Cora.

"Would you please guide her in her role as mistress of this house? I'm afraid Miss Cora's a little overwhelmed. She wasn't expecting slaves."

Menasha finally looks at Cora, but there's no warmth in her stare. It's all matter of fact. *"Yes, ma'am."*

It's not the answer anyone was expecting, so a silence falls about the group.

"Thanks, Menasha," Nancy finally says. *"That'll be all."*

When Menasha is out of earshot, Mel shakes her head. *"Not sure what help she'll be able to offer, so stand your ground and tell her what you want."*

They begin discussing travel arrangements to New Orleans when sounds of a horse entering the front yard can be heard. Teresa and Nancy head to the window.

"That must be our overseer," Mel says, also standing, "although he looks a bit worse for wear."

Cora remains seated, twisting the calico fabric of her skirt into knots. I sense that Cora was hoping to find a small plot of land to farm, something she would manage herself, maybe hire a farm hand or two when needed. She would cook her own meals, decide whether coffee had chicory added or not.

Now, this burly man is waltzing through the front of her home like he owns it and she must put him in his place to establish order. How many times have women been forced to act like someone they're not only to prove themselves to men?

"What's this?" the giant of a man asks.

The witch trio are about to introduce themselves when, to their amazement, Cora stands. She's unsteady on her feet but she's determined.

"I'm Cora Schumacher, your new boss."

The overseer pauses in his manliness for a minute, then rubs a beard as red as his thick curly hair and takes her in from head to toe. "Pleasure."

Cora's still not comfortable, especially since this man is taking liberties with his gaze, but she knows her duty so she straightens her back and introduces the trio. "These are my friends and traveling companions."

"I'm Tyson McDaniels," the man says, and it's then I recognize a slight Scottish accent. "I run the place."

"For now," Nancy says with a smile.

This disarms McDaniels and I want to cheer.

"What the hell does that mean?"

He begins a long discourse of how Walter Schumacher hired him and he's been running things for the past two years. How Walter assured him that no matter who inherited Briarwood Plantation, he would always be the boss.

"Did my uncle also allow you to freely use the main house?" Cora asks. "I hardly think it's appropriate for an overseer to simply walk

through the front door without a knock or introduction."

"In this house, it was appropriate." He's starting to get defensive, which feeds Cora's confidence, what little she's pulling from. But he adds snidely, *"Not like there were women about to fuss about etiquette."*

"And was it also appropriate for you to steal from this house?" Nancy asks, her eyes narrowed and her arms crossed about her.

"Who the hell are you?"

"I've already informed you, these are my friends," Cora inserts. *"And do not use that kind of language in front of us, sir."*

McDaniels straightens so that he towers over petite Cora, but I must give the girl credit for she stares right back.

"We found my uncle's furniture in your house, Sir," she tells him, nodding to the pieces in the parlor that weren't there before. *"In addition, we found my uncle's ledgers and personal items. I was also told by my uncle's lawyer of an inheritance belonging in the house, but no money was found here. However, close to one hundred dollars was found...."*

"You know nothing of running a plantation." McDaniels is shouting now, losing control. I would conclude that Cora owns the winning hand but I fear this oversized man may become violent. *"That money was needed to run things, needed to purchase items for the place. That's where I've been all this time, Missy, but I don't need to be explaining that to you."*

"I think you do," Mel says, *"because stealing is a crime punishable by law."*

"And you smell of whiskey, Sir," Nancy says. *"So, I doubt Cora's money was well spent."*

This quiets McDaniels down a bit. He looks at Cora and his tone softens, but he's still in fighting mode. *"Look, I know you're new here, so there's lots to be explained. We'll get to that in due time. But I run things and I run things good and no one stealed nothing."*

At this point, Cora's scared this enormous man will never leave, even if she does fire him. She glances at the other women as if to say, *"What do I do now?"* They don't appear to know either.

"You stole that money and you knows it."

Everyone turns to the parlor door to find Menasha standing there, coffee pot in hand.

"Stay out of this, Menasha," he retorts.

"I ain't staying out of anything. I seen you taking this furniture. I seen you stealing that money from Mr. Walter's frock coat. I wouldn't put it past you to have killed that kind ole man trying to find the rest."

McDaniels raises a hand to strike Menasha, who amazingly enough doesn't move, head held high.

"Don't you dare touch her," Cora shouts.

"You need to leave," Mel says, moving to Menasha's side, her voice quivering with fear. *"Now."*

"You're fired," Cora adds, although her courage has faded and those shivers have returned.

McDaniels wants to fight back, but he knows he's surrounded. He looks from one woman to another but can't find words to defend himself or restore his dominance. Finally, he smirks and grabs his hat.

"To hell with this," he says and moves toward the back door.

"You leave with what you have on right now," Nancy says. *"The overseer's house is locked."*

"I have belongings in there," McDaniels shouts, his voice found.

"Not anymore," Cora says softly. *"Now, git."*

McDaniels lunges forward toward Cora and she steps back. I worry he's about to be physical but he's just trying to scare her.

"You haven't heard the last of me," McDaniels says.

Those tears return and pour down poor Cora's face but she's not backing down. *"The sheriff knows of this so if I were you I would leave this area."*

I'm not sure Cora tells the truth or if McDaniels buys her story. One appears too frail in the telling and the other too suspicious. But McDaniels places his hat on his head, looks from one woman to the other, then leaves out the front door.

"And don't you take that horse neither," Menasha shouts at him. *"That ain't yours to take."*

Teresa hauls out the front door and down the steps to grab the reins of the horse but McDaniels doesn't try to steal the chestnut pony. His long legs make good time across the front of the property, heading out the road that leads to the Natchez Trace. *"You haven't heard the last of me,"* he shouts at them, then turns a corner and disappears from view.

The women release a collective exhalation, smiling at each other that for once they conquered the wills of a man. Menasha appears uneasy in *their company, but Cora touches her shoulder and offers a thanks.*

"Yes ma'am," is all Menasha says, then hurries off to the kitchen. Cora appears disappointed for I sense she wants to be this woman's friend.

"She'll come around," Teresa says. "She did come through for us today. That's encouraging."

Nancy puts an arm about Cora's shoulder and one about Teresa. Mel joins the semi-circle, taking Cora's hand.

"We can move mountains when we women stick together," Nancy says.

My heart soars watching these women. I can almost feel the love emanating through their psyches. Then, a voice asks, "Do you get that, Vi?"

I'm suddenly standing right behind this group, although they aren't acknowledging my existence. That voice comes again.

"Do you understand, Vi?"

"What?" I ask.

"Vi!"

It's TB shoving me awake.

"Shelby came by, said dinner's in ten. I didn't know if you want to shower or anything."

I sit up, knowing I've been sleeping for there's a dollop of spit on the side of my mouth. I wipe it off with my hand, trying to pull out of the haze. The room's dark so I know the sun's gone down.

"You okay?"

Am I? I feel lost. Even though I must have been napping for at least an hour, these visions of ghosts demanding entrance into my sleep interferes with my ability to rest. Many times, when I've dealt with these mysteries I've gone days without a good night's sleep because the ghost tales invade my dreams until I find them peace. Am I closer to solving Cora's murder? With Reynald and McDaniels in the picture, I have at least two prime subjects. I wouldn't recuse Menasha either. Something about that passive-aggressive countenance makes me suspicious.

"Did you see Cora again?"

I nod, recalling that last scene, but I don't feel like discussing it. I'm still pissed at him. I look up and my husband's showered and changed, looking smart in a royal blue shirt and string tie over Levis. He's rarely out of jeans but the top half of him prefers flannel shirts in winter and T-shirts in summer.

"Is this dressy?" I ask.

"No, just thought I'd wear something different for a change."

I reluctantly slip into a nice shirt and slacks with a cardigan sweater. I'm doubly tired and irritable from the day's event and lack of a restful nap and keep grumbling about having to dress up for a rural property dating back to the early 1800s.

"We're probably going to have barbecue over a pit anyway," I spit out as we leave our warm cabin and emerge into what has become a frigid night. Now, I really wish I were still in my LSU sweatshirt and jeans, topped by my warm winter coat.

"I never said you had to dress up," TB counters.

We join the rest of the group in the Council House Cafe where staff members are ready to serve up items that smell heavenly and no, it's not barbecue. Carmine's back from the police station, huddled in a corner with Winnie and the Pennington couple. All three give me a stare, which adds to my discontent. Pepper, too, eyes me suspiciously, turning her back when she catches my eye. Naturally, Dwayne's charming Shelby who's laughing heartily — until she notices me enter and then her smile fades.

"Great," I tell TB. "Everyone's happy to see me."

TB heads toward Carmine and touches him on the back. "Everything okay?"

I follow along but I'd rather get a plate of whatever smells so good and head back to my cabin. If vibes were knives in this place, I'd be the one in the hospital, not Kelly.

Thankfully, Winnie saunters up and whispers in my ear. "Dang it, girl. You only broke her leg."

I want to laugh. So badly. But the last thing I need is people thinking not only did I push that woman over a cliff, but I'm relishing it. I bite my lip and rein it in.

"Shut up," I tell her.

She sobers up a bit. "Don't sweat it. She probably tripped trying to get at Dwayne and was too embarrassed to admit it."

I glance over at Lucifer and he sends me a wink.

"Jesus," I say in reaction, then feel several dead ancestors berating me for taking the lord's name in vain. "Sorry."

"Sorry for what?" Winnie asks.

"What is his story?" I whisper to her. "I can't for the life of me figure him out."

"Then don't."

When I look at Winnie, she's suddenly deadly serious. "You heard Carmine. You've seen how this man acts. What more proof do you need?"

"I can't help it, Winnie. I was an investigative journalist before this. I have to know."

Shelby announces it's time to take our seats, that another local historian is here to explain French Camp. We head to our tables but Winnie leans close and whispers, "Then you'll likely be the next once being pushed."

Over plates of fried chicken, mashed potatoes, greens and cornbread, Robert Blake, a historian at Mississippi State, takes us back to the early 1800s when Louis LeFleur started trading with the Choctaw Indians a few miles south of where we are today. He moved to the present location around 1812 and set up a "stand," much like Buzzard Roost, a place for people to rest on the Natchez Trace. LeFleur hailed from France so his stand became known as French Camp.

"That's ingenious," Winnie says under her breath.

LeFleur later married a Choctaw native, Blake tells us with a smile like it's going to be some great revelation, and their son was Greenwood LeFleur, a Choctaw chief and a Mississippi State Senator.

"The town of Greenwood was named for him," he says proudly.

Pepper's disappointed that the big reveal wasn't someone she might know, the Pennington's are confused, no doubt because they don't know where Greenwood is, Dwayne's still charming up Miss Shelby, and Carmine's busy indulging in banana pudding. Winnie looks like she's the only person who thinks this is cool.

"Greenwood's in *LeFleur* County," she says.

Robert lights up. "Yes, you know your history."

"Well of course I do," Winnie retorts. "I went to Ole Miss."

The two schools are apparently rivals for Robert and Winnie start sparring, affectionately of course. The rest rise for more banana pudding, except for me. I'm not a fan of bananas or the way they slip Vanilla Wafers along the sides of the bowls and said wafers get soggy. I instead head for the pecan pie by the coffee carafe and bump into Pepper while I snag the last slice.

"How could you do such a thing?" she whispers.

"Sorry, do you want the last piece?"

She gives me the evil eye and moves off. Next thing I know, Shelby waits behind me for coffee.

"How's Kelly?" I ask.

"Her leg's broken but she'll be out of the hospital in the morning."

"That's good news," I say softly, wondering if Shelby believes me.

"She said you all have history."

I'm taking a sip of coffee and snort, a bit going up my nose. "History? We shared a car ride to the airport once."

"And you abandoned her on the side of the road."

I want to shake my head and make this nightmare go away. It was a late-night ride from Eureka Springs, Arkansas, where we had attended a press trip, to Springfield, Missouri's airport. I was freaking out about seeing ghosts for the first time and losing my temper at another travel writer, worried that I might never be asked back on press trips. Kelly made me drive and then immediately fell asleep. If anyone should be mad, it's me.

"You're mistaken. I was driving, we went through Branson, and I decided to get out and see my aunt who lives there. I was in dire need of family at the time. It was Kelly's rental car and she continued to the airport. I didn't abandon…."

Shelby utters "Whatever" and walks away.

I lean against the table and take in the room. Carmine and TB are deep in discussion, TB glancing my way with a guilty look. No doubt they're discussing me. Pepper's doing the same, only to my dear friends Joe and Stephanie, the latter of whom is shaking her head in wonderment. Shelby's laughing again, with you know who, and Dwayne manages a sly smile when he, too, looks back. Winnie's the only friend tonight, and she's busy talking SEC football with Robert.

I leave my coffee cup behind but take the pecan pie with me, grab the salt shaker, and head toward the door. Just before my hand's on the doorknob, I feel a touch at my shoulder.

"Watch out for the ghosts," Dwayne whispers in my ear. "I heard that Andrew Jackson came this way after the Battle of New Orleans and some soldiers died and were buried here."

I don't turn around. "Sure, Dwayne. Whatever you say."

Someone calls his name and when I turn, it's Shelby. Her face is pinched in that jealous look women have, as if Dwayne's about to choose me, the cliff pusher, instead of her tonight. Pepper, too, watches me alarmed, and it's then I realize what he's doing.

I finally look him in the eye. "Divide and conquer. Is that your plan?"

"What?"

He's still smiling that annoying confident grin and for the life of me I can't understand why men do the things they do. I could bang my head on the concrete sidewalk and it would never make sense.

"We're powerful in numbers," I say, remembering the

witch tribe of Briarwood Plantation. "I wouldn't forget that."

With those final words, I steal into the cold, dark night of French Camp.

CHAPTER TEN

When I return to the cabin, Stinky sits perched in the middle of the floor, as if he's both expecting me and waiting to have a talk. He reminds me of my mother when I stayed out past curfew, she smoking on the front stoop, the tip of her cigarette the only light I spotted when I stumbled drunk to the door.

"Got a good excuse, young lady," she used to say, right before she took away the keys to the family car.

I close the door and throw my jacket on to the bed, then sit down in front of my tabby cat. Tonight, I'm looking for advice from this freakish feline.

"What am I supposed to do?" I ask him.

The cat gets up and jumps on the bed, making himself comfortable. He begins a slow bath beginning with his right paw.

"That's what I get for talking to a cat," I say to myself.

I rise and place the pecan pie and salt on the table. Where once that pecan and sugar concoction was to be the salve to my horrid day, the dessert doesn't appeal anymore. Instead, I lay on the bed next to Stinky and scratch his head. The cat leans into my massage and purrs and the action shifts his body so that I spot what he's been laying on. It's a brochure titled *The Wild Herbs of The Natchez Trace Parkway*. I pick up the brochure the same time Stinky gives me a wink.

The list mostly contains wildflowers and edibles travelers would have consumed as they headed along the trail. But there's a few in here I recognize, plants that may come in handy. A light bulb goes off.

I grab my cell phone and call the one person who can help. Aunt Mimi picks up instantly.

"Well, this is a surprise," she says in her sweet Alabama accent. "Hi, Sugar Baby."

Even though my mother attended the finest universities of the world, and eliminated her linguistic roots along the way, it's startling to hear a relative this close to our family talk like Paula Deen.

"Hey, Aunt Mimi," is all I can manage before the tears start falling.

"Oh, Honey Chile, tell me everything."

I relate the events of the past few days, explaining how Dwayne gave a talk at the SCANC convention, then surprisingly became part of our press trip. I mention Carmine's weird but elusive conversations about angels, TB showing up unannounced, and the horrid incidents of the past twenty-four hours. My aunt listens intently and only utters an occasional "Oh dear" or "Uh huh" and I relish the fact that I have one family member who lets me talk.

She's also the only one sharing psychic DNA, so there's that.

I end my spiel with Stinky sitting on an herb brochure.

"That cat's not normal," I conclude.

"That cat's special and if I were you I'd keep him close."

I look over at my purring tabby and he winks.

"What do you think?" I ask her.

She exhales a long breath. "First of all, stay away from that man. Your friends are right. There's something evil about him."

Now, it's my turn to sigh. "You know I can't do that. I'm too curious. And if he is evil, then none of this is going to stop."

"Vi, you don't have to be the superhero here."

I think of the Briarwood quintuple standing up to McDaniels.

"Someone has to."

"How about that nice policeman?"

I laugh, more at the way she asked that question than the question itself. "That *nice policeman* thinks I pushed Kelly off the side of the so-called mountain."

There's a pause, then, "I don't see that."

She's referring to her second sight so that gives me hope, but if someone else takes a bad turn on this trip I may be doing time in rural Mississippi.

"I'll be careful, I promise," I assure her.

"Vi, stay away from him."

I change the subject.

"What can I do to protect myself?"

There's a lengthy pause and I know my aunt's shaking her head, thinking that the one family member who shares her "gift" is too stubborn to take logical advice and may get herself killed.

"I'll be careful," I assure her. "But I can't remember which herbs to use. The grimoire you gave me is at home."

Aunt Mimi's reluctant but she rattles off the necessary information. I jot it all down on the pad by the side of the bed.

"Thanks," I say when she's finished.

"Last resort," she commands.

"Yes, ma'am."

"After this trip, we should meet up at the old homestead and I can teach you some more."

"That would be awesome." I would love a weekend in rural Alabama with my favorite aunt. Even though she's my only aunt.

Stinky meows and when I look over at him I spot the salt shaker on the table.

"One more thing," I say. "Should I put a circle of salt around my cabin for protection?"

"You have enough?"

"Yes, ma'am."

"Just the thresholds. Doors and windows. Anyplace someone could get in."

We catch up a bit but it's late and Mimi manages an active senior living establishment in Branson so she heads to bed early. I promise to call more often.

"Call me every night until you get home," she insists.

"Yes, ma'am."

After I hang up, I grab the salt shaker and head outside. I lay a stream of salt across the front door threshold beneath the doormat — I don't want anyone to spot this and imagine witches visited this Christian academy. I place some along the windowsills, again trying hard to be inconspicuous. There's a back door so I slip around to finish off the salt shaker, trying not to be afraid of the dark woods surrounding my cabin. After I lay a line of salt I straighten and turn and run right into a body.

I can't help myself. I'm so startled I yell.

"Vi, it's only me."

I attempt to compose myself and TB moves to hug me, but I'm not in the mood. I'm still reeling from the idea that he thought I slept with Dwayne, not to mention him discussing me with Carmine at dinner.

I move away. "You scared me, is all."

His shoulders drop. I can't see his face but I know he's disappointed I didn't rush into his arms.

"What are you doing back here?" he asks.

"Protecting myself."

I head to the front of the house, TB following behind. We move into the warmth of the cabin and Stinky meows from the bed.

"Why did you leave dinner?" TB pulls off his jacket.

Suddenly, that pie looks mighty good. I pull off the plastic wrapping, grab a fork, plop down at the table, and dig in.

"Had no reason to stay," I say behind mouthfuls. "Besides, everyone probably felt safer with me gone."

TB sits across from me with Stinky in his lap.

"And no, you can't have a bite."

"Why are you so angry with me?"

Why *am* I so angry at my sorta husband? The world's turned upside down and I can't really blame him for falling for Dwayne's evil, as Aunt Mimi called it. On the other hand, yes, I can. I did cheat on him this summer, even if we were technically separated at the time. He cheated on me, too, I might add. Since we've been back together we've been loyal to each other, so to think I would do such a thing now really dills my pickle.

"Why were you so quick to believe Dwayne?"

He looks down where his fingers are scratching the top of Stinky's head.

"I don't know, Vi. I swore I saw him coming out of the trailer."

I'm about to slide the last part of the pie into my eager mouth — that wonderful buttery crust with just enough pecan pie attached and the bottom offering a hint of crystalized sugar — when that light bulb turns on again. I place my fork down and slide it across the table within TB's reach, then head for my laptop.

"What is it?" TB says and I can tell he's enjoying my last bite.

I open the laptop and start Googling fallen angels, Lucifer, and the devil. I can still hear Carmine insisting Dwayne wasn't the latter, but the information that's popping up does mention folks of this persuasion being able to tap into people's fears and emotions, and can cause them to see things that aren't there.

"Kelly and I have history, like Shelby said," I tell TB. "Nothing crazy like Shelby suggested but Kelly's the kind of person who holds a grudge, especially if she thinks a woman's stealing her man." With an afterthought, I add, "Which I wasn't."

TB's eyes narrow and I know he's not following.

"Pepper adores animals. Her greatest fear is seeing harm done to them, hence viewing that horrific scene in the back of her cabin."

TB shakes his head, still not getting it.

"If Dwayne's as evil as Carmine makes him out to be, then he's playing on their emotions. In the case of Kelly, making her see things that aren't there."

I'm about to include the man sitting in front of me, but I hate admitting that TB's fear is that I will leave him for another.

"What about that girl in the woods?" he asks. "The one you helped cross over."

I shake my head. "It was strange that she accepted our help so easily and moved on, but she must have been real. Why else would I have felt the electricity of that light and feel so strange as I did the next day?"

Unless Dwayne used it as a means to violate me.

I push that idea away, but another one takes its place.

"Dwayne said he would call that girl's family, to let them know what happened and that she's at peace."

"Did he?"

"I have no idea."

TB and I stare at each other, that thought floating around our brains. Then, TB joins me on the bed and grabs the laptop, asking for input. I tell him Natalie Stephens, Jackson Street, Tishomingo, and he types this into Google and several articles emerge, one with the same girl's face.

Poor Natalie disappeared one day while the family was enjoying a picnic in the park. The entire town of Tishomingo, and several Mississippi State Police officers, searched the park to no avail. After two months, police gave up.

"That poor child," TB says, both of us feeling the pain the parents must have experienced never knowing what happened to their little girl.

TB switches to the White Pages and looks up Stephens on Jackson Street and one entry comes up. John and Debbie Stephens.

"Should I call her?" I ask.

TB nods but he's likely feeling like I do. How will these parents react and will they believe me? And did Dwayne make the call earlier?

I take a deep breath and punch in the number on my cell. It rings twice and then a woman's voice answers. "Mrs. Stephens?" "If you're trying to sell something you can hang up right now," she says in a stern Southern voice.

"No ma'am, I'm not."

"You'd be the third one tonight and I'm not in the mood."

I swallow and gather up my courage. "Mrs. Stephens, it's about your daughter."

Silence follows and I swear I can hear that woman's heart beating across the line.

"What about her?"

I exhale. I can do this.

"This may sound strange but I'm a medium and I was at Tishomingo State Park recently and I think Natalie drowned in the creek near a red tree marker. I was about two hundred yards on the trail past the cabins, where the first rock outcropping is."

"How do you know her name?"

That's what she chooses to focus on?

"She told me, told me where she lived, then I Googled her and found out she disappeared."

More silence.

"Mrs. Stephens, I'm not trying to scam you or sell you anything. I just want you to ask the authorities or the park officials to look in that area of the creek. They might find something that'll give you peace."

She's crying now and my heart breaks.

"I lost a child, too," I whisper and TB turns away. "I know your pain and I just want to help. Natalie wants you to be at peace."

She keeps crying and after almost a minute manages to say, "Thank you" and hangs up.

I flip the phone closed and drop my head into my hands. Losing Lillye comes back so hard I can't breathe. I knew at the time of her death I would never recover but life kept going and so did I. But sometimes that heartbreaking, raking pain takes over and I wonder how I'll survive. It's as if someone stole my heart when she died and times like these I'm reminded of that hole, so dark, giant, and all-consuming.

TB's rubbing my back and whispering comfort in my ear. I grab his hand on my shoulder and hold tight, as if it's a rope thrown to keep me from drowning. Finally, I rest my head on his chest and we silently grieve the dearest thing we had in our lives.

After what seems like an eternity, we straighten, compose ourselves, and get ready for bed.

"You didn't say if Mrs. Stephens had heard from Dwayne," TB says, crawling under the sheets.

I join him and the warmth of his body comforts me on this cold, cold night. I can't say for sure, but I'm fairly certain Dwayne lied. There's a bigger question here as well. How did he know Natalie was at that spot in the creek in the first place?

"I don't think he did tell her," I say as I turn out the light.

Cora's sitting in the parlor working on needlepoint, pausing as if she's waiting for me. I'm outside the action again, but I can't help feeling that she's showing me her life for more reasons than solving the mystery of her murder. I almost expect her to turn and welcome me to Briarwood.

Menasha arrives with tea and places it on the table in front of Cora whose body language changes immediately. Cora doesn't trust this woman, I sense, or resents having to be in charge of an enslaved person within her household, someone living so close.

"Thank you, Menasha," she says.

"Yes, ma'am."

Menasha moves to leave but pauses on the room's threshold. "Will Mister Wendell be requiring anything specific?"

This takes Cora aback. She turns and looks Menasha in the eyes, and Menasha bows her head. I've heard that slaves weren't allowed to gaze into the eyes of their owners, must keep their eyes downcast. It's one more thing that disturbs Cora.

"What exactly would Mister Wendell need?" Cora asks.

"Men like cigars and whiskey. Sometimes we kill a chicken when company comes."

Cora digests this. "Do we have cigars and whiskey? And yes, let's kill a chicken."

Menasha heads to a cabinet in the corner of the room and taps the top lightly. A door opens and behold, there's whiskey and a box of cigars below.

"I'm surprised McDaniels didn't raid that as well."

"Yes, ma'am."

Menasha leaves the room and Cora rises to see what her kitchen slave had in mind. Behind the whiskey, in a hidden drawer, lies several bills, apparently Uncle Walter's financial stash. Cora studies the bills, then slips them into her skirt pocket.

The vision fades and we move to a rainy day and the home's dining room. Cora and a man are enjoying a roasted chicken with various sides and glasses of wine.

"Lovely dinner, cousin," the man says.

"Wendell, we're not related."

The man smiles affectionately. "After all those years living near each other in Kentucky, we're practically family."

Cora places her glass on the table and becomes serious. "I want to sell this place, Wendell. I aim to take the money and return to Kentucky, purchase a small farm there."

Wendell leans back in his chair. "Are you sure? You have a wonderful situation here, good soil, people to till it. According to your uncle's ledger, Briarwood has been quite profitable over the years. Not to mention that the climate is so agreeable."

"I have to admit, the balmy winter suits me well."

"Then why not stay?"

Cora looks around the room to make sure Menasha is absent. "I can't bear owning slaves. It goes against everything I believe in."

"I understand your feelings, Cora, but they are necessary to running a farm."

Cora frowns and looks down at her lap. "Surely, you don't believe that. Mary's farm in Kentucky was run by the family, along with hired hands, and they all lived quite well. In fact, well enough to take in an orphan like me."

It's obvious Cora detests living off the kindness of strangers. She had been so hopeful with Briarwood.

Wendell reaches across the table and takes Cora's hand, which surprises her. I'm thinking it's an impertinent gesture for the time.

"I understand," he says.

She pulls her hand free and rests it in her lap. "I thought about selling the plantation and freeing the slaves, giving them the option of following me home to Kentucky and working as hired hands."

Wendell takes a long drink of his wine. "I don't think that's a good idea."

"Why not?"

"Because this is the Deep South, Cora. You can't free slaves because you don't like the institution."

Cora crosses her arms. "They're my property now. I can do as I wish."

Wendell rubs his face thoughtfully. "We are about to go to war, Cora. Congress is fighting over what states will be slave states and which ones will not. People are not going to take lightly to a woman wanting to upset the apple cart at this time."

"I'm not upsetting anything."

"By freeing your slaves, you're sending a message that you don't approve."

She huffs. "I don't!"

"But you do see how this will come across to those who do in this state. Besides, in Mississippi a freed slave can be sold back into slavery after living ten free. Will you be able to move your people to Kentucky in that short of time?"

"I could free them once I get to Kentucky."

Wendell shakes his head. "It's not possible."

Cora stands and begins pacing the room. "Why are you fighting me on this? I thought you would understand."

Wendell rises and moves to her side, places his hands on her shoulders.

"I do, Cora. I don't see this as the right course of action."

She folds her arms about her. "And what is? Gaining prosperity at the hands of people in bondage?"

Wendell takes her hand and leads her back to the table. They both sit down, facing each other.

"I have a better idea. Marry me."

Cora's eyes enlarge and she smiles as if he's jesting. "You're not serious."

"I am."

Cora's smile disappears. "Wendell, you're an old friend but...."

"I'm a man, and this is a man's world, especially here in Mississippi. Together, we run this farm and help send those who live here

into freedom."

Cora catches her breath and her eyes light up. "The Underground Railroad," she whispers excitedly.

"Exactly."

There's a catch, however. Cora must now head into bondage herself, one of a feminine sort. Her smile disappears and Wendell squeezes her hand.

"Think about it. We could do good together. Or, if you'd rather, you can sell the farm and all the slaves on it and return to Kentucky."

It's a huge decision. If she marries Wendell, they may be able to set her slaves free. On the other hand, she will be tied to a man she's only known as a friend, a man ten years her senior. In truth, she barely knows him. If Mary hadn't insisted on sending her cousin down to Mississippi to assist her in selling the plantation, Cora would have sought consultation locally.

The vision shifts once more and Cora's standing behind the main house, watching slaves work on their cabins. The sun warms her face, her head free of the restrictive bonnet, and her bare feet relish the cool, gumbo mud.

"Miss Cora," a slave named Jackson calls out. "It's getting close to planting time."

Cora looks up at the budding dogwoods, their pink and white flowers raining petals everywhere. She must decide soon, for to let her fields go fallow will decrease her asking price on the plantation. And without an overseer, she doesn't know how she will instruct her slaves to plant cotton and indigo, to even purchase the seed. Her experience veers toward small fields of corn, vegetables, and hay.

She's also come to love her new home, the soft winters, the Spanish moss lilting in the breeze beneath the massive oak trees, the camellias showing color in January.

She says nothing but I know what her decision will be. She'll marry Wendell, either allow him to run the plantation or hire an overseer to do the job. They'll live as husband and wife and secretly find ways to send their property north to freedom. It could work.

She will have to lay with him, of course, but it's a wife's duty, is it not? Likely children will be born. Cora has always wanted to be a mother.

Still, she doesn't love Wendell and she will exchange her freedom for those of others. She looks at the slaves around her, many smiling and enjoying the spring day as much as she. Since her arrival, she has instructed the slaves to improve their cabins, add insulation, attend to their cedar-shingled roofs. Their diet has improved, even though Menasha insisted they were quickly running through the food resources. Cora even dug through her uncle's closet and passed out his clothes so that the male slaves would be warm over the winter months. They appear before her well fed and clothed, almost happy, and she knows this is what freedom will look like once they escape the bonds of their situation.

It's important, she tells herself. It's worth the sacrifice.

Yes, she will marry Wendell. And she would help move her people to safety.

I awake and find it's still dark outside, glance at the clock beside my bed and realize it's two a.m., the witching hour as some like to say. More like the ghosting hour, I think.

I look over at my husband, a man who could sleep through the world ending. Those blonde curls fall across his forehead and there's a slight smile on his lips.

Times have changed since Cora's age but do I fear being together again with TB. Is it because I fear losing *my* freedom? We married so young, so insistently since I became pregnant. We remained together for two years following Lillye's death because neither of us was motivated to do anything except sleep, eat, and work. Katrina pushed me to action, which is how I ended up living in a potting shed two hours west of New Orleans and changing careers. And now…?

He's a good man.

I feel this rather than hear someone say it out loud, but it's like a message from another world coming through, similar to the ghostly images I see on occasion. I get the sudden urge to touch TB's face, let my thumb roam across his cheek, enjoy those soft, stubborn curls.

He's a good man.

I almost imagine it's Lillye whispering in my ear.

TB would help me send slaves into freedom, I think, as my eyelids grow heavy. And he wouldn't demand I marry him for the task.

Morning comes way too soon and I'm desperate for coffee. TB's been up for a while and has showered and shaved, looking good in his blue flannel shirt and jeans. I used to love watching him walk through the door after work, his tool belt hugging that slim waist. I had admonished him about not removing it before driving home and TB, with his usual innocent smile, would shrug and say, "It takes too long."

Lillye would come bouncing up to greet him.

"I'll do it," she would exclaim, then remove each tool while TB lovingly caressed her head.

"Where are you?"

I look up to find TB leaning against the door jamb of the bathroom. How long have I been standing here?

I shrug. "Just remembering something."

TB walks over and starts to give me a morning hug but then thinks better of it. Now, it's my turn to be disappointed. Have I caused my husband to doubt my affections? Of course, I have.

Before he can pass me by, I grab the front of that flannel and pull close. I breathe in his heavenly scent and wrap my arms about him. He returns the hug instantly.

"What's the matter, Boo? Were you having a ghost vision again?"

I nod, which is a lie, although watching Cora decide to marry a man who's almost a stranger has made my pity come, as Aunt Mimi likes to say.

After I dress, we head to the Council House Café for breakfast and who should be there but Kelly, a cast covering her right shinbone. She gives me a hostile stare but then thinks better of it, fiddling with the hem of her shirt. It's now or never, I think, and head her way.

She's perched on a comfortable chair, her leg extended

over a soft ottoman. I sit down in the chair opposite her.

"How are you?" I ask, and immediately kick myself for such an insipid question.

"As well as can be after falling down a mountain."

Her tone isn't as accusatory as I expected.

"Kelly, listen, I didn't...," I say playing with my own shirt's hem.

"I know."

My head pops up. "You do?"

She looks around the room but the others are all gathered around the coffee, like buzzards on road kill. "I swear I saw you behind me right before I took that tumble. Like clear as day."

"I wasn't there...," I insist but she raises a hand.

"I know."

She glances around the room again and it's then I notice than everyone — and I mean everyone, including the woman putting out silverware — is watching our conversation. One person is absent, however, and it's you know who.

"I thought about it in the hospital," she begins. "I know you probably don't like me very much."

"I don't dislike you, Kelly. I wasn't in a good place when we were in Eureka Springs and you offered a ride to the airport but then let me drive while you napped, and the weather was so awful, and I needed family." I'm rambling. "I had an aunt who lived in Branson...."

She raises her hand again. "I know. I thought about that, too. I tend to take advantage."

More likely used to getting your way being rich and beautiful, I think.

"Anyway," she continues, "I can't imagine why you'd push me off a cliff. I mean, you're here with your husband."

I know where this is going so I lean in close. "I have no designs on Dwayne. If you must know, he and I share some psychic abilities and that's what we talk about."

This perks up Kelly, much to my surprise.

"What? You're psychic? Wow, that's so awesome."

I pull back. "Yeah, I guess. Didn't get much sleep last night."

Now, it's her turn to lean close. "Why, what happened?"

I don't feel like explaining my gifts or my relationship with Cora right now. As Dwayne throws the door of the café open and we all get a burst of cold air, I know my mission is something more important.

"I'll explain later. Just know that I'm on your side and that we women have to stick together."

Kelly looks confused. "Stick together, how?"

I look at Dwayne who sends me a warning glance.

"He's not right, Kelly. If my intuition's correct, he slept with Shelby last night and Pepper the night before."

Kelly's head jolts up, her stern gaze traveling from one woman to the other.

"It's not their fault," I quickly add. "Which is why we need to stick together."

I'm not sure Kelly understands or if her jealousy still dominates her senses, but Shelby calls us to sit and enjoy breakfast so I assist Kelly to the table, then take a chair by TB and Winnie. Thankfully, Winnie fills the morning conversation with tales of her children who have been calling constantly since she left, the goats she's raising are eating her hydrangeas, which might die anyway if the temperature keeps falling, and her farmhouse that's a massive work in progress. I relish the reprieve of thinking about fallen angels and plantation ghosts. Before long it's time to resume our trek down the Trace.

We all haul out the door to retrieve suitcases and meet the van, but I'm ahead of the game. My suitcase is packed and ready to be loaded. It's one thing I'm super proud of, being able to pack in record time. If there was a suitcase Olympics, I'd win gold every time. I wait in the cold morning air by the van, inhaling my coffee, while the rest go back to their cabins.

It's then I spot Dwayne, standing in the Parkway, taking photos of the mist of morning. I hear Aunt Mimi's warning in my ear but I ignore it, my curiosity getting the better of my logical mind.

I follow him, standing on the perpendicular street to provide distance between us. He turns and smiles, as if he knows I would come, and we stare at each other on the crossroads.

"We need to talk," he says.

"Yes, we do."

I'm not afraid of this man. I know I should be but something deep in my soul wants to take this guy down. I know he's going to ask me to join him in some dark woods tonight, prove his evolution theory, or worse, hurt Shelby along the way. But I'm not falling for his charm. Not anymore.

And then, she appears.

It's Lillye, standing next to Dwayne in her favorite outfit, a purple and gold dress we bought at the LSU gift shop one Sunday when we drove up to Baton Rouge. She's even got on her purple ballet slippers my mother thought was too tacky but Lillye adored them so we let her wear them everywhere. Her curls hang loose about her shoulders, harking back to the time when she had her own hair, before chemo took it all away.

I'm so shocked, I can't speak.

"Are you ready to evolve?" Dwayne asks me.

I'm here to disavow this man, to tell him off, to fight back at whatever evil he's springing forth on this trip. I can't trust him, should not follow him anywhere.

But all I can do is nod.

CHAPTER ELEVEN

Shelby cheerfully points out historic sites on the map, places we will pass as we make our way south along the Trace but no one seems interested. Joe and Stephanie examine photos on his Nikon and Carmine and Winnie are deep in conversation about editors with a publication they both write for. Kelly's busy trying to figure out how to walk on crutches and Pepper's thumb beats out a marathon texting on her cell phone. Dwayne has already entered the van, taking an entire aisle in the back and it appears he's starting a nap.

"Well, perhaps we should make our way to the boardwalk outside Jackson, then," Shelby says, clearly disappointed.

"Great idea," Pepper says, and jumps on board, heading to the back to talk to Dwayne. Shelby watches and frowns.

Still working the women, I think, as I watch Dwayne perk up at Pepper's approach. On the other hand, some women carry that stubborn kink in their armor, always falling for the wrong man. I'm no stranger to that scenario, having had a dalliance with a co-worker when reviewing hotels this past summer. He was charming, arrogant, and a fun romp in the hay. But he was a jerk, and even though I followed in his arrogant footsteps for a while, I came to my senses. I hope these three will do the same.

"Okay then," Shelby says to me and I notice her eyes glistening. "Just follow us to mile marker one twenty-two."

I touch her arm and lean close. "She's a kid. It's not her fault. Blame him."

She doesn't answer, nods slightly, and herds the others on to the van. TB and I enter the pickup and head out. Stinky makes himself comfortable in my lap.

"You're quiet," TB says after a few miles.

I'm too busy thinking of my meeting with Dwayne and the

vision of Lillye. I want so badly to share this with TB, to try to make sense of it all, but he'll likely talk me out of tonight's rendezvous with the devil. We're spending the evening at a plantation close to Natchez and Dwayne insists there's a ghost in need of a crossover nearby. It sounds like another walk in the woods which I'd be crazy to do but I want to see him in action. I want to know how he does what he does and if I'm able to do something similar to evolve. How I will handle this, I haven't a clue.

And Lillye…she was so incredibly real. Her vision only lasted seconds but it was enough to give me hope I never would have imagined before.

"Vi?" TB asks.

"Wondering about Cora," I lie.

"I forgot to tell you, I did some research on her and Briarwood," TB says excitedly. "The place is now a museum and bed and breakfast."

This perks me up. "Wow, maybe we can visit it when we hit the city."

"It's not in Natchez. It's about twenty minutes north of town."

"Cool! The next time we stop, let's tell Shelby we want to pause at Briarwood."

"It's not called Briarwood."

This doesn't make sense. "Then it's likely not the one Cora lived at."

"It's the one."

"TB, I know for sure she lived at a plantation called Briarwood."

He looks over at me and that enthusiasm drops. "It's the same one, Vi. I did the research."

He's been awesome helping me investigate my ghostly mysteries but I fear his lack of education and experience with this kind of thing works against him.

"If there's no modern Briarwood, it may have fallen into disrepair and been torn down," I explain to him. "We will have to use what we have on Wendell and try to figure out where he lived and compare that to maps today."

TB looks at me again, this time like a fussed-out puppy.

"I appreciate your help, but it might be a lot more complicated than you think."

He turns back to the road, but I can see him biting the inside of his cheek, something he's prone to do when aggravated, like when LSU is down by two, it's twenty seconds to go, and they're almost in field goal range.

I touch his arm. "I really do appreciate your help. Let's look at all the information the next time we stop and we'll see if we can piece this together."

TB says nothing, which isn't like him. Stinky takes this moment to stretch his claws, digging deep into my thigh. I yelp and move him on to the seat. TB looks down at the feline and I swear they're both sharing a smile.

"Okay, I could be wrong," I admit, getting the message. "Show me what you've found at the next stop."

We hardly say a word until we reach the boardwalk that stretches through a tupelo and bald cypress swamp along the edge of the Ross R. Barnett Reservoir outside Jackson. Through the trees, I see the bright blue of the lake glistening in the autumn sun but the boardwalk disappears through dense woods.

"Keep your eyes open," Shelby says brightly as we join the group. "You might see an alligator."

TB and I share an "Oh goodie" look; we've seen plenty growing up in South Louisiana. We tell Shelby that since we're well acquainted with swamps and wetlands we'll hang back and help Kelly hobble along. Shelby hesitates, no doubt thinking TB and I will throw Miss Georgia to the gators.

"It's fine, Shelby," Kelly assures her. "We're all good now."

I was hoping to snag Carmine during this stop and get some answers, and I catch him lingering by the boardwalk entrance, looking my way. When he notices Dwayne put his arm around Shelby and lead her off down the trail, whispering something in her ear, no doubt assurances, he exhales and follows behind. I wonder if he fears for her safety since she's the current Dwayne girl.

"Bitch," Kelly says softly. I give her a look and her shoulders fall. "Okay, Mom. Bastard then."

I laugh. "That works."

Poor Pepper watches the interaction with Dwayne and Shelby, stuffing her hands inside her black leather jacket and walking silently behind. Joe and Stephanie, bless their Yankee hearts, come up on either side and distract her. I assume they share a joke for Pepper's laughing.

"Can you manage those crutches down this walkway?" TB asks.

We all gaze down the trail through the wetlands and I get the feeling that TB and Kelly think as I do, that we'd rather sit in the warm sunlight at the trailhead than traipse through nature. At least this morning.

"Wanna just hang out here?" TB asks Kelly.

"Oh God, yes."

We plant ourselves on the bench and do exactly what I envisioned, hang our heads back and let the morning sun bathe our faces. After a while, TB straightens and turns towards Kelly.

"I have a friend you need to meet."

I realize he means Stinky and I'm wondering if he has a leash somewhere in the back of his cab. Instead, he walks to the pickup, opens the door wide, and lets the cat saunter out. I bolt upright.

"TB, what are you doing?"

"He's fine," my agreeable husband says.

"He's not fine. Are you crazy? He's not a dog."

TB bites the inside of his cheek again. "I know that, Vi."

Meanwhile, Stinky approaches Kelly and rubs up against her good leg. I gaze at Kelly with wide eyes, hoping she agrees that having a cat wonder free on the side of the Natchez Trace Parkway is as crazy as I think it is.

"Shouldn't he be on a leash or something?" Kelly asks, and I take the time to give TB a stern look.

"He's fine," TB insists, volleying that look back at me.

Sure enough, Stinky doesn't go far, sniffing out the bushes around us, checking out a small section of boardwalk, using the outdoor kitty litter behind a bald cypress knee. When he starts veering off toward the road, TB whistles and the cat comes right back.

"That's amazing," Kelly says. "How did you train him to do that?"

"I didn't do anything," TB explains. "Vi found him hanging around her apartment and when he stays with me — when Vi goes on press trips — he does everything I say."

I'm still not convinced. "Tell me you don't take my cat walking through the neighborhood."

"*Your* cat?" TB asks.

I never thought about who owned Stinky. He came to me as a stray and I always assumed he would never call anyone his owner; he's that independent. He ping pongs back and forth between TB and me like a divorced child and seems to like that arrangement.

"Don't y'all live together?" Kelly asks.

A silence falls as I wonder how to answer that.

"Vi stayed in Lafayette, the town we evacuated to, and I'm in New Orleans renovating our house," TB says.

He leaves out the part about me filing separation papers following the storm.

"You poor things," and with that she asks the hundred questions people do when they find out you spent two days on a roof after the nation's worst disaster flooded your home. I listen patiently but I want none of it. TB, on the other hand, loves to tell his "Katrina story," much like everyone else in New Orleans these days. Thankfully the group returns and I scoop up Stinky as inconspicuously as I can and place him in the pickup. When I close the door behind him and look for TB, I find my sorta husband carrying Kelly back to the van, heavy cast, crutches, and all. She's grinning like she's being carried up the stairs by Rhett Butler.

I climb in the cab and scratch my sorta feline behind the

ears. "Daddy's something else, isn't he?"

Stinky winks.

Once again we're heading south, skirting the capital city of Jackson, although civilization remains hidden behind the park-like setting of the Trace. The van pulls over several times at historical markers and we all read the signs. I'm sure the van occupants aren't willing to get out for we pause for a few minutes and then take off again.

"You want to talk about Briarwood?" TB offers. "Or would you rather do the work yourself?"

He sounds testy and defensive.

"I'm not doubting you."

He smiles sadly and shakes his head. "Aren't you?"

Yes, I really am. I went to journalism school and he dropped out of college to become a carpenter. I don't think I'm off base here but I really should give him the benefit of the doubt.

"I'm sorry about before. What did you find out?"

"I followed Wendell Meyers through the census records and he always lived in the same place. He shows up in the city directory of Port Gibson, which is the town next to Natchez, same address for years."

"Does it mention Briarwood?"

"They don't record names of homes, Vi, just addresses."

"So, how do you know this B&B is the same?"

He pulls several pieces of paper out of his laptop bag and hands them to me.

"When did you manage this?"

"The French Camp office has a printer."

I'm impressed.

"Anyway, there's Wendell's death certificate, a couple of court records from when he bought additional acreage, and a story on when he ran for mayor of Port Gibson."

I'm *seriously* impressed. I underestimated my husband and feel bad about my earlier admonishment.

"This is awesome, TB."

He begins to rebound and there's a happier glow about him. If I'm not mistaken, he loves doing this. The first time I asked for his help was on my initial press trip to Eureka Springs and he practically bounded out the room to the local library. He, and the librarian who assisted him, are the main reason we solved that case.

"There's more," he continues. "The article about Wendell running for office states that he lives in a home with a different name. Something-in-a-field. So, I called them and that's how I found out it's the same as Briarwood."

I laugh. "Something-in-a-field?"

TB grins and shrugs. "I can't remember. Something with field in it."

"Did you talk to anyone there?"

"I did, spoke with the owner. It's not just a bed and breakfast. They give tours, said he did a lot of historical research, and he insists that Cora went a little nuts and they had to put her away."

"What?" I practically yell.

This can't be true. I feel it deep in my soul. I know what I saw, Cora sitting by a stream while someone came up from behind, lifting an arm to deliver a blow.

"It sounded fishy to me, too," TB continues. "So, I checked it out. There were a couple of mental hospitals in the state at that time and neither one had a Schumacher or a Meyers as a patient."

Again, I can't help but question my husband's research. "How do you know this?"

"I called the archives department in Jackson and they have all the old records. Had to tell them I was a descendant, though. I said I was her great great grandson."

Damn, he's good. But the injustice pisses me off.

"Do you have the number of this something-field?" I ask TB.

He digs in his bag and pulls out a note with a number scribbled on it. I flip open my cell and call them. A man by the name of Ricky Esteban answers on the third ring. I introduce myself as a travel writer and ask if he's the owner.

"Yes, I am," Ricky says proudly. "How can I help you?"

"I'm Viola Valentine and you spoke with my husband yesterday, Thibault Boudreaux. About Wendell Meyers's wife?"

"Yes, I did. Sorry I didn't have more information."

"Well, I think what you have is wrong. What makes you think she died in a mental hospital?"

"Oh, that's well known," he insists.

"And you have research to back this up?"

He stumbles a bit. "Uh, that story's been carried down for years."

"Did you ever think that maybe it's just that, a story?"

Where once we were cordial and Ricky believed I was a travel journalist about to make him famous, now his tone turns quiet and a bit defensive.

"The family that owned this place told me so when I bought it."

"But that's not necessarily fact, is it? What if they were hiding something?"

I hear TB calling my name, telling me to calm down. I realize my voice has been raised a notch, but I can't help it.

"How many times have stories like this been tossed around erroneously and ruined a good woman's reputation? Y'all couldn't see to double-check your information?"

"Excuse me, ma'am, but how does this concerns you?"

My blood boils hotter. "It always concerns me when a woman's being maligned, as it should concern *you*, especially if you live in the house that once belonged to her. She inherited it, not some Wendell Meyers."

There's a pause and I'm starting to think I went about this wrong.

"Ma'am, I have business to attend to. If you're that concerned about Mrs. Meyers and her death, I suggest you do your own research and get back to us."

"You bet I will."

"Good day."

I flip the phone closed and find my blood pressure a bit too high. TB's looking at me like I'm the one who's gone crazy.

"What?" I say to him.

"Why are you so tense?"

"Because I'm tired of women being ignored in history. And this guy, who's done all this 'historical research,'" — I use my fingers to imitate parenthesis — "is convinced of this woman's insanity simply because he heard a rumor in the family."

TB rubs his chin thoughtfully.

"What?" I ask.

"I was going to stop by and talk to the guy but now we're probably not welcome."

"Unless I find out more."

"I can't use my laptop driving," TB says. "There's no internet connection."

"I have my own internet," I say, and pull out Cora's photos.

It's nighttime and Cora's lingering on the back porch while sounds of men laughing drift out from the parlor. It's clear she's unhappy, has been crying. As I inch forward — I'm again an outsider — I see she's several months pregnant.

Menasha steps on to the porch and brings Cora a tray of tea, placing it on the table in front of her.

"Don't you want some light out here, Miss Cora?"

Cora doesn't say anything and Menasha moves to leave. She's not turned around when Cora grabs her wrist and holds tight.

"Please stay," she says, her words choked with emotion.

Menasha appears uncomfortable and looks toward the kitchen.

"For God's sake, Menasha, look at me."

Menasha does as she's told but reluctantly. At least I think so for it's difficult to make out their faces in the darkness. Finally, Menasha pulls away and I feel Cora's disappointment. But the kitchen slave doesn't leave. She lights a nearby lantern, and sits next to her in a nearby chair.

"It's the baby talking," she tells Cora. "You'll feel better once he comes."

Cora shakes her head. A silence lingers.

"Does he hurt you?" Menasha whispers.

Cora nods her head, still saying nothing.

I see Menasha's body tense. "I believe I've heard him not following doctor's orders, to leave you alone."

Again, silence, but it's understood Menasha heard right.

"I wanted to help y'all," Cora whispers, the candlelight casting eerie shadows across her tear-streaked face. "I wanted to take y'all to Kentucky and free you there."

Menasha straightens, alert. "What's that, Miss Cora?"

"He talked me out of it, said a woman couldn't do that, that I would never get away with it in Mississippi, never make it to Tennessee before we were all stopped. He convinced me to marry him, said we would do it together. To free y'all another way."

A round of laughter rises up in the quiet night and Cora tenses. It's clear she now despises her husband.

"He's like the rest of them now," she continues with disdain. "Always fraternizing with the other plantation owners. Talking crops and trips to New Orleans. He knows that slavery makes wealth and money buys you friends and whiskey. He's even bragging about increasing the acreage and buying more slaves."

Like I did moments before, her voice is rising with the injustice of it all. Menasha moves to sit by her side on the porch settee.

"Don't get excited, Miss Cora. It's not good for the baby."

"How do I bring my child into this horrid world?" she whispers. "How do I live in it?"

To my surprise, Menasha takes her hand. "That's a question I ask myself every day ma'am."

Cora looks at Menasha, who this time doesn't turn away. In the darkness of the night, the two women share their pain. Cora gazes down at their entwined hands and smiles, but Menasha turns Cora's hand over and slips the cuff of her shirt up her arm. Numerous bruises are evident.

"I can help with that, Miss Cora."

No words are spoken but I instantly understand. She's not talking about first aid. It's exactly what Aunt Mimi and I discussed the night before, certain herbs that cause drowsiness, sickness, and some, even death. Which ones these women will pick and brew is the question. Obviously, Wendell survives whatever they are contemplating.

The vision fades and I'm almost blinded by the light of day. Cora's once again sitting on the back porch, gazing out at the back forty, a warm blanket across her lap for the sunny day contains a chilly nip. She doesn't care and the son she's birthed is swaddled tight in her arms, warmed by his mother's love.

"He's going to catch the death of cold," Wendell says emerging on to the porch, unsteady on his feet. Instead of the clean-cut dapper man I saw sitting at Cora's dining room table, Wendell's sporting an untrimmed beard and ruffled hair and his clothes are wrinkled although finely made.

"What do you care?" she retorts, still gazing lovingly at her son. "You haven't spent two minutes with your son since he's been born."

"I've been busy."

"Busy drinking and gambling with your friends." She gazes toward the slave quarters. "Among other things."

"How else am I going to satisfy my needs, since you're off limits?"

Cora looks up now. "You're despicable, a sorry excuse of a man. I rue the day I ever let you into this house."

Wendell's eyes narrow and he moves toward Cora like he's about to strike. Cora braves herself for the blow.

"Breakfast is ready," Menasha calls out from the kitchen, interrupting the action. Wendell grunts and heads inside.

Cora leans down to smell the head of her sleeping son, reveling in his sweetness. But her smile fades, knowing that he, too, is now a victim of this nightmare.

I open my eyes to see that the van's slowing down and turning into a sunken driveway, the mud banks almost as high as our cars.

"What did you see?" TB asks.

I explain the vision and how Cora entered a marriage of convenience that has backfired, how she's now a mother of a baby boy and thrilled, but worried about both of their futures. I don't mention the conversation between she and

Menasha, about how I believe the two may be conspiring to drug the man, or worse; I can't be sure that is what I heard.

"I can see how she would go crazy living with a man like that."

"Maybe you shouldn't have yelled at that B&B owner," TB answers. "He might have been right."

Doubtful, I think. I still see Cora lingering by the water's edge, an arm raised, ready to kill, just like Wendell on that back porch. Did Wendell kill his wife? Did Cora and Menasha attempt to drug him and it backfired? Or was there someone else who reappeared in her life — Reynald, McDaniels? And yet, anyone or all of the above would drive a woman to enter an institution.

I admit there may be more to this story than I realized.

We drive through thick woods until the road forks, one side rolling down to a lovely pond with a fountain in the middle, the perfect setting for a wedding, and the other towards an expansive lawn leading up to the house. The antebellum home sports a wrap-around porch filled with rocking chairs, windows that stretch from floor to ceiling, and a massive front door that must open into a wide hallway. Two live oak trees drape their branches across the porch and roof as if to shelter the horrors of the world away from those who live there. And all along the driveway the owners have planted Knock-Out Roses which, because of warm weather leading up to this week, have caused them to bloom in vibrant shades of crimson and pink.

"It's gorgeous," I whisper.

As we pull up to the front steps I get the immediate feeling I've been here before, that *deja vu* sensation that sweeps through you and quickly disappears, leaving you to wonder if it's all your imagination. Like maybe you've seen the place on a postcard or something. Which I probably have, since I've never driven the Trace, nor visited the surrounding area of Natchez. In fact, the last time I came to Natchez, the town, was in high school, when Dad and I visited for the Spring Pilgrimage, Natchez's annual tour of historic homes and associated events such as the Confederate Pageant, which, I'm embarrassed to admit, I really enjoyed.

I close my eyes and sigh. Once again, I'm reminded of my sister's insistence to call my father, a man who's been out of our lives for years now. I'm still angry at my father's disappearance, but I promised Portia I would make an effort.

I'm so busy thinking of my father and the pain he left behind that I fail to realize everyone has exited the van and are being greeted by the plantation's owner who's standing in the center of the circle of journalists. Even TB has left the cab, walking over to join the rest.

"Guess, it's time to put on my travel writer hat," I say to Stinky, who purrs.

After the emotional vision of Cora, I want to sneak my cat inside, find my plantation bed and take a nap, but we're scheduled for lunch in the main dining room, then a tour of the house and grounds. After that, it's hiking at a nearby site, a ghost town called Rocky Springs. Despite the name and what specters I might find there, I'm anxious to visit the old town that was once so prosperous about two thousand people lived and worked in this remote village.

TB turns and sends me a worried look.

"I'll be back soon," I tell Stinky. "I'm being summoned."

I climb out of the pickup truck and head towards the group. It's then that I hear a familiar sound. As I make my way through the crowd and spot the source of the voice, my fears are realized.

Ricky Esteban's the owner of this establishment.

CHAPTER TWELVE

"Welcome to Richfield," Ricky announces to the group once we're inside. "One of the few accommodations on the Natchez Trace besides campgrounds and one of the finest plantation homes in Mississippi, if not the Deep South."

"Thank goodness," Kelly says. "I'm all for a real bathroom."

"We've stayed in cabins at Tishomingo and French Camp and in retro Airstreams at Davis Lake," Shelby says, a bit defensive.

"All wonderful places," Ricky says, coming to her rescue.

Shelby's smile returns, Pepper frowns at the memory of her trailer, and everyone else looks ready for a nap. Dwayne's casing out the place. I'm hanging back of the crowd because sooner or later someone will start introductions or maybe Ricky will hand out our room assignments and my name will emerge. I'm trying to remain invisible while I can.

Ricky, on the other hand, is beaming having travel writers visit his plantation which, he announces to us, he purchased several months ago and is excited about the publicity. A short, petite man with salt and pepper hair wearing small, round glasses, he reminds me of a shy history professor I had at LSU who was so enamored with Huey P. Long that he failed to realize half his audience were asleep and the other half doodling away.

"There's so much to see here at Richfield," Ricky says, looking around the massive hallway filled with antiques, portraits, and elaborate crystal chandeliers. "But don't worry, I'll explain all in good time."

Jeff arrives and begins placing luggage inside the hallway. The journalists scramble for their suitcases, anxious to spend any amount of time in private repose; we have so little on these trips. Ricky's enthusiasm drops.

"Why don't y'all get your bags and I'll see you to your rooms," he finally says, realizing his audience has disintegrated. "You can refresh before lunch and then we're have our tour."

"Lunch is in thirty minutes," Shelby calls out.

Ricky pulls a set of key cards from his pocket and TB sends me a glance and I wince knowing what's coming. Ricky starts with Winnie, then hands Shelby her card and gives them both instructions on how to open the keypad on their room doors. They grab suitcases and head to bedrooms at the end of the hallway. Ricky calls out Dwayne's name and informs him that he has the bridal suite at the back of the house on the second floor.

"Well, isn't that special," Dwayne says with his trademark smile and glances at Pepper with a wink since Shelby has gone to her room. I feel Kelly tense at my side.

"Easy girl," I whisper to her.

Carmine's next and it's then I realize that Ricky is going in alphabetical order. Carmine, the Penningtons and Kelly receive their keys and are located by what I assume will be next to our room on the second floor. Kelly balks at the stairs but Ricky shows her the way to the elevator. Everyone heads off and Ricky returns, holding the final card in his hand. He starts to call my name, then pauses and looks up. I smile tentatively and do a little wave.

"You're the one who called," he says, and it's not friendly.

I start to explain but TB steps forward, hand outstretched. "I'm Thibault Boudreaux. I'm the one who originally called."

This derails the man. He looks down at the card and can't figure out how he missed TB.

"He's my husband," I offer.

"And so honored to be here," TB adds with a bright smile.

Ricky hands TB the card and explains that we're in Room 102, which opens on to the second-floor balcony.

"If you'll follow me, I'll show you to your room," he says softly.

Ricky turns and heads for the elegant staircase that ascends gracefully to the second floor. I glance at TB for support but he only shrugs, grabbing our suitcases and following the man. No one says a word while we walk up the long staircase, the ancient wood floors creaking every step of the way. Once we get to our room, Ricky explains the keypad, then opens the door to our room, an exquisite bedroom with four-poster bed, fireplace, antiques, and those floor-to-ceiling windows opening to a tree-sheltered porch with rocking chairs.

"It's lovely," I say, running a hand across the chenille bedspread.

Ricky tells TB how to control the temperature, shows him the bathroom, and then heads back into the hallway. "You access the porch through this hallway door. There's also a staircase to the rear of the porch on the house's left hand side, in case you want to explore the grounds. Just be mindful of the others; their windows open to the porch as well."

"Thank you so much," TB says, but Ricky looks down and shuttles away.

"You're got some feathers to smooth," TB says to me once he's back in the room, door closed.

Thirty minutes is next to heaven on a press trip. I could take a warm shower with expensive toiletries and super-thick towels, rest in this glorious old bed, or linger in a rocking chair on the porch and watch birds flit by on the live oak branches. Or I could head downstairs and make amends with Ricky Esteban.

I let out a deep exhale and leave the room.

"Be nice," is the last thing I hear my husband say.

I slip down the staircase, hoping to be delicate in my approach but the wooded floors built over a hundred and fifty years ago practically scream my entrance. I find Ricky in a sunny room off the back of the house, standing behind a bar checking in an African American couple. He's sees me coming and frowns so I look around the room that's been fashioned as a social gathering place for guests, complete with tables sporting board games and a bookshelf full of titles dedicated to Mississippi and its diverse history.

"Nice room."

You'd never believe I was a writer by the astute things that emerge from my mouth.

Ricky explains the lay of the land to the couple, asks where they're from, where they're going, do they need restaurant recommendations, and the like. I feel like he's taking his time here, but I guess I deserve it.

"My family's from around here," the man says with an accent-free tone. "Hoping to do some genealogy research."

Must be a trend, I think, or Ancestry has opened up a whole world of fun to people who like that kind of thing.

Ricky brightens and mentions how he's a local historian and happy to assist, all the while sending me a snarky look.

"Thank you," the woman says. "We appreciate the help."

Finally, the couple head to the one room on the ground floor that isn't occupied by our group. I'm ready to apologize but Ricky spends a good minute or two filling out a form before he looks up. I try not to get exasperated.

"What can I get you, Mrs. Valentine?" Again, no sense of friendliness here. "Something to drink?"

I offer a smile. "I'm fine, Mr. Esteban. Thank you."

We stare at each other for a moment, me standing awkwardly in the middle of the room and Ricky behind the bar poised like a soldier at a barricade. Finally, I approach, hoping he doesn't shoot.

"Look, Mr. Esteban, I'm really sorry about before."

"You were very rude on the phone."

I take another step forward. "I know, TB told me what you had said to him and it took me by surprise. I didn't mean to get so upset."

Ricky relaxes a little. *A little.* As if his name being mentioned caused him to appear, I see my husband coming down the staircase, sending me a look and then heading for the front door.

"Why does Cora Meyers mean anything to you, anyway?" Ricky asks. It's obvious I touched a nerve with this man.

"Why *doesn't* it mean anything to you?"

He shrugs. "She lived here for a very brief time. Wendell Meyers owned this place from the time of the Civil War until the 1930s. He helped bring slaves to freedom. He's the story."

Now, it's my turn to bite the inside of my cheek. "How do you know that?"

Ricky looks offended. "I'm a local historian and when I bought this place I learned everything I could from previous owners and their families. I think I know more about my property than you do."

"Don't be so sure."

I hadn't meant to go there, but my defiant tone has come back. Ricky's back straightens and he pushes his glasses up his nose and looks at me in contempt. "Mrs. Valentine...," he starts.

I decide to get back to civility. "Viola, please."

"Viola, I don't know why this means so much to you but I can assure you that I am the foremost authority on the Meyers family, including his first wife and son who both died young."

I gasp. Loudly. Which takes Ricky aback.

"Her son died?"

He must have read my emotional reaction for his tone softens. "Yes, not long after he was born."

My old friend heartache returns and I feel Cora's pain deep in my soul. The loss of a child. Is there anything worse in life? "Mrs. Valentine?" Ricky calls out to me, but I'm back in that black hole of despair.

The front door opens and I turn to see TB sneaking inside with Stinky in his arms. He puts his index finger to his lips to command me to be quiet, but as he comes closer he must see the pain lingering in my gaze for his forehead burrows and he mouths, "What's wrong?"

I shake my head, as much to resume composure as to make sure Stinky gets to our room without Ricky noticing; pets are not allowed at Richfield.

I look back at my host and change the subject, trying to swallow the lump in my throat. "Why is this plantation called Richfield? It was originally Briarwood."

Now, *Ricky's* forehead is twisted in curiosity. "Why do you want to know all this?"

There's no way around my inquisition. I step forward to the bar and place the two photos I found of Cora on top. After Ricky looks at them both, I turn them over.

"Are you related?" he asks.

I remember TB saying he had lied to the Archives Department so I decide to take that track. "Cora Schumacher's my great great grandmother."

The tension in Ricky's shoulders drops and he picks up the photo of Cora with the baby. But he's still skeptical, looking at me curiously.

"She had no offspring so how can you be related?"

Good question.

"Actually…," I pause, searching my *brain's* archives for an answer. "Cora had a brother who stayed in Kentucky and I'm descended from him."

"Why didn't you say so?"

Why not? Think Vi. Then TB's conversation comes back to me.

"Uhm, well, Cora was my great-great aunt but when I tell people that they don't take me seriously. Like when I did some genealogy work in Jackson, I had to tell people I was a direct descendent to get information. Apparently, they don't always divulge information to those who are not in the direct line."

I don't know if Ricky's buying this for that wrinkled forehead remains.

"And what do you know about her?" he finally asks, and I wonder if he's beginning to have an open mind.

I hear Winnie and Pepper laughing about something and heading for the stairs. A door opens downstairs as well and I realize my time is up. I grab the photos and put them back into my pocket, then lean across the bar.

"I think she was murdered," I whisper.

Ricky's eyes enlarge and he's about to inquire further but Winnie enters the room and starts exclaiming how much she loves the place. Pepper's not as enthusiastic; it's not her thing. But when Ricky suggests drinks, she perks up.

"What are you offering?" Pepper asks.

"Anything you want," he answers. "We have wine and locally brewed beer, plus soft drinks and sweet tea. Cocktails will be served before dinner."

Winnie and Pepper hesitate. It's only noon, after all. But when Dwayne waltzes in like he owns the place and loudly proclaims, "A cold beer sounds perfect," we all join the bandwagon. By the time the rest show up and we head into the dining room, we're either sporting glasses of beer or wine. All except Shelby, who asks for a Diet Coke, and Carmine, who takes a sweet tea.

"That's not like you," I say to him in jest.

He's not smiling. "Have to keep my wits about me," he says, and heads into the dining room, sitting next to Shelby.

For the hundredth time on this trip, I feel like Carmine's avoiding me or blowing me off. He's one of my best friends and his constant dismissal hurts.

We enjoy a lovely meal of chicken salad over fresh greens with candied pecans, cheese straws, deviled eggs, and pie for dessert. It doesn't get more Southern than this. Afterwards, we're aching for a nap, but Ricky rallies us for a tour of the plantation.

I've done my share of these old Southern homes, oohed and awed at the Mallard four-poster beds, the portraits of family members, the ugly ceramics people value as art, and the elaborate crown molding, as well as other architectural elements some — not Ricky, thank goodness — fail to mention were crafted by slaves. Richfield, on the other hand, captures my entire focus for it was this house that once belonged to Cora.

But it doesn't resemble anything from my visions. These are not the rooms where Cora sat with the witch tribe, or listened to Wendell offer marriage. The kitchen has been modernized, which is to be expected, and that sunny room where Ricky and I discussed the family might have been the back porch where Cora cried that night while her husband drank with fellow slave owners.

"Where is the original house?" I interrupt Ricky in the middle of his explanation of the European tapestry hanging in the front parlor. I didn't mean to blurt that out.

"The house was enlarged several times," he says.

He starts to return to that God-awful tapestry when I ask, "But where did the original house exist?"

Ricky gives me that semi-hostile look he bestowed on me in the back room, and sighs.

"The original house was your standard farmhouse back in the day. It consisted of a parlor on one side, a dining room on the other and a bedroom and kitchen behind. The original home had a front and back porch. When Wendell Meyers enlarged the home in 1861, he tore down walls and added on to either side. Most of the original house, Mrs. Valentine, is the massive hallway."

I'm standing on the threshold of the new parlor, so I step a couple of feet backwards and gaze into the hallway. There's nothing here to remind me of Cora, nor is there a feeling that she lingers in this space. It's just another expansive plantation.

I also consider what Ricky said, that Wendell enlarged the house at the beginning of the Civil War. Where did he get the money?

As we walk through what used to be Wendell Meyers' office I spot a familiar face on the wall. It's Wendell many years after Cora's demise for he looks about twenty years older.

"So that's the old man?" I say, then realize I said it out loud.

Ricky gives me what is now the familiar look. "Yes, that's Mr. Meyers," he says, and proceeds to tell the audience the history of the Meyers family. I'm not interested in what that man did either before or after Cora died so I wander around the room gazing into glass cases and checking out Wendell's reading material. Out of the corner of my eye I notice Dwayne studying me. I'm about to say "What?" but I hear Ricky gushing about how Wendell sent a mother and her son to freedom right before the Civil War.

"He sent the slaves to Kentucky, where Mr. Meyers had family, and they were set free," Ricky says proudly.

Again, I react before I think and let out a huff. Everyone turns and looks my way.

"I'm sorry," I begin, trying to explain my actions, "but I can't imagine a man who made this much money off slavery, enough to build this exorbitant home, simply giving away two of his slaves."

At this point, Ricky's about to chew my hide. "Mrs. Valentine, I know what I know," he says defensively, his voice almost cracking with emotion.

"I'm sorry, Mr. Esteban, but it doesn't make sense to me."

Ricky ignores me, Shelby exhales, and Winnie sends me a mom look while we all move into the hallway so Ricky can show off the enormous chandelier encircled by elaborate crown molding. I pause in the library, waiting for everyone to pass, including TB who gives me a half-smile. I half-smile back.

Just as I'm about to join the others, I notice Dwayne studying the Wendell portrait.

"Friend of yours?" I ask.

He smirks. "Funny, I was going to ask you the same question."

"I didn't mean to sound impertinent. I don't like misinformation."

"I think it's more than that."

Dwayne turns around so I can fully see his face and something in my gut tells me he knows I'm lying. My intuition also tells me to keep quiet about Cora.

"Like what?" I ask.

"Like it's someone you're channeling and you're close to a

crossover."

There were times when I couldn't get Lillye to eat certain foods, things like collard greens and scrambled eggs. I would do the fork airplane, bribe her — even disguise the offending food to trick her. I always got the same answer. She would look at me sternly and utter, "No, Mommy."

I'm getting that image now. The memory falls out of the ether like dust but the image's clear. Either my intuition is demanding I keep quiet or Lillye's coming through.

"I don't know what you're talking about," I say and move to join the others.

Dwayne catches my elbow and places his lips near my ear. "This is perfect. Meet me tonight and we'll send her up the ladder and you can watch me in action."

I pull my elbow free and say nothing, head over to stand by Winnie, but I catch TB watching.

"Let's say after dinner, then?" Dwayne whispers to my back. "Just you and me, love?"

I watch my husband tense and can't help wondering if Dwayne did that on purpose.

The tour wraps up after that and, because it went longer than expected, we have fifteen minutes to regroup or wander the grounds before heading over to Rocky Springs. I grab my camera and head outside, searching for something that tips me off to Cora's demise, but all I find are landscaped gardens, expansive lawns, gorgeous ancient oak trees, and a gazebo and reception area for weddings. To say I'm disappointed is an understatement.

"What was that all about?"

Winnie comes up from behind, shooting photos no doubt for the wedding publication she writes for. I look around and make sure no one's in sight, then lean close. "This is the plantation of the woman whose pictures I found at Tom's Wall."

"No shit," Winnie exclaims, then, because she's a mom, adds, "Pardon my French."

"That would be *merde* if it was French."

She rolls her eyes. "Whatever."

"But Mr. Esteban has a few facts wrong and I couldn't help myself."

"Like what?"

"He said she died in a mental institution."

"How do you know she didn't."

I don't.

"She's haunting me, Winnie. That means water was involved. And from what I've seen in my visions, I believe she was murdered."

Shelby calls to us and we head towards the van.

"The trouble is," I confide in Winnie, "I have no proof of this."

Winnie lets out a snort. "Then maybe you shouldn't pick fights with historians."

We go our separate ways, Winnie to the van and me to TB's pickup. When I jump in the cab I can feel the tension in the air.

"It's not what you think."

TB bites the inside of his cheek. "What is it then?"

"He asked me back at French Camp to accompany him on a crossover so I can witness how he does it."

TB shakes his head. "Are you kidding me?"

I knew he wouldn't understand but the force of his exasperation takes me by surprise. "You don't know the half of it."

The van takes off and we follow. "Oh, I understand all right. This crazed individual has convinced you that you will see our daughter and now you're going to walk to hell and back even though you know in your heart that he means you harm."

TB's voice has elevated; I haven't seen him this angry since the nurse was late with Lillye's pain medication.

"I've got to know, TB. I have to know."

"Know what, Vi? That this man is a fruitcake? He's slept with every woman on this trip, and probably killed that fox and broke Kelly's leg." He looks at me with big eyes. "Do you remember what happened when he talked you into the last crossover?"

I look down into my lap, wishing Stinky was here. The trouble is, I still don't remember what occurred that night and that hole in my memory haunts me. But then there was Lillye, standing in the middle of the street, beckoning me to reach her. Her image haunts me more.

"I can't help it," I say softly. "I need to see her."

TB pulls over to the side of the road, shifts the truck into park, and turns to look me dead on. He takes my hand, but from his tone I know this will not be a sympathetic conversation.

"Vi, you are not the only one suffering here."

This isn't what I was expecting.

"I buried my child and I grieved. But every time you go running after some pie-in-the-sky belief, I feel like I'm burying her all over again."

Definitely not what I was expecting.

"TB, I…."

"Nothing," he commands. "If you want to talk to Lillye, just do it. She's right here." He moves his hands around the cab. "Always. Why can't you see that she's right in front of your face."

I think of the message I received in the library and want so badly to believe what TB is saying, but I did see her. Dwayne showed her to me. She was as real as flesh and blood.

I say nothing and TB calms down. After a few moments, we get back on the Trace and head south. When the Rocky Springs sign comes into view, we pull into the parking lot behind the van. Shelby runs over to the driver's window, hands TB a brochure on the place, instructs us to read it and returns to the van.

"That was brief," I say.

"Might have something to do with you arguing with our accommodation's host."

Again, he's not happy, so I take the brochure and read about the town that began in the 1790s and peaked about

1850. Rocky Springs was a bustling town with a church, school, Masonic Lodge, post office — you name it — and it's all gone save for the church. First, the Union Army had thousands of troops stationed here, then yellow fever hit, followed by boll weevils ruining cotton crops and the springs drying up.

"Pretty sad," I say.

We follow the van through the woods, crossing streams and spotting deer and rabbits by the side of the road. I want to exclaim how beautiful this place is but the tension remains. The van halts at the beginning of a hiking trail and the other journalists emerge. When TB spots Kelly struggling with her crutches, he jumps out of the pickup and comes to her rescue.

"This trail leads up to where the old town was located," Shelby says. "There's a beautiful old church on one side and remnants of the town on the other."

We take off down the trail, pausing here and there to read the signs, admire the stream beneath the bridge, and assist Kelly who's struggling with the rugged path. When I spot the church, I know what lies behind, so I make my excuses to TB and Kelly and veer to the right.

Sure enough, behind the church built in 1837 by the Methodist congregation, there's a graveyard. I spot old tombstones and cast-iron enclosures inside, once an elegant homage to the dead but now a creepy spot probably frequented by teenagers driving the back roads looking for places to scare their dates. The grass is overgrown within the cemetery and bees buzz loudly from a hive high up a water oak. Most of the tombstones are discolored and in bad need of a cleanup — in New Orleans we do this every year at All Saints so I'm admonishing these people in my head — but none of this stops me. I've always admired old cemeteries and the histories they contain.

For instance, there's a tall elegant monument to Sarah, daughter of John and Harriet Stevens, who died in 1854. Sarah was twenty-five, at least entered adulthood, but it's obvious the pain her death caused her parents for they spared no expense at her funeral.

"Thus, the human heart bereft," the monument states. "And nothing but memory is left."

Is that true, I wonder? Is all that's left of our time on earth nothing but a memory? Or is Lillye still here, as TB insists, existing on another plane, waiting to communicate? And what of Dwayne's conjure of Lillye? Was that real or was he playing with my fears and desires?

The bees buzz around my head, much like the confusion running through my mind. I sink to the ground, not worrying that the overgrown weeds are still damp from the latest rain. What is the truth, I wonder?

I sit in this sacred space for several minutes before I begin. Since no one else has braved this rugged piece of land — and people are forever scared of cemeteries and I've never known why; I find them beautiful — I think of what TB said in the truck. I close my eyes, take a deep breath, and think of my once special child. And I begin to speak.

"I miss you," I start, but the pain's too deep for words. Tears pour down my cheeks but I try to focus, imagine she's here, believe that she can hear me. Like my experience at Tom's Wall, I swear two tiny hands touch my shoulders, and that sweet smell that was all Lillye invades my senses. I breathe it in, tell her in my mind how much I love her, will always love her, and ask that she guide me.

In an instant, the moment passes, the bees, a lone cardinal call, and a slight breeze rustling the overhanging tree branches the only sounds. Once again, the dark hole reappears, threatening to swallow me whole.

Before I fall inside, before I descend into the familiar pain, that cardinal perches on a tombstone in a lone area of the wooded graveyard. It seems to beckon me so I wipe away the tears, gather my emotions, and wander over. The tombstone's badly discolored, covered in a brown and beige dirt layer, so I lean down to remove as much of the grass and grime as I'm able.

Here, in this lonely place that history has forgotten, lies the son of Cora Meyers, aged three months old.

Right behind his stone is a smaller one, that of Cora Meyers.

CHAPTER THIRTEEN

"April twenty-third," I tell TB. "Cora's death date is September the ninth."

We're back in our room and TB's writing down what I'm rattling off nonstop.

"Did you get all that?"

He doesn't respond and he's biting his cheek again.

After my foray into the Rocky Springs cemetery, Shelby gathered us together for a hike, a chance to enjoy the natural side of the Trace, she said, adding with a laugh that it'll also help walk off that big Southern lunch. Kelly raised her hand to remind our host that she couldn't walk far so I grabbed the opportunity.

"I just got an urgent message from my editor," I said. "I really need to go back to the B&B and send over edits. Kelly can ride over with us."

Half the group gave me a look that said, "Take me with you," and Kelly practically squealed with glee. Talk about a pack of weary journalists.

The three of us — TB, Kelly, and I — squeezed into the pickup cab, Kelly talking nonstop all the way back to Richfield about her latest cover feature and her upcoming press trip to New Zealand. For once I was not feeling jealous; my trips usually stick to the Deep South and I can't help turning green when I hear of journalists heading overseas. This time, I was too busy contemplating what I had witnessed in the cemetery.

"What did you get?" I ask TB.

He looks up from his laptop. "Seriously? The Internet is great and all but it does require human research."

I shrug. "I thought you just pulled it up on Ancestry."

TB shakes his head. "How did you get through journalism

school?"

This smarts, because I never was good at research. "I got As in writing. The other stuff wasn't as much fun. Besides, look where it landed me, following cops around in St. Bernard Parish. I'm good with police procedure, little good it does me now."

"It might," TB mumbles, "if you keep solving murders."

I start pacing the room because I'm excited. Finding out when Cora died might bring up information on what happened.

"This is 1860," TB says, reading my mind. "Don't get your hopes up. They didn't record everything like they do now."

I pause. "It won't tell me how she died?"

TB exhales, looks up, and crosses his arms about his chest. "Okay Miss College Graduate, you need to leave me alone and let me do my work."

There's something about his tone. Resentment? All this time I thought he didn't mind not having a degree. His well-paying job certainly took the sting out of being interrupted in college by a baby. Or maybe I was too blinded by money — journalism pays squat so I was always jealous of his salary. Did I fail to realize he had dreams? But just what are those dreams?

I almost ask about him going back to LSU but I'm still hurt he didn't tell me. Now, I wonder if I say something he will think I'm patronizing him.

"I'm going for a walk," I tell TB and he grunts affirmation, studying his laptop.

I was hoping he'd find answers quickly and we could traipse through the plantation grounds together. It'd be a good time to explain what happened with Dwayne at French Camp, how I saw Lillye, and what I plan to do tonight. Maybe it's best, I think, as I watch my husband digging through the Internet. The less he knows, the less he'll try to talk me out of it.

I grab my jacket and scarf and head out the door.

"Take Stinky with you," TB says without looking up. "I

ran out of kitty litter and he probably needs to poop."

I don't have two seconds to respond to this insane suggestion when Stinky goes flying out the door, heading down the hallway to the second-floor balcony entrance. There are so many logical problems with this scenario but I'm thinking it's time to roll with it. I open the balcony door and Stinky takes off around the corner, me following right behind. We pass Kelly's room and I see her through the window talking animatedly on her cell phone, her broken leg prompted up on a pillow, she leaning back on an elegant four-poster bed. The next room before the back staircase must be Dwayne's and I attempt a peek inside but the curtains are pulled tight. Stinky leaps down the stairs, heads to a group of nearby shrubs and does his business.

"That cat's not right," I say to myself, hoping that he continues to be strange and doesn't run off into the woods.

When my feet hit the ground floor, Stinky emerges from the bush and meows. I look around to make sure my host doesn't see. Have no idea how to explain me walking my cat in a no-pet accommodation. Stinky meows again and walks off toward the woods and my fears are realized.

"Stinky," I call out in a whisper.

He looks back at me for a second as if waiting for me to follow. And, of course, I do, thinking the whole while that I'm following a cat! But then, I see dripping wet ghosts and my friend believes in fallen angels so why not?

We enter woods consisting of pine trees, oak, and a few other hardwoods so there's a mixture of year-round greenery and bare branches. A chilled breeze makes my cheeks tingly and the fallen leaves crackle under my feet. A blue jay cries out and another answers a few yards away. The trees sway in the breeze and hum, much like those bees did earlier. I exhale my worries and enjoy the moment, following my orange tabby down a solitary path deeper into the woods.

"Where are you going?" I figure I might as well have a conversation with him.

Stinky turns his head slightly and meows, as if to say shut

up and follow. And I do. I look back at the big house and it's barely visible now through the trees. There's something similar about this scene, however, as if I've been here before. I think back on when Cora helped her slaves fix their cabins, the spring sun beating down on her face, she happy with her new home. When I look back again, I realize it's about the same distance from the main house.

I nearly trip over Stinky, who's come to a halt. He lets out a yelp as I step on his tail.

"Sorry, but what's the big deal?"

I look up to see a group of bricks sticking out of the ground, as if an old wall once stood here. As I get closer, I find more bricks in the shape of what must have been a building of sorts, the wood rotted and disappeared leaving behind remnants of a foundation. I lean down and study several of the bricks, rectangular but not perfect, and all sporting slightly different colors. I suspect they were made by hand.

Stinky falls on his side and rubs up against a few bricks, purring away. He makes himself comfortable among the leaves and brick debris while massaging his head against one of the larger bricks. Taking his lead, I sit down among the ruins, too.

"I wonder what used to be here?" I ask him and he meows.

I decide to enjoy the solitude of the woods, so I lean back against what's left of the wall. In an instant, the vision comes to me.

I'm standing outside a slave cabin that's located next to a brick smokehouse and the smell of roasting meats invades my senses. I'm busy studying the brick building with the tin roof, imaging what delicacies lie inside because I'm so very hungry, when I see Cora and Menasha walk up, heading toward my home.

"I didn't do nothing."

I look up to find a beautiful African American slave woman and feel an instant connection.

Menasha holds up her hands. "We're not saying you did, child."

Cora comes into the light of the candle that I'm holding and she appears to have aged ten years, which couldn't be possible considering she died a few months after her three-month-old son. As her face becomes clearer, I know why; I spot the familiar pain. She's carrying a parcel in her arms, held tight against her chest as if a balm for her now empty arms.

The slave woman named Rebecca Hamilton backs up a step nervously and is almost inside our cabin. "He made me do it."

Cora steps closer, and before Becca can slip away Cora grabs her hand. "I know that. I want to help."

Menasha turns to me. "Jacob, go make yourself scarce."

Jacob? I look down and find I'm wearing rough trousers that reach above my ankles and a torn calico shirt. I'm barefoot and dirty and my stomach growls from emptiness. This body can't be more than twelve.

"What the...?" I begin, but Becca gives me a stern look so I quickly say, "Yes, ma'am."

"Let's go inside," Menasha says and the three women enter the cabin and close the door.

I must know what's going on so I crawl underneath the house — it's raised for better circulation in the humid south — and sit quietly beneath where the women are gathered inside. The floorboards are rift with holes so I can make out their faces. I hear my mother offering them something to eat, but instead Menasha pulls a couple of biscuits and a small tin of coffee from her pockets.

"We have to be quick," Menasha says. "We've given the master something to keep him sleeping for a while."

Becca looks scared, afraid of what these women will do to her, but she nods.

"The mistress has arranged for you to travel with someone she trusts, an old friend of hers from Kentucky."

"Travel?" Becca says with alarm, looking from one woman to the other. "You selling me?"

Menasha rubs her hands on the front of her dress and gives Cora a look.

"His name is Bertrand Willis and he's a good man," Cora says. "You can trust him. He's the brother of Mary Willis Tillerson, my dear

friend, and they are both children of a man who helped raise me when my parents died."

Becca stammers, "Are you selling me?"

"Listen, child," Menasha says sternly. "It's for your own good."

Becca calls out my name and I can hear the fear, sense her panic from beneath the floorboards. I'm ready to call back and assure her I'm okay when Cora takes my mother's hands.

"He'll be going with you," she assures her. "You'll both be safe where you're going. Safe from the likes of...." She looks down at her feet, gathering up what little fortitude she has left since her child died. "...my husband's ways."

A horse neighs outside the cabin and all three women jump.

"We have to hurry," Menasha says. "We haven't much time."

Cora hands my mother the package she's carrying.

"There's money here. Some food. A blanket. Salt."

Becca takes the package but she's still confused.

"Bertrand has the papers on both of you. I can't free you from here but he will once you get to Kentucky."

"I don't understand," Becca says. "Where's this Kentucky."

"Far from here," Menasha inserts, "but don't you mind that. You're heading to a much better place."

"And Jacob...."

Cora nods and attempts a smile but it's feeble. "Of course."

Menasha places a hand on Becca's back and moves her to the front door. "Grab what you can. I'll fetch Jacob. But you must leave now."

I scurry out from underneath the house, dusting myself off before the women open the front door. I instantly spot a nicely dressed gentleman in the seat of a wagon, a healthy mule in front.

"Howdy, young man," he calls to me with a smile.

I'm speechless in front of this well-to-do white man but he appears friendly enough. Will he be taking me to this Kentucky? I shake my head because it's becoming unclear the difference between me and this young Jacob. Of course I know where Kentucky is!

"Jacob," Menasha calls to me. "Help your mother get her things into the wagon."

Momma is pulling items from the cabin and I take them, shoving them over the wagon's side. This white man has already filled half of the wagon with barrels and sacks of something but there's room for us. At my back, I hear Menasha assuring momma that everything will be all right.

"You're still a slave," Cora tells Becca. "I sold you to Mr. Willis at the courthouse in Natchez so he will have papers on you and Jacob as y'all travel through Mississippi. Otherwise, it wouldn't be safe, someone might grab you both."

Momma nods and hangs her head. I sense she feels that the mistress is getting rid of us because of what happened between her and the master. Cora gently places a finger beneath her chin and raises her eyes to hers.

"Mr. Willis will set you free when you get to his farm, you understand me?"

Momma looks down at her feet again but Cora repeats the chin raising. "Rebecca, I'm trying to help you."

"Yes ma'am."

Cora sighs. I don't think she believes momma. "I want what's best for you and Jacob. And the new one on the way."

What? Momma's having a baby? I shake my head again, realizing that this new life might be the product of Rebecca and Wendell Meyers.

"Yes, ma'am," Momma says.

"Once the master goes to New Orleans, I'll be on my way to y'all." Cora looks up at the nice man in the wagon. "Thanks to my dear dear friends in Kentucky, I might now have a future."

The man in the wagon smiles back.

"You have my word, Mrs. Hamilton," the man says to Momma, the first time I've heard a white man call my momma by her last name. "Mrs. Meyers and I have an agreement. Once you're free, you're welcome to stay and work on my farm. For pay, of course. In fact, my wife has three young'uns and she sure could use some help in the kitchen."

Something about this man and his warm way of talking relieves the tension in Momma and she braves looking up at him. "I'm right good at cooking, Mr. Bertrand."

He tips his hat. "Well, then, that'll do just fine."

Holy Moses! A white man tipped his hat to my momma.

Cora slips a letter into Momma's pocket and leans close. She's whispering so the man won't hear but I catch what she's saying.

"I trust him completely. But I want you to send this letter back to me *when you get there. Put a swig of rosemary from his garden inside so I know for sure."*

Momma nods quietly.

"And please," Cora whispers. "Name the child after your late husband and not mine. He deserves a better father."

"Yes, ma'am."

The nice man in the hat helps my mother into the wagon seat and Menasha looks at me, nods for me to jump in the back. I turn around thinking she's looking at someone else.

"You child," she fuses. "Get along now."

I do as I'm told, remembering I'm a young African American child, but once I'm settled Menasha touches my hand where it rests on the wagon's side and squeezes. I'm surprised because I never thought that woman liked me, always yelling at me from her kitchen in the big house.

"You take care, you hear?"

The man kicks the mule into action and we take off through the slave quarters, then on to the road that leads to the Natchez Trace. I look out the back and watch sad Miss Cora, Menasha, the slave cabins, fields of cotton and indigo, and the main house of Briarwood disappear.

Suddenly, I'm standing next to Cora and I'm back to being Viola. I look down at my hands to make sure I'm seeing right but they blur in front of me.

"Vi," a voice calls out.

I look up and spot young Jacob in the back of the wagon, waving at me through the fog.

"You can't trust him," he yells out.

"Who?" I ask, wondering if it's Wendell Meyers he's speaking of.

"Don't go anywhere with him," Jacob answers. "He wants you, but if he finds out about us he'll take us with you."

I'm confused and I look to the women at my side for guidance but they're fading away. In fact, the whole world is now covered in gray fog. And yet, somewhere in the dark ether I hear Jacob still calling out.

"Remember the kitchen herbs."

I awake with a start, the kind where you snort and find dribble on the side of your mouth.

"Taking a nap?"

I look up to find Dwayne casting a shadow over me. I bolt upright and lean back against those bricks that I now know made up the smokehouse. "I must have dozed off."

He laughs and that charm emerges. If I didn't know better, he'd be a perfect man, good looks and all. Right now, his shadow gives me the chills and I pull my jacket tight about me.

"I thought you had an urgent edit assignment," he says.

"I did," continuing the lie. "When did y'all get back?"

Now that I think about it, the sun's lower in the sky and darkness descends.

"About ten minutes ago. Thought I'd go for a quick walk, see what's around here." Dwayne nods towards the bricks. "Guess you found something."

"Old smokehouse, I think."

His eyes narrow. "You've seen that in a vision."

That chill runs through me again and I shake it off. "Read about it somewhere."

He gives me a sly grin as if he knows I'm lying. "Dinner's in twenty minutes."

Startled, I jump up realizing it's much later than I imagined and I may have lost my cat. I call out Stinky's name.

"Stinky?" Dwayne asks.

"Long story."

I look around the woods but my cat's nowhere to be found. A horrible thought flits through my mind, that Dwayne may have hurt him in some way. I search through the brick remnants, behind the surrounding foliage and trees, and am just about to panic when my tabby comes strolling out of the woods.

"Thank God," I say, but Stinky immediately halts, the hairs on his back at full attention and his back arched skyward. He's spotted Dwayne and begins a deep low growl that makes the hairs on my own neck rise.

"Where the hell did that cat come from?" Dwayne asks, trying to appear unfazed.

"Long story," I repeat, then begin down the path toward

the house, as far away from where Dwayne's standing as I can get without struggling in the brush. I call out to Stinky but he's still starring down Dwayne, that growl growing louder and fiercer.

Dwayne reaches down and grabs a branch so I call to Stinky once more, this time more urgently, and the cat reluctantly trots off behind me, his back hairs still standing at attention. Once we're a good way down the path toward home, I lean down and give him a pat the length of his spine.

"Good boy."

He meows but there's fear laced in that tone, and I'm pretty sure his heart is beating as fast as mine.

We saunter up the steps to the second-floor balcony, passing the Penningtons shooting photos in the late afternoon light, that sweet moment for photographers. They look at Stinky, then gaze up at me.

"Long story," I say as me and my cat head towards our room.

Before I'm around the balcony corner, TB's there, eyes wide with concern.

"Are you okay?" he asks as he picks up Stinky, who's happy to be back in TB's care.

"Weird experience in the woods."

I don't go into detail because one, the cat needs to get inside ASAP and two, what I've learned remains for TB's ears and no one else's.

"What's going on?" TB asks once we're inside our room.

"What's the dress code for dinner?"

"Kinda fancy. Shelby stopped by and said the mayor's coming to dinner."

"How much time do we have?"

"Fifteen minutes."

I need to shower, wash my hair, and change but my heart's still in action mode. I exhale deeply, wishing I had a glass of wine.

"You going to tell me what happened?" TB asks.

I look up at my darling husband, dressed in that nice royal

blue shirt tucked inside his best Levi's. The man doesn't own anything dressier than this look and I wouldn't want it any other way. I long to grab him, pull him on to that four-poster bed, and send those clothes flying but work beckons.

"I have to shower. But I got a name. Rebecca Hamilton used to be a slave on this plantation and Cora sent her and her son Jacob to Kentucky with Bertrand Willis, a member of the Kentucky family that took Cora in when her parents died."

I see the wheels turning in TB's head and I hope he's getting all this. I grab some clothes from my suitcase and my ditty bag. "Do you think you can check that out while I get dressed?"

He silently heads to the bed and his laptop and as I watch that adorable blonde head pull up the Internet, I wish with all my might I didn't have to be somewhere in fifteen minutes. What heavenly things we could do in that time. Stinky jumps up on the bed and nestles close to him, and TB scratches behind an ear while he studies the laptop screen.

In a flash, I realize I love this man. I always did, both during and after our life with Lillye, the question always being was I *in* love. And yet, in this moment watching TB work, his blonde curls falling about that boyish face, my crazy cat by his side, I know it's more than sharing a life and a child, that even though Lillye forced us together and we made the best of it, that I cut the cord when Katrina arrived and I started a new life, my love runs deep into my soul. Am I ready to commit? To stay with him forever? A feeling so sublime pours through me, like flipping on a switch in the darkness. Yes, I think. I am.

Fifteen minutes later I'm clean and dressed and feeling punchy from the realization of before. I take TB's arm and hug him close as we descend the stairs, wondering if we could renew our vows in some glamorous place such as this. He glances at me wondering what's going on, but I don't make eye contact, simply savor the moment and the feel of his arm on my cheek.

"Hey guys," Winnie calls out and joins us.

We ask about the hike and what they saw while waiting for the rest to join us. The Penningtons arrive, and Joe leans close to my ear and asks about the cat.

"He's our baby," I whisper. "We couldn't leave him at home and he travels like a dog so why not?"

Joe laughs. "I wish our cat would do that."

I shush him. "Don't let Ricky know."

"Don't let Ricky know what?"

I turn to find my host impeccably dressed, standing behind me.

"That I'm going to spotlight your place in my publication," I blurt out, hoping my editor feels the same. "It was going to be a surprise."

He brightens. A bit. The man's a tough cookie. He pushes his glasses up his nose and motions for us to go into the dining room and, like cows to the barn, we follow because something smells incredibly delicious.

The others are already there, gathered about the table and speaking with a tall drink of water that Ricky tells us is the mayor of the small town nearby. Ricky makes announcements, formerly introducing us to the mayor, and we gather around the table to sit. Just then, the couple I saw from before enter and look at both the journalists and the spread before them with hesitation.

"Come in," Ricky says to them with a big smile. "Please, join us."

"Are you sure?" the woman asks. "We don't want to intrude."

"Absolutely," Shelby says. "We're a bunch of travel writers visiting and the mayor's here to talk about the town. You're in for a treat."

The man and his wife relax and head to the table where two chairs are free. As they move into the room, I get a good look at them both. My breath catches and I audibly gasp, for standing before me is the spitting image of Jacob Hamilton.

CHAPTER FOURTEEN

TB, the Jacob look-alike, and his wife all stare at me like I've gone mad. I look around the table and find that most everyone else is staring as well.

"Love this crystal," I gush, grabbing a glass and holding it up. "Mr. Esteban, where did you find this beautiful set?"

Ricky turns on like an iPod and starts discussing the history of this ugly crystal set — did I mention antiques outside of the twentieth century don't interest me? I sneak a peek back at the man now seated on my right and he's looking back with curiosity.

I can't help but stare. He resembles the boy in my vision, what I managed to see once I got out of his body. It's those chocolate brown eyes, the tilt of his head — even his hands look the same and I saw those plain as day.

"Uncanny," I say out loud, not meaning to.

"What?" the man answers with a tone. "You've never seen a black man in Mississippi before?"

"Jacob," the woman admonishes him.

For the second time, I gasp, and once again the whole table notices.

"Do you like the dishes too?" Dwayne asks with a knowing grin. What he realizes, I can't imagine. I want to tell this Jacob he reminds me of a former plantation resident but of course this will come off odd and I don't want Dwayne to know what I've discovered in the woods.

"They're spectacular," I lie. They look like something my great aunt Gertrude used to have.

I get the feeling everyone senses something else is going on but after an uncomfortable pause, they all start talking again, mostly asking the mayor questions about the area. I turn to the couple who are still studying me with a quizzical expression. I lean in close to Jacob so I don't garner anyone else's attention.

"You remind me of someone," I say in little more than a whisper.

"Your gardener?" Jacob asks.

His wife sends him a serious look. "You are being rude," she whispers.

Jacob looks down at his plate and begins playing with his knife. "Sorry, Ms…?"

"Valentine."

"Ms. Valentine." He looks up and smiles but it's more for show. "First time visiting the great state of Mississippi."

He knows his ancestors lived here as slaves. I can feel it. And he doesn't like it one bit.

"No worries," I say. "I get it."

He leans in close and his attitude is anything but friendly. "Get what?"

"Jacob!" His wife places a hand on his forearm and squeezes.

"Y'all alright down there?" Ricky asks.

I smile and assure Ricky all is well, but Jacob's still not smiling. I lean in close to my table partner and say quietly, "Mr. Esteban doesn't like me much because I don't agree with his history of the place."

Jacob's countenance changes immediately. "And what might that be?"

I feel a burning sensation on my left side and look over to find Dwayne studying me.

"Tonight," Dwayne mouths with a sexy smile.

Next to me, TB tenses. He's noticed the transaction between us. I sigh because I feel like that goldfish in a bowl. And then there's Carmine, who keeps looking my way as if he's checking on me.

The salad course arrives and a nice African American lady places my dish in front of me and I notice Jacob giving his wife a knowing look as if to say, "See, things haven't changed." When the nice lady announces that she's a local caterer, and what we're eating was farm raised at her place, his wife gives him another stern look.

I decide to focus on my salad for a while and Jacob remains silent, too. After a while, however, his curiosity gets the best of him. "What history?" he asks.

I turn my head so my voice resonates within his earshot only. "Mr. Esteban thinks that the owner, Wendell Meyers, helped slaves to freedom. But I believe it was his wife, Cora, who sent a family to Kentucky."

As I suspected, Jacob reacts to this news. I add, "The slaves she sent away were Rebecca and Jacob Hamilton."

His wife must have heard that part for she drops her fork on to her plate.

"You know about the Hamiltons who lived here?" she asks loudly.

Everyone at the table stops talking and looks our way once again.

"You must know our history," Ricky steps in. "I was going to explain all that when I give you a tour in the morning but it sounds like you've read about us already."

Dwayne studies me again and that knowing smile returns. I clear my throat, remembering young Jacob's warning. But what is it that Dwayne might want to take control of?

The wife starts to say something, but Jacob grabs *her* forearm this time and says, "We're looking forward to that."

"Mrs. Valentine here is related to Cora Meyers," Ricky announces, and I wince. TB, who had a fork of greens heading upwards, stops mid-bite and gives me a funny look. Jacob and his wife also gaze upon me with a surprised look. I smile and shrug. But it's Dwayne's comment that ruins my appetite.

"Cora's descendant," he says. "I can't wait to hear all about it later on."

Dwayne gives me a wink and TB throws down his fork, his appetite apparently disappearing as well. I try to get my husband's attention, to reassure him he's being played, again, but he won't look my way. Instead, he begins a discussion with the couple about Natchez and its many attractions.

When the chicken course arrives with its farm-to-table beets and mashed sweet potatoes, my favorites, I'm not hungry at all. Still, I manage a few bites listening to the mayor go on and on about the travel opportunities of the region, the new brewery and rum distillery in Natchez, and how places such as Richfield tell more of the antebellum story than plantations of the past. I feel Jacob stiffen to my right and Ricky sends me a worried look, I suppose waiting for me to announce that Wendell raped slaves, not sent them to freedom.

When the crème brûlée arrives, and the conversation at the other end of the table heats up, I turn toward Jacob. "I'd love to talk to you about the Hamilton family."

"I'd like that as well," he says quietly and I'm thankful no else is privy to our conversation. "After dinner?"

I look over at Dwayne who's busy charming up Kelly. Back to girl one, I think. Kelly catches me staring and I shake my head, hoping she gets the message that falling for this man once again is not a good idea.

Watching this interaction also makes me determined to discover who this man really is, what his intentions are toward me and my SCANCy talents. How did he make Lillye appear? Will I be able to do it as well? Why does Carmine fear him, and Jacob the younger feel he's a threat? Against my better judgment, I must know.

"I can't this evening, I have to meet someone," I tell Jacob and notice TB stiffening at my side. "How about over breakfast?"

"That would be lovely," Jacob's wife says, and I realize I don't know her name.

I hold out my hand to them both and introduce myself.

"Jacob Summerland," Jacob says, giving me a hearty handshake. "This is my wife, Melissa."

"Nice to meet you."

"We have to leave around ten tomorrow," Melissa says. "We're meeting a genealogist at the library in Natchez."

I so wish I could tag along. "We're leaving around ten as well, heading to Natchez for a bus tour."

"When is breakfast?" Melissa asks Ricky.

"Are you hungry already?" Ricky answers and everyone laughs.

"Just making plans," she answers with a sweet smile.

"How's eight sound?" Ricky says. "Then we'll have our tour and the travel writers can explore the grounds if they like."

"Or sleep in," Pepper adds.

I know that everyone will be down at eight, so I suggest meeting the Summerlands at seven-thirty in the back room and they agree. It's close to nine when we finish, and even though any other night I'd be raring to go, all I want to do now is slip inside that beautiful bed and close my eyes. The others appear to have the same idea and head off to their rooms, but even though my body is demanding I join them, I hang back.

"Your date's waiting for you," TB says as he passes me in the hall.

I start to dispute this but my husband's long strides are eating up the staircase. I look for my buds Winnie and Carmine but they're ahead of TB, now on the second floor. Within what seems like seconds everyone has disappeared into their rooms.

All except Dwayne.

He's hanging out on the back veranda waiting for me to join in whatever weird thing he has planned. I catch the red glow of his cigarette as he takes a puff, watch the cloud swirl about his head. My logical mind is screaming to join TB but my feet keep walking toward the back room, my hand opening the parlor door and entering the dark, cold night.

As I do memories come flooding back. Lillye's sweet little hand in mind, struggling to walk across the living room floor. An older Lillye on the swing set in the back yard, singing *You Are My Sunshine* as she swings back and forth, her head wrapped in a scarf because she lost all her hair. Her looking up at me from the hospital bed, telling me it would be alright.

But the image that stands out as I walk down the stairs to meet Dwayne at the fountain is Lillye in her high chair, arms crossed as I try to get her to eat collard greens.

"No, Momma."

In a flash, she shakes her head and says sternly as if she's right in front of me now.

"No, Momma!"

I stop at the edge of the fountain and Dwayne greets me with a smug smile.

"I knew you'd come."

He throws the cigarette on the ground and stamps it with his toe. He zips up his jacket tight and starts off toward the woods.

"Where are you going?" I ask.

He stops and looks back at me but since he's left the penumbra of the porch light all I can see are the whites of his eyes. "To show you how it's done."

I cross my arms. "Show me here."

He cocks his head. "You want to do a crossover here in the middle of the patio where everyone can see, SCANC girl?"

That old thought that's been roaming around my head returns. "I don't have anyone to cross over, Dwayne. You're a SCANC, you show me."

This derails him a bit; I barely make out his eyes narrowing. "Fine. Let's go in the woods and do this."

"Do what?"

Yes, I can really be stubborn when I want.

"You know what."

"You're going to suddenly find a ghost in need, have them climb the ladder, and while they're at it touch the light and that makes you evolve?"

He comes closer and I can now make out his face by the house's back safety light. He's impatient with me. "What's the problem?"

I take a step back. "The problem, Dwayne, is I don't think you're a SCANC at all. Just who are you planning to cross over here? And are you going to promise to call their loved ones like that poor girl in Tishomingo and then fail to do so?"

When he reacts to my last statement, I add, "Yes, I know. I called them."

"What you don't know, SCANC girl, is I called them after you did."

He's lying. He's tired like the rest of them, full of good food and wine, and was hoping to get this over quickly and his defenses are down. I feel it.

"What's your specialty, Dwayne?"

He steps closer. "The question is who are you channeling, Vi? Cora? Her dead baby boy? Or one of the slaves? Maybe all of them. What a boon that would be."

I remember Jacob's warning from the back of the wagon and Lillye's voice echoes in my head.

No, Momma.

"I'm not offering anyone to you, Dwayne. And I don't think I will evolve by stealing other people's souls as they cross over. In other words, I'm not going in those woods with you."

Dwayne realizes I'm not moving and he pulls his hands through his dark black hair. He looks around the patio and notices the wedding reception hall off to the right. "Fine, we'll do it over there."

For the first time in days, I'm not scared of this man. I step closer. "Do what, Dwayne? What is it exactly you do? And what is your SCANC ability, you never said."

I can tell he's getting *really* impatient with me.

"I showed you your daughter, you ungrateful bitch."

His language is like an unexpected slap to my face but I sense it's worse for him. He's losing control, something he's not used to.

"Do you want to see her or not?" he asks.

Of course, I do, I think to myself, but I just did. Maybe

TB's right. She's right here and ready to be with us. All we have to do is ask.

And yet, that black hole emerges when I remember the smell of her petite head, her soft fine hair that was constantly unruly, flying every which way. The sound of her feet as she trotted into our bedroom on Saturday mornings, begging us to rise so she could watch her cartoons. Her laughter watching *Sponge Bob*. How she smiled even in the worst of her pain.

I close my eyes hoping to stem the darkness about to swallow me whole.

"You see, it's right there." Dwayne's voice is getting closer, its tone soft and seductive. "You have the ability to be with her. Let me show you how."

No, Momma.

I open my eyes and find Dwayne right in front of me.

"Come with me and you'll be able to be with your darling Lillye."

He's messing with my fears and desires again. How he does this, I'll never know, but I swallow hard and call forth the greatest mother of all. I ask for strength, feeling my resolve rise from my toes to the top of my head. I straighten my back and stare him straight in the eyes.

"Don't you ever. Say. Her name. Again."

And with those final words, I turn and head back toward the house.

"You're missing out on a great opportunity," he yells out to me.

"You're wrong," I say to the darkness as I head inside. "I already had the greatest opportunity."

My adrenaline is racing from the experience and I pause at the staircase railing to catch my breath. Once my heart has resumed a steady beat, I head upstairs. But I'm not going to bed. I need answers and it's time Carmine Kelsey gave them to me.

I don't just knock on his door, I demand entrance. "Carmine," I practically yell.

He opens the door dressed in *Star Wars* pajamas, the kind a kid might wear. Who knew? But I don't waste time contemplating this.

"I want answers," I tell him. "And I want them now."

Carmine quietly closes the door, pulls his robe's belt tight around his waist and looks at me. After several seconds, he nods. "Okay, but first we need bourbon."

I make myself comfortable in the nearest chair and watch my friend and mentor pull one of the finest bottles of bourbon from his suitcase.

"Where did you get that? You couldn't have possibly brought that on the plane."

"Never you mind." He throws two ice cubes in a glass and fills it up.

"Water please."

Carmine places a hand on his chest in astonishment. "*Mon dieu.* That's sacrilegious."

"I don't care and neither should you. I'm rather pissed at the moment."

He heads into the bathroom and I hear the water running, then returns with my drink with a sour look on his face. "I thought better of you, being from New Orleans."

I take a large gulp, savoring the burn on my throat and the warm feeling that's on the way. Anything to get my heart beating normal again.

"I thought better of you for not leaving me in the dark about that creepy man from Texas."

"Don't blame Texas," Carmine says, sipping his drink.

I lean forward in my chair and look him straight in the eyes. "Forget Texas, what the hell is going on?"

Suddenly, he looks concerned. "Did something happen tonight?"

"Carmine!" I'm so frustrated I could nab one of those frilly pillows and beat him senseless.

He raises a hand in appeasement. "Fine. I'll tell you everything but you have to have...."

"An open mind, I know."

He takes another sip and leans back in his chair, getting comfortable. "Remember how I told you there are theories why certain people are psychic."

Images of vomiting in a bathroom come to mind and my stomach turns. "Right, angels had sex with humans and those with their DNA are psychic."

"Some people."

I wait for more but he's hesitating. "And?"

His face furrows. "Do you believe me?"

"I'll let you know when you're finished."

He leans forward, elbows on his knees. "It's like when you have a flat tire in the middle of the desert and a nice person comes along and fixes it for you. Or you're about to get hit by a bus and someone appears in the nick of time and gets you out of the way."

I nod. "Angels among us. My Aunt Mimi loves that song by Alabama."

He raises a finger. "Not angels, but their descendants."

This is heading in a strange direction and my face must show what I'm thinking for Carmine leans closer. "You still with me?"

"Trying to be."

That must be good enough for Carmine for he continues. "There are different types of descendants based upon their paternity. Some people rally for injustices, others are protectors. I'm a messenger, which is why I felt the need to explain how you're a SCANC when I first met you on that press trip to Eureka Springs. Well, that and your aura."

"My aura?"

"Descendants can read auras. That's how we recognize one another."

I take a long drink and place the empty glass on the table by my side. This is getting good. "You're saying I'm an angel?"

Carmine sits silent for a beat, then places his own glass down. "No, darlin'. I'm saying TB and I are angel descendants. You're a witch."

At this point, I know he's pulling my leg. I don't know what angers me more, that he would tell me this cotton-picking story or use this moment when I'm so frazzled to play a joke. I stand and head for the door. "Screw you, Carmine."

He grabs my hand before I can get far. "Vi, I'm not kidding."

He says it with such force and certainty, I pause and study his face. I'm waiting for some smug smile to emerge or for him to start laughing, but he's as sober as a priest on Sunday morning. Besides, Carmine has never been one to play tricks on me. Winnie, maybe, but never Carmine. He was always the serious one, the dad telling us to behave.

"Sit down, Vi," he says. "Please."

I head back to my chair and slip my legs under me, get good and comfortable because if he's for real, I want the whole enchilada.

"When you said you had left your camera behind," he begins, "I called TB and suggested he bring it up, asked Shelby if TB could join our press trip."

"I know, because you wanted us to have quality time together."

"Not at all. Because he's a descendant and I needed him here to protect you."

I shake my head. "You're saying my husband's an angel?"

"Descendant."

"And you wanted him to protect me from whom? The devil from Dallas?"

Carmine exhales. "I don't believe in the devil. I think hell is here on earth."

"Well, whatever. I assume from that drunken escapade the first night, where you blabbed on and on about fallen angels, that Dwayne's not one of the good guys."

"No, he's not."

Carmine rises and gets the Woodford Reserve, sits back down and pours us both a glass. He doesn't add water to mine, but I let it slide. Think I need it straight up at the moment.

"But, *you're* one of the good guys."

Carmine blushes and I nearly fall out of my chair. This is a first. "I'm a messenger. That's all."

"And TB?"

Carmine sits back down and gazes at me hard. "He's a protector and a warrior. Has it on both sides of his family."

I shake my head and smile. This is too much. "What? No."

Carmine downs his bourbon much like I did moments ago. "His aura is as bright as lightbulb, Vi. I need sunglasses looking at him."

"TB?"

"Yes."

"My husband?"

"Vi, yes."

"If this is true...," and I give Carmine the stink eye because if he's ribbing me I will knock him into the middle of next week looking both ways for Sunday, "...then why hasn't he ever said anything?"

Carmine pours us another. "He doesn't know. At least I think he doesn't. He's a sweet man, your husband, but he's a little...."

"Now you're saying it."

"Okay, so he's a little simple-minded. In a good way."

"But if y'all can read auras...?"

He leans back in his chair, back to sipping his bourbon. "I don't know, Vi. He's never mentioned it to me. My way of thinking is to let that dog lie. A man like TB, who offers nothing but unconditional love, it's probably best not to let him know he has such power."

"Power?"

"Well, like I said, it depends on paternity. I'm just a messenger, but TB, he's got some strong stuff going on there."

Which brings the conversation back to my lack of angel DNA. "So, why isn't he psychic?"

"Not all descendants are psychic. And maybe TB's holding

back."

I think of our conversation about Lillye, how he talks to her, feels her presence.

"And me?"

"Like I said, there are two theories here."

"And one is being a witch?"

I rise and begin pacing the room. I detest labels, and the word witch travels with enormous baggage.

"Please don't tell me you're still in the broom closet," my gay friend says.

I shrug. "I love stones and herbs and the power of nature, and I believe there is much healing to be gotten there, much like my ancestors who were burned at the stake for that word. Which is why I don't like 'witch.'" I emphasize witch using fingers for quote marks.

"People today now own that word."

"Do they?" I send him a sad smile. "So, hags on broomsticks and stirring cauldrons at Halloween are all positive images of our history?"

Carmine reaches out and takes my hand again. "We all have our negative images to overcome. But we have to wave our weird flag proudly."

I squeeze his hand. "I'm not a witch, Carmine. I don't know anything about all that. I definitely don't wear capes and wave wands at witch-a-cons and create altars at home."

He laughs. "Now you know why I don't like SCANC gatherings." He sobers a bit and adds, "But those people are still authentic, Vi, and so are you."

I think about Aunt Mimi and her herb garden, how people would show up and purchase herbs when she lived in Alabama and I'd visit in summer. She taught me a lot about tinctures, poultices, and brews to heal what ails you, but the word witch was never spoken. Heck, back in those days, we never talked about speaking to the dead either. It wasn't done. It wasn't until after Uncle Jake's death that she came out to me about her psychic abilities.

Then there was Grandma Willow, supposedly the finest

soothsayer in Alabama.

I shake my head. "Buying crystals in a store and carrying gris-gris bags around for protection doesn't make me a witch."

Now, it's Carmine squeezing my hand. "Honey, your aura is deep green. Trust me, I know who you are."

I sit back down across from him, and we both sigh.

"What does all of this have to do with Dwayne?" I finally ask.

Carmine looks down at his lap and rubs his hands up and down his thighs. "I never wanted to get you involved in this, Vi. He's here for me, something we never finished in high school and have been battling ever since."

"Here for you, how?"

"I don't know what his plans are, but I have friends like me — descendants — who are hoping to catch him in the act when we get to Natchez. Word on the street is that something's going down at the Angels on the Bluff event tomorrow night."

"Wait, the what?"

Carmine smiles. "It's the name of the annual candlelight tour of the old Natchez Cemetery. I didn't make it up. It's a fabulous event, sells out every year. You'll love it. But we've heard Dwayne has something planned."

I think back on the last few days, the horrific scene at Pepper's cabin, Kelly's broken leg, my lack of memory from the night at the creek. Whatever's coming must involve the group somehow. I share my worries with Carmine, confess my conversations with Dwayne, including tonight's. He's not happy with me, but he listens and takes it all in.

"He loves messing with people," Carmine finally says. "He's probably trying to keep us all at odds."

"And the God Light?"

Carmine turns silent and I know there's more to this crossover magic than he's letting on. I wait to see if he'll explain but he suddenly looks exhausted.

"Can I help?" I ask.

Carmine looks up as if he's seeing me for the first time, then shakes his head and smiles. "You can go to bed and stay close to that sweet husband of yours. And for god's sakes, stay away from Dwayne."

"Carmine," I say sternly, "you can't do this alone."

He takes my hand and stands, pulling me up with him and leading me to the door. "I'm not alone, sugar. No worries." He gives me that daddy look. "Keep this to yourself. Not even TB. *Especially* not TB."

"But you haven't told me all."

We're already at the door, which I find open. I feel a hand at my back pushing me into the hallway.

"Carmine," I protest.

"Good-night, Vi."

With those final words, Carmine closes the door.

"I saw your *Star Wars* pajamas," I say to the wood staring me in the face.

I stumble to my room and find TB sitting in bed working feverishly on his laptop. He looks adorable in his reading glasses, a big dollop of blond hair cascading over one eye. I'm flooded with feelings, a warmth that spreads through me like wildfire, something so needed after this crazy night.

And, I must admit, I'm looking for a halo.

"I don't want to hear about it," TB says sternly and whatever joy I felt at seeing him disappears.

"It's not what you think."

He remains silent, typing away.

"I wasn't with Dwayne." I'm reminded of our heated conversation at the patio fountain so I revise, "Well, I was with Dwayne but not for long. The rest of the night I was with Carmine."

TB glances briefly at me over his glasses. "Are you drunk?"

I kick off my shoes and try to pull off my socks without falling over. "Maybe. Carmine wouldn't cut my bourbon with water like I asked. He's such a snob but then he has great taste in alcohol."

"Carmine?"

I want to explain everything, about my rendezvous with Dwayne and how Lillye's memory kept me from doing something incredibly stupid, Carmine's talk of angels, and how something serious is about to happen in a Natchez graveyard tomorrow night. But Carmine insisted I remain quiet so I do.

TB senses I'm holding back. He shakes his head and returns to his work.

"I'm leaving in the morning," he says.

I'm halfway removing my pants but I jolt up, almost toppling over. "What? No!"

"There's no reason for me to stay. I'm in the way of whatever you're doing."

I finally pull off the offending pants and throw them at the chair, and miss.

"TB, I need you here." In more ways than one.

He closes his laptop and pulls off his glasses, placing both on the side table. "I don't know what you need anymore, Vi. But I need to go home."

I haven't seen him this despondent since I asked for a divorce after Katrina. When we got back together this summer, I thought things were moving along nicely.

"I need you," I tell him. A small voice inside my head insists I add how much I love him, too, but the words fail to come. I'm too drunk.

He smiles sadly. "Do you? Then tell me what's going on."

I want so badly to explain, to ask about his angelic ways. Does he even know what he is? More than anything, I want to jump that long trim body and make wild love in an antebellum bed. But I hear Carmine's insistence in my head, to keep everything under wraps. That maybe it's best my simple-minded husband who loves unconditionally not know of his powers. That in order for him to keep me safe, I must do the same for him.

So, I say nothing.

"Good-night, Vi." TB turns off the light on his side of the

211

bed. "I'll be gone after breakfast."

Standing in the middle of that enormous plantation room, I feel like Scarlet O'Hara at the end of *Gone With the Wind*, when she finally comes to her senses about Rhett Butler but it's too late. Maybe not, I think. I grab my nightgown and TB's keys to the pickup and head for the bathroom. I change for the night and brush my teeth, then dig in the bathroom cabinet until I find the appropriate item. I pull out a roll of toilet paper and place TB's keys inside the cardboard tube, then replace the roll in the back of the cabinet and cover it with a box of Kleenex.

I climb into bed and turn off the light, slip an arm about my husband and place my face upon his back. I inhale the delicious smell of him, a mixture of musky soap and something sweet that's all TB. As I fall into Lala Land I wonder if that special smell comes heaven sent.

Just before I fall asleep, I feel his hand on mine.

CHAPTER FIFTEEN

I wake to find two faces staring at me, one looking down standing by the side of the bed, and the other on my chest. I bolt to a sitting position which causes Stinky to dig in with his claws.

"What time is it?"

"Time for you to get up," TB says, and I realize he's fully dressed.

I grab my cat that's about to puncture holes in my chest, hold him close, and pull my feet over the side of the bed. I glance at the clock and realize I have fifteen minutes to get dressed and downstairs for my talk with the Summerlands.

"Why didn't you wake me?"

TB's pacing the room, looking under chairs, behind pillows. "I've been too busy trying to find my keys."

I say nothing, drop Stinky on the bed, grab some clothes, and head to the bathroom. I can still hear TB tearing up the room while I dress, wash up, and brush my teeth. Before I join him, I reach into the bathroom cabinet and retrieve his keys within the toilet paper roll and slip them inside my jeans pocket. I head into the bedroom like nothing's happened.

"Ready?"

TB shakes his head looking around the room. "I have to find my keys."

I grab his sleeve. "Let's go get breakfast. I'll help you find them when we return."

We're a few minutes early but the nice lady who served us last night is busy in the kitchen; I hear her moving pots and pans. I stick my head inside and find Menasha's rugged kitchen with the wood-burning stove and pie cabinet now looking like something from *Southern Living*. There are stainless steel appliances, a commercial stove, a fridge that could hold a cow, and gorgeous granite countertops.

"Wow, nice digs."

The nice lady looks up and smiles. "Isn't it? Wish I had this spread at home."

Not me, I think. My idea of cooking is watching someone else do it.

"By any chance is there coffee available somewhere?"

The catering lady brightens with a huge smile and I'll bet she's this cheerful all the time. "Yes, ma'am. It's just about brewed. I'll bring it out."

"Thank you. We're in the back room, thought we'd get together a little before breakfast."

"Yes, ma'am."

I cringe. I'm only thirty so hearing people call me ma'am, even though it's the polite thing to do down south, makes me feel old. So, I decide to nip this one in the bud. "I'm Vi," I say, holding out my hand.

"Carol," she answers, then hands me a card that says, "The Long Hot Simmer, catering by Carol Zimmerman."

"Cute."

That big smile returns. "Thanks."

After Carol assures me caffeine relief is on the way, I head to the back room and find the Summerlands talking to TB about their early morning walk. Apparently, they ran into each other by the pond, TB walking Stinky for his morning constitution.

"Your cat is something else," Melissa says to me.

"That's one way to call it."

We sit around one of the room's tables and make ourselves comfortable, Melissa pulling off a jacket.

"It's actually warm out there," she says. "I don't know what happened but it's warmed up and the wind's blowing like crazy."

"Probably a front coming through," I explain. "It sucks up warm air from the Gulf and then rains. Once the front rolls in it'll drop several degrees in minutes."

"Weird," Jacob says.

I'm about to repeat that stupid saying we love to tell visitors — "If you don't like the weather in the Deep South, wait five minutes" — but it's so trite, I don't. I'm ready to start discussing Jacob's ancestors. Instead, TB beats me to it.

"I did some research." He opens his laptop. "There was a Rebecca Hamilton and her son, Jacob, reported as runaway slaves by Wendell Meyers of Briarwood Plantation in 1860. I found it in the courthouse records."

Jacob looks at TB's laptop and his eyes light up. "That's fantastic."

"If you give me your email, I'll send y'all this document."

"That'll be amazing," Melissa says, equally excited.

So, that's what my husband was doing last night. I'm so impressed I remain quiet and watch him in action.

"I did find some bad news, however." TB turns the laptop to Jacob and I see Jacob's excitement fall.

"Oh no."

"Yeah, sorry."

"What?" I ask.

Jacob turns the laptop toward Melissa and she sighs and frowns.

"What?" I repeat.

"Rebecca's son died of fever on the Trace," TB says to me quietly. "I found an old newspaper story about it. They got sick at Buzzard Roost Spring near the Tennessee border. She and the man she was traveling with survived, but the son did not. He stumbled into the backyard to get to the creek, must have gotten dizzy because he fell in and drowned."

Oh my God. That child I spotted at Buzzard Roost. That was Jacob. Explains why I also channeled him here at Richfield.

"But Rebecca lived," I say to Jacob, the one in front of me. "And she was your ancestor?"

He nods, but that sadness remains. I feel it, too. Poor Becca, travels out of slavery and rape to freedom only to lose her son in the process.

"She ended up marrying my great-great grandfather in

Kentucky and they owned their own farm, had nine children," Jacob says. "She lived a very good life."

He's holding something back, and I think I know what it is.

"Your ancestor was conceived here," I quietly say, and everyone looks at me startled.

Suddenly, Carol and her sunshine enters the room. "Coffee!" she announces cheerfully.

We all try to regroup emotionally and allow her access to the table. She places a huge platter in front of us.

"There's real cream, sugar, that horrible artificial stuff." She chuckles at the last part. "And some tea bags and a pot of hot water if anyone wants tea."

"Wow, thank you so much," TB says.

The two exchange enthusiastic smiles and I wonder if Carol's an oblivious angel, too. It warms my heart watching this pair until TB catches me staring and his smile disappears. Now, my heart plummets. He still thinks I traipsed off into the night with Devil in a Blue Suit. Which, of course, I did.

"Let me know if you need anything," Carol says and hurries off to the kitchen where something smelling unbelievably good is cooking.

"Thank you," we all say to her wake.

When the kitchen door swings back, Jacob crosses his arms and sends me a stern look. He wants to know why I think he's descended from someone else, pre-Kentucky. I decide honesty is best.

"I'm a medium."

This isn't what they're expecting. Even TB is surprised.

"I know it sounds crazy but I can sometimes talk to those who have passed on."

Melissa does the sign of the cross, which could go either way. Sometimes Catholics are open to souls walking the earth and sometimes they see it as the work of the devil. Speaking of, I wonder where Dwayne is this fine morning. I look around to make sure he's not listening in.

"And who are you speaking *to?*" Jacob studies me hard.

He's not sure he believes me but I sense he's open to the idea.

I need coffee first. I pour myself a cup and add a dollop of cream, take a sip and sigh. "I have seen the mistress of this house and her kitchen slave helping Rebecca and Jacob escape by way of a man named Bertrand Willis."

"Yes, we know about that," Melissa says enthusiastically. "They have been friends of the family for generations."

I smile at this news but inwardly I'm grimacing, wondering how to breach this painful subject.

"Go on," Jacob says.

"Rebecca was with child when she left. I believe it was Wendell Meyers' and Cora was helping her escape because Wendell had threatened to sell them off."

No one says anything for several moments, until Jacob nods.

"We knew there was someone else," Melissa says. "His great grandmother's birthdate was before her parents' marriage although we didn't find that out until we started doing genealogy research; they always lied about her age. Some people in the family said she was a product of Rebecca's first husband but when we found his death certificate, that didn't jibe."

"There's also that white glow about me," Jacob says with a sad smile. "My line was always a bit paler than the rest."

"I'm sorry," I say.

"Also explains how my great grandmother's name was Cora."

Cora had a namesake? This warms my heart. "Cora would have been so pleased. She was an avid abolitionist."

"What happened to her?" Melissa asks.

I look at TB but he shakes his head. Obviously, his research pulled up nothing on the house mistress.

"She died in a mental institution."

We all turn at the sound of Ricky's voice. He's standing at the threshold of the back room, holding a vase full of flowers.

"If y'all are ready, we're meeting in the dining room for

breakfast."

And with those few words, he leaves.

Melissa and Jacob rise, thank TB for his research, me for my whatever you want to call it; that's how Melissa describes my channeling. The couple head to breakfast and TB closes his laptop.

"Wow, that was great what you found."

He gives me a hesitant smile, like he's not sure he's allowed such compliments.

"TB?"

He places the laptop under his arm. "I'm going to find us a seat."

I'm about to follow when I remember something Jacob said as he traveled through the darkness in that wagon so many years ago. Before he lost his life halfway up the Trace.

I head to the kitchen and hope that Carol is busy serving the others breakfast in the dining room. She's nowhere to be found so I start digging through drawers. I find some cloves and bay leaves, search through jars of herbs and spot some fennel. Nothing that can do damage but protection might be more what I need.

"Can I help you?"

I jump and turn, smiling nervously. Carol heads to my side, still sporting enthusiasm but her forehead creases as she gets closer and sees what I'm doing.

"I was looking for herbs," I say.

She glances down at my collection, then studies me hard. "You have some bad mojo following you around?"

She says it half-jokingly as if she's not sure that's what I'm doing. I straighten. "Yes. How did you know?"

She shrugs and looks at the three herbs I have placed on the counter. "Don't see you putting those on your eggs."

"But...?"

She waves her hand and reaches into her pocket, pulls out a weird looking thing resembling a nut.

"St. John the Conqueror root," I say, marveling at the item before me. I've been having a hard time finding this legendary root because my favorite botanical shop in New Orleans flooded during Katrina and has yet to reopen.

"Named for an African prince," Carol tells me proudly. "Was sold into slavery but he routinely tricked his master and made it back to Africa one day."

"I've heard the stories," I tell Carol, "always wondered if the legend helped those in bondage keep faith or if there indeed was an African prince named John. I usually keep one in my protection gris gris bag, although I didn't bring one with me on this trip."

She places the root in my hand and closes my fingers around it. "Take it. I have more at home."

I'm speechless at her generosity, especially since she barely knows me. And yet, I feel like we're soul sisters.

"I love the stories, don't care if they're true or not," Carol continues, placing biscuits on to a tray. "My favorite is John falling in love with the devil's daughter, Lilith, but the devil told him he had to plow sixty acres in half a day before he could marry her. Lilith told John that her father would kill him regardless, but John finished those acres, stole the devil's horse, took Lilith, and they escaped back to Africa."

I smile, savoring the feel of this magical man in my hands. The fact that his wife had a similar name as my daughter isn't lost on me, either. "Good story."

Almost as good as Carol's smile; it's enough to brighten the world.

"Keep it," she says. "John left his magical powers in this root because if he used them on his own, the devil would find him and Lilith. So, the root's ours now to protect us." She pats me on the arm. "And you."

I have no idea what I'm up against with Dwayne, what evil he has intended for tonight or what Carmine hopes to conjure to counteract this event. But I place my root in my pocket and vow to Carol that I will keep it there.

"Now, hurry up and get a seat before the eggs get cold."

I do as I'm told, enter the dining room, and sit next to TB, who chose two chairs as far away from Dwayne as possible.

Good thing, too, for Dwayne's sending me the evil eye big time. I reach into my pocket and hold my root tight, but to my surprise TB wraps a protective arm about my shoulders and gives Dwayne a defiant look. It feels good, although I know I still have road to travel to convince my husband I didn't do what he suspects I did.

"Where's Carmine?" Winnie asks, and I realize my buddy's not present.

"On the back porch on his phone," Pepper mumbles, her head bent over her eggs.

Someone woke up on the wrong side. But it's been a long trip with plenty of drama for all of us so we mostly eat breakfast in silence. All except the Summerlands, who talk excitedly to Ricky about what TB has found and how Jacob connects to this place. I notice Dwayne listening closely, asking questions here and there. Jacob responds and I long to kick him under the table but he has no idea of Dwayne's intentions, whatever they may be.

Ricky, on the other hand, is blanching. He has a few evil glances for me, as well.

Shelby arrives all bubbly and gives us fifteen minutes to pack up and meet the van out front. Half of us groan and several of us — you know I'm one of them — gulp down our coffees and head to the rooms. When no one's looking, I slip two of those fabulous biscuits into my pocket and nab a slice of bacon for Stinky and a to-go coffee for me.

"How are we getting the cat out of here?" I whisper to TB on the way up the stairs.

"How are we driving home is the big question?"

I pull the keys out of my pocket and hand them to TB.

"Where did you find them?"

I think to come clean, express my love and appreciation, and beg him to stay but I'm surrounded by cynical journalists. I shrug instead. "They were right on the bed."

When we reach the landing, I spot Kelly struggling to exit the tiny elevator. Her crutch catches the elevator threshold and she's about to lunge head-first into the nearby wall and a table full of miniature ceramic dogs when TB bounds forth and catches her within inches of disaster. Kelly gushes her thanks, Winnie expounds on TB's quickness to action, and I'm downright astonished. I saw the accident about to happen but couldn't have saved her in time. TB wasn't even looking in that direction.

Carmine passes me on the staircase and I hear Winnie explaining to him how my husband saved the day. Carmine catches my eye and smiles, that lone eyebrow raised to the heavens.

"I get it," I say under my breath.

It takes us several minutes to return to our room for everyone's enthusing TB's actions and Kelly's pouring forth gratitude. As usual, when TB's in a situation like this, he appears uncomfortable, constantly telling everyone that it was nothing, that anyone would have done the same. I stand on the periphery sipping my coffee, taking it all in, wondering how the hell I never saw this before.

"You're my angel," Kelly says and I nearly spit coffee all over the place.

Once again, my husband takes it wrong and his smile disappears. I'm about to regroup and say something, wipe the coffee from my face, when TB announces that we all need to get going and everyone moves to their room to pack up. TB and I slip into ours and he immediately starts throwing clothes into his backpack.

I close the door and lean against it, wonder how to get out of the pickle I'm in. I'm so proud of him right now, for the work he's done, for going back to school —heck, for being an angel without having to announce it to the world. I cringe on that last thought, still can't wrap my mind around that one, wonder why I never suspected, although how on earth would someone know? I'm also in love with a man who I thought I needed distance from, thought we weren't compatible, imagined that after Lillye died that that would be the end of it.

And yet, how do I tell him this? If I brag about his

research, will he think I'm patronizing? Or worse, patting him on the head that he's finally got some smarts? He imagines I think he's dense, which, I admit, he has grounds to do. All those years raising Lillye while we worked different careers, followed by endless silence between us, he retreating to the television and me to that black hole, did I label him that to justify what was as much my failure to communicate as well as his? We lost a child, most marriages don't survive that heartbreak. I could have at least tried. On the other hand, maybe we're both struggling to survive the worst heartache imaginable.

"I'm sorry," I say.

TB turns and looks up. "For what?"

"Everything," I whisper.

Again, I suspect he thinks I'm talking about Dwayne, who's the farthest thing from my mind.

"Whatever, Vi. We're married in name only. You made that clear long ago."

He throws his backpack over his shoulder and heads for the door, but I grab his arm. I lean into his shoulder and breathe him in, let my cheek fall on his upper arm.

"There's no other man. There never was." I look up into those baby blue eyes, his gaze curious and longing. "It wasn't about Dwayne as a man. It's about me and this weird situation I find myself in."

"And what situation is that, Vi?"

This surprises me for he knows how it all went down on August twenty-ninth three years ago.

"The storm, the trauma, the ghosts I have to save."

"And what goes down tonight?"

"Tonight?" What does he suspect, I wonder?

"What did you and Carmine talk about?"

I avert my eyes, TB closes his and grimaces, and I long for all the world to explain what Carmine told me but I have specific instructions to remain quiet. Finally, TB exhales, pulls the backpack over his shoulder.

"I'm going to take Stinky down the back staircase. You go

out the front with the rest and hopefully no one will notice."

He grabs Stinky under one arm, checks the hallway for people, then leaves, the antique door creaking in his wake.

I pull my stuff together and follow, hoping to see his pickup in the parking lot when I leave the building. But it's nowhere to be found.

"Where's your husband?"

Dwayne stands confidently, dressed in jeans and a neat T-shirt, slipping on sunglasses. I touch St. John in my pocket more to ease my broken heart that protect me from this man, who I won't give the satisfaction of answering.

Shelby calls us to order and we all say our thanks to Ricky, who avoids me, then we all climb into the van. Everyone's lethargic so you'd think we're climbing the stairs of Gibraltar. I find a seat next to Winnie with Carmine behind and they both look at me surprised.

"He left," is all I say.

This concerns Carmine. Greatly. He gazes out the window searching for TB's truck but it's gone.

"What did you do?" Winnie asks.

I'm about to say I failed him but the words get stuck in my throat, lodging there like food you were too quick to enjoy. I look out the window at that sleepy pond, the burnt orange cypress trees and the majestic oaks, that old Southern porch with its rocking chairs, and everything starts to blur. If only we had one more day to pause and enjoy this place, TB and I making love before breakfast, spending the afternoon on that porch reading, talking. Taking a long walk through the woods. I know why Cora decided to keep this place, to stay in a convenient marriage instead of returning home to Kentucky an old maid with coins in her pocket. It's magical.

It's also incredibly sad. Too much ugly history and heartache stain these magnificent houses. One reason why I can't blame Ricky for believing those family stories about Cora, instead of the horrific truth about Wendell.

That lump in my throat finally passes. Well, yes, I can. Before this trip ends, I will be setting Ricky's history straight.

"What was all that about Cora being connected to that nice couple?" Winnie brings me back.

Dwayne sits up front, trying to cheer up grumpy Pepper while Shelby looks downcast. The man never stops. Knowing he can't hear me, I fill Winnie in on what TB and I found, how we believe Cora was the savior of Rebecca and Jacob, how she lost her son at an early age and died not long afterwards.

"And not in a mental institution," I add, although I still have no idea how she died.

We enter the Natchez city limits and Shelby announces that we have now exited the Natchez Trace, the end of the line. We drive through the quaint, riverside town that's home to hundreds of historic homes, thanks to Union General Ulysses S. Grant, Shelby tells us, who refused to burn the town belonging to the nation's millionaires at the time of the Civil War.

"Natchez was one of the richest cities in America, if not the richest," she says proudly.

We pass delightful homes and churches, mostly nineteenth century architecture with a few late Victorians thrown in. Before we hit the downtown area, Shelby points out a couple of massive antebellum homes. And I mean massive.

"The city was founded by the French in 1717 — the oldest city on the Mississippi River," she says.

"Oldest *European* city," Pepper adds. "Wasn't it named for a tribe?"

Shelby straightens her blouse and her smile fades. "Yes."

We park at a hotel by the river and disembark. The plan is to check in, break into groups, and experience a horse-drawn carriage ride through the historic town, then have lunch in a tavern claimed to be the oldest surviving building. After lunch, we're visiting a distillery and a brewery, then heading to the annual "Angels on the Bluff" cemetery tour. At the latter being mentioned, Pepper finally brightens.

Once again, I wish TB was here. I'm not the only one.

"Where is your husband?" Carmine whispers to me

heatedly as we grab our suitcases.

When the carriages arrive, the Penningtons take a carriage to themselves while Dwayne offers his hand to Shelby who blushes, then sweeps Kelly off her feet and places her in the back. He then jumps inside and sits between the two, an arm stretched over each shoulder. Both women smile for all the world.

The rest of us — Carmine, Winnie, Pepper, and me — groan collectively, then enter our own carriage, although two on one seat and two on the other. I find myself next to grumpy Pepper, who still, no doubt, is thinking I murdered a helpless animal or stole the man of her dreams. Or maybe it's the fact that she's left out of Dwayne's arms, once again.

"He's a jerk," I whisper to her.

"Doesn't help that they flirt with him all the time," she says so low I barely hear her.

I take her hand, and those heavily mascara eyes look at me, surprised. "He's playing you all. *They're* not the enemy. He is."

The carriage driver, a delightful man named Steven Winn, introduces himself and we're off, our hair flying madly since the wind has picked up again. I'm ready to hear a tale of hoop skirts, pageants, and the "War of Northern Aggression" but our tour guide delivers a well-balanced story of Natchez, starting with the French building Fort Rosalie on the Mississippi River bluff and the native tribe resisting and being annihilated by the French.

"Uh huh," Pepper utters next to me.

Holding on to his hat, Steven explains the history of the town, how its wealth grew on cotton from neighboring plantations, and how these fancy homes were built for owners who'd rather be socializing with other rich families than isolated on rural farms. Natchez sits on a dramatic bluff, a protection against the river's annual flooding, and below the town at the river's edge steamboats arrived and products loaded and unloaded. Called Natchez-Under-the-Hill, the mini town owned a reputation for violence and prostitution, so when our poor horse navigates the steep road down to the

Mississippi, we see both sides of the city.

We cover a lot of ground, including some pretty impressive churches and a synagogue; apparently some Jewish bankers and merchants came in at the turn of the century and gave an economic jolt to the town. Steven pauses at the Forks of the Road where slaves were auctioned off.

"To give you an idea of the prosperity of Natchez, slaves might have cost twelve hundred in Virginia before the war and sixteen hundred and up here in Natchez," Steven tells us.

"That's disgusting," Pepper says.

"Another tragedy," Steven says as he turns his horse toward the tavern and lunch, "is the Rhythm Club fire where in 1940 a fire broke out in a nightclub and hundreds of people were trapped inside. Two hundred and nine people were killed."

As we pass the site of the former nightclub, a sadness pours over me. I look to Carmine and know he's feeling it, too.

"But not all is sad," Steven says. "Natchez is also home to novelist Richard Wright and many other African Americans who were successful."

The carriage finally stops at King's Tavern, a building that definitely appears to be the oldest in town, something dating back before Gone With the Wind architecture. Steven thanks us and we disembark.

"Y'all going to the Angels on the Bluff tonight?" he asks.

"Yes," Pepper says enthusiastically. "Can't wait."

"Great event and a gorgeous old cemetery," Steven says. "Right on the river. If you get a chance, go back during the day and walk through."

We all nod but when you're on a press trip, your time's not your own.

"If you're really adventurous, head a little further north and visit the Devil's Punchbowl," he adds. "It's an old ravine back there where pirates and other nefarious people hung out."

Pepper beams but Carmine and I share a glance. We'd

rather not.

The interior of King's Tavern is even more interesting, a few tables surrounding a bar, a roaring fireplace to our left, wooden beams interrupting a low ceiling, and a brick floor that looks like it might have been here since its inception. I can easily picture Trace travelers, pirates, and Cora herself enjoying a hot meal and beer after a long walk from Kentucky, thrilled to be finally back in civilization.

The owner gets us situated and takes our orders, offers us local beer which I choose, wanting to be in the spirit of the place. He then explains how the tavern was the end of the road for most or the beginning for others, depending on which way people were heading on the Trace.

"Because there were so many travelers coming through, it also attracted thieves and murderers," our host tells us. "Many times people rested here until others arrived and then went out on the Trace in groups. But many people lost their lives traveling through Mississippi with money in their pockets after selling their goods downriver."

"We don't have that problem anymore," Shelby pipes in with a smile.

I savor my beer and some delicious flatbread but I can't keep my eyes off that fireplace. I notice Carmine glancing there as well, so I slip close to his side.

"What happened here?"

He's a gay SCANC and his ghosts are few and far between so I'm casting my line way out there. Sure enough, he shakes his head. But we still feel it. As if someone was murdered here.

Afterwards, we visit the rum distillery next door, listen to more tales of gypsy, tramps and thieves, and then we're off to the Natchez Brewery and a fleet of beer samples. Pepper's in hog heaven, perks up nicely, and heads outside to play lawn games with other millennials. The rest of us, however, are getting sleepy and I'm longing to call TB and find out where he is. Shelby gets the message and offers to drive us back to the hotel, but Pepper asks to remain.

"It's only a few blocks," Pepper says. "I can walk back."

Shelby hesitates and I wonder if it's because she's our press mother — they're anal about knowing where we are at all time — or if she's worried about our youngest member and the incidents that have plagued us on this trip. That strange sensation I felt at the tavern returns so I encourage Pepper to come with us and get some rest before dinner. She glances over at Dwayne and shivers, then surprisingly, agrees.

Once back at the room I open my curtains and admire the rich amber colors of the sunset over the Mississippi. Storm clouds are gathering in the west and the wind rattles my window and lets out a howl. According to The Weather Channel, the rain's due close to midnight so our stroll through the cemetery should be blustery.

I flip open my cell and call TB but it immediately goes to voice mail. I lay back on the bed and try a nap, hope to receive a visit from Cora and discover how she died, but sleep won't come. The air sizzles with electricity with the incoming cold front and my sinuses are going crazy. Finally, I pull on a jacket and head to the lobby for a Diet Dr. Pepper. Who should I run into but Jacob Summerland.

"Well, hey there," I say.

"Hey, yourself." He gives me a hug that surprises me because I thought only people south of the Mason Dixon Line did that.

"I've had the most informative day." He reaches into his bag and pulls out several sheets of paper. "Your husband is a whiz. First, we went to the courthouse and found all kinds of information. Then, the library, where we found lots more. He's really good at this genealogy stuff."

"That's awesome," I say, trying to keep the hurt from my voice. All this time he was in Natchez. "What did you find?"

Jacob pulls me onto a lobby couch. "After Cora died, Wendell enlarged the house for the first time so he came into money somehow. TB looked for a probate that showed Cora had some kind of inheritance but we couldn't find any."

I'm thinking of the cash her uncle hid behind the whiskey,

the money her overseer didn't find. Then there was the money from the sale of Rebecca and Jacob. Or maybe her friends in Kentucky gave her money to escape her husband and Wendell found it. Or, all of the above.

"He also worked deals with the Union Army after the War, made a fortune out of some government contracts."

Jacob starts discussing plantation documents, slave schedules, another house expansion and the like, until I touch his forearm. "Did you find out how Cora died?"

Jacob shakes his head. "Sorry, no. But I did find this."

He hands me a newspaper clipping of Wendell's funeral. The article mentions Wendell's former wife and Cora's date of death, which will come in handy, but the piece's primarily about how wonderful this abusive slave holder was. My heart sinks.

Then, I gaze closer into the pixelated photo. There, standing behind what appears to be the mayor, is a familiar face.

Dwayne Garrett.

CHAPTER SIXTEEN

It's not long after Jacob and I relate what he's found and he heads off to dinner with his wife when it's time for our cemetery outing and the other travel writers start appearing in the lobby. Winnie grabs me and begins a long diatribe about problems with her kids back home, the Penningtons are rushing around looking for camera batteries, and a group of Girl Scouts flood the lobby checking in for a district meeting. In all that chaos, I can't grab Carmine and explain what I'd learned and every time I call TB it heads to voice mail.

I look for our time traveler and, for the first time since the trip began, spot Dwayne enjoying company with a man. He's talking to our van driver Jeff, both of them laughing about something like old friends.

Once the Penningtons have their batteries and Kelly struggles in with her crutches, Shelby herds us on to the van and we head to the Natchez Visitor Center. Apparently, our carriage driver was right, this Angels on the Bluff tour is widely popular for there are several school buses there to haul us out to the Natchez City Cemetery. Since we're late arriving at the shuttle spot, Shelby grabs our tickets and tells us to load the first school bus heading out. I'm one of the last to get on board and seats are few and far between, so I grab one close to the front. When I look around, Carmine's several seats behind.

"Keep close," he mouths to me.

We travel through town on a road that parallels the river, meandering through a neighborhood of Victorian homes before reaching the cemetery that began in 1822. Shelby was right, this place is enormous. The tombstones stretch over acres of hills and roads finger through to allow access. It's too dark to make out many of the statues and monuments, but several are lit for the occasion, and luminaries line the roads. The wind's still blowing hard so as the live oak trees sway dramatically, shadows are cast about revealing statue faces, then concealing them again.

"Awesome," I hear Pepper saying in front of me.

Someone else mentions how spooky this is, but I agree with Pepper. I love cemeteries. The crazy weather, on the other hand, can go.

A tour guide named Linda who's dressed in a reflective vest and carrying a lantern introduces herself and tells us to stay together and follow the path. She will lead us to several places throughout the cemetery where costumed actors will tell the stories of those buried there. In the distance, I see other groups in different stages of the tour, wavering lights weaving through the tombstones. In several places, there are small campfires bursting with activity due to the erratic wind and generators lighting small stages where actors are addressing groups.

Before we start, Linda points to the Turning Angel on our left, a lovely statue of a female angel writing something in a book in her lap. At her feet are several graves, young women who died in a horrific gas explosion at the turn of the twentieth century.

"She's called the Turning Angel because people have said when you approach the statue at night and turn your headlights on the statue, she will turn and look at you," Linda explains.

This reminds me of my own angel, so I check for Carmine. Instead, Winnie appears at my side.

"That's ridiculous," she mutters in my ear. "It's a play of light."

"Where's Carmine?"

I must have sounded concerned for she gives me a puzzled expression. I don't wait for an answer, scan the crowd but it's so frickin' dark. If there's a moon, it's covered by the approaching storm clouds which are billowing around us. I spot Pepper who's hanging close to Linda — good —

and the Penningtons are busy setting up photo shots on the side of the road, illuminated by the paper lanterns at their feet. Winnie is by my side and Shelby takes up the rear of the crowd, helping Kelly on to a motorized scooter. Dwayne's nowhere to be seen, but again, it's too dark to tell.

"Where's Carmine?" I ask again and find my heart beating rapidly.

"What's with you?" Winnie asks, unconcerned. "You his mother now?"

And then we're off, following Linda down the road, the wind wiping around us, my jacket billowing as if I'm pregnant, then deflating, then filling up again. I keep searching the crowd for my SCANC friend but a school busload of people is too difficult to dissect.

Finally, we pause as a woman in a hoop skirt tells us the story of Katherine Grafton Miller, the founder of the Natchez Pilgrimage, one of the oldest home tours in the country and an annual event that spurred tourism that continues to this day. I glance around and spot Carmine off to the side talking to someone on his cell phone, which makes me breathe easier, even though he seems to be having trouble with the phone. I try to head in his direction and find out what's happening but I'm unable to once the crowd starts moving again.

Another long walk through the darkened cemetery paths and we meet Florence Irene Ford, a doting mother who comforted her daughter who was terribly frightened of thunderstorms. When the child died of yellow fever at age ten, Florence buried her next to steps with a glass window at the coffin's head. Florence would sit at the base of the steps, watching her daughter's coffin, and continuing to console her during storms. The window has since been removed due to vandalism but we can view the steps if we like, Linda informs us. I'm too busy searching the crowd for I've lost Carmine again.

The next stop features Lilly Ann Eliza Granderson who was born into slavery in Virginia, but moved to Kentucky when she was young and learned to read and write from the master's children. When her master died, she was sold to a Mississippi plantation and ended up in the hot cotton fields, which caused her health to fail.

"Figures," I hear Pepper say somewhere to my left. I scan the crowd but in the intense darkness cannot find her.

The woman portraying Granderson explains how she ended up in the kitchen because of poor health and it's then I realize I know this voice. I'm unable to maneuver closer to the front so I walk to the edge of the crowd and peer over. It's Carol from Briarwood and she proudly tells how Granderson taught numerous slaves in her secret night school.

As she concludes, she adds, "I'm proud to say that I'm a descendant from another slave who did heroic things. Menasha Walker was also a kitchen slave and was taught to read and write by Mrs. Granderson. Menasha helped move others to freedom and taught former slaves in her later years."

I'm so captivated at hearing that Carol is related to Menasha and how her ancestor spent her life that I fail to notice the crowd shifting to the next stage until the glow of Linda's lantern falls away and I'm suddenly enshrined in darkness. I step lively to catch up with the crowd but the path eludes me and I stumble on a tree root, realizing that I've missed the road by a few steps. I make out the luminaries up ahead so I'm not worried that I will be unable to find my way. I take the moment to rub my knee that feels warm and sticky beneath a tear in my jeans.

"Dang," I say to the darkness. At this stage of the trip, I don't have another clean pair of jeans to wear.

I stand and shake myself off, but I'm not two seconds on my feet when my head explodes. Did I hit my head, too, I think as the world spins and I tumble on to the ground. But that's impossible, since I went down knees first and the pain seems to be emanating from the back of my skull.

I feel hands lifting me up by the armpits and dragging me

into the darkness and for a moment I imagine someone saw my fall and has come to my rescue. But then the hands disappear and I fall lying on the ground, my head hitting the dirt and feeling as if it's made of glass bursting into a million pieces. I hear a car door open and those hands return, dragging me into what feels like our van, up three steps and then thrown on the floor between the two aisles. Once again, pain shoots through my skull like lightening.

I hear the door close and someone starts up the van. I'm about to ask what's happening but a groan sounds from above. I raise up on my elbows high enough to keep the throbbing head pain at bay and get a look around. Someone's sitting in the seat to my right, their head pressed against the window like they're sleeping.

"Vi?" I hear Carmine whisper, but the world tilts again as the van starts moving and all turns to darkness.

I'm back in Briarwood and once again I'm Cora. My head no longer hurts but I feel a tightness around my middle, enough that I can hardly breathe.

"What is this?" I ask Menasha, who's helping me dress.

She looks at me like I've lost my mind. "Your corset?"

I feel Viola flow away from the scene and Cora take over and I now know that whatever comes out of her mouth will not be me. I'm a participator in someone's else body.

Menasha pulls a dress over my head and starts lacing me up in the back. Downstairs, I hear men laughing.

"How will I get through this night?" Cora asks.

"Like you always do," Menasha says, straightening out my skirt. "Smile and play along."

"He's going to kill me when he finds out."

"If he hasn't already."

That damn corset feels like a prison made of cloth, but I slip on my shoes and make my way downstairs. I stand at the doorway, hands clasped tightly together. Menasha gives me an encouraging nod so I take a deep breath and enter the parlor. Wendell sits on the settee as if he's king, drinking his whiskey as usual, no doubt pouring our profit down his throat if he hasn't gambled it away in New Orleans. He's surrounded by two men I've never met and won't likely this night for Wendell never introduces his friends to me. Lingering over at the bookshelf in the corner are two men I do recognize and my heart stops beating. Tyson McDaniels, my former horrid overseer, and Reynald, my guide down the Trace, are whispering about something important while another man sits by their side, his hat pulled low about his face and his body covered by outer wear he failed to remove when entering the house.

I feel like Daniel in the lion's den and wonder if my faith in God will save me this night for Wendell turns toward me and I see the hatred in his eyes. He knows I have sold Rebecca and Jacob and sent them away.

"Y'all have met my delightful wife," he says with a sneer. "She's quite the businesswoman."

The two men I don't know are polite enough to tap their hats but my enemies in the corner do not. I curtsy and ask if the men need anything. The two gentlemen thank me and say no but Wendell hasn't taken his glance off me.

"I need the money you received for those two slaves of mine you sold," he says. "Not to mention some pile of money your uncle left behind that I'm now learning about."

A silence falls about the group and the gentlemen look uneasy. I hear a snicker at my back where McDaniels stands.

"It's late," says one of the gentlemen, grabbing his hat. "I really must be going."

Now, I recognize him. He's the clerk of court, the man who registered my sale of Rebecca and Jacob at the courthouse. It's a man's world, after all, a confederation of masculinity desperate to maintain control.

The other man agrees and retrieves his hat and the two scurry out the door faster than our field cat spotting a rat. I suddenly feel surrounded with Wendell in front of me, those two at my back, and that silent man sitting there, so I ask my leave and turn toward the door.

"Leaving so soon?" Wendell asks and that smug tone remains.

I squeeze my hands together and close my eyes. I know what's coming. He'll beat me — or worse. I don't say a word, simply nod my head and leave the parlor, closing the door in my wake. I head down the back porch stairs and walk towards the slave quarters, slip a hand inside my skirt pocket and feel the sharp kitchen knife hidden there.

"Don't forget this, Vi."

I hear the voice as if it's Cora's but I rub my hands across my dress to make sure I'm still in Cora's point of view and not talking to myself. I'm still Cora, but I'm puzzled who said that and why.

The sun's setting behind the slave quarters, all of whom are out working in the fields save for an elderly woman looking after the small children. I recall Wendell insisting that when planting time arrives, these children will be sent to work and my pleas on their behalf fell on deaf ears.

I head down to the pond, and know instinctively that I've been here many times before, my place of solitude. There's a sweet little spot next to a willow where I have attempted to escape the pain of losing my son and the abuse my husband inflicts daily, whether verbal or physical. Now that he's returned from New Orleans and found Rebecca and her son gone — not to mention that there's inheritance I failed to tell him about and he can't locate where I've stashed it — the abuse will surely intensify. And yet, I don't care. Since my darling boy perished, nothing matters anymore.

I sit next to the willow and watch the sunlight play upon the water, wishing the sublime sight would provide some semblance of comfort. The ground feels cold beneath my clothes and there's a chill in the late spring air as the sun descends upon the horizon, but nothing compared to the coldness of my heart.

Footsteps sound and I sense a body behind me, but I don't turn. If Wendell wants me dead, then so be it. I begin to sing my favorite hymn as a shadow falls upon me and I make out an arm rising above my head, its hand carrying a tool of some kind. I close my eyes and welcome death. The blow arrives instantly.

The pain shoots through my head and I'm blinded by the impact, feel myself falling forward and the world turning dark. The last thing I register is falling into the pond while the cold water greets my face.

I gasp as the water jolts me awake.

"Get up SCANC girl."

Dwayne stands before me, an empty Big Gulp in his hand.

I shake my head and wipe my face with my sleeve, shivers running through me for that horrid wind has dropped several degrees with the cold front pushing through. My head still pounds and I'm dizzy as hell. Something sticky lingers in one eye and the ground feels cold and damp beneath me.

"Where are we?"

I hear a murmur to my right and look over to find Carmine, bound and gagged, sitting on the ground. I instinctively try to stand and head to his rescue but both the intense pain in my head and Dwayne's hand on my shoulder knock me back down.

"What's happening?" I ask him. "Are you mad?"

Dwayne starts pacing, those perfect teeth inside a sly smile and those cold blue eyes the only things I make out in the darkness of these woods, wherever we are. Not far away I see our van, so I know the man has kidnapped us and taken us away from the group.

Finally, Dwayne squats down and I can make out his face.

"You know, SCANC girl, I had high hopes for you. I could have showed you the world but you just wouldn't listen."

"Showed me how to steal souls is more like it."

His smile fades. "I'm not what you think I am."

"You're right." I lean in close. "You're no Lucifer."

The slap comes fast and hard; I didn't see it coming. Now, my left cheek burns along with the throbbing in my head and I taste blood on the side of my lip.

"Nice," I say. "Beating up girls."

"And faggots," he adds with a smirk, which makes me hate him so much more.

He stands and looks down at me with contempt. "All I wanted was your dear friend Carmine. He's been dogging my steps for years, him and all those silly friends who think they're the guardians of the earth."

He looks at Carmine. "Where are they now, Carmine? Little help they're offering tonight. Of course, it helps when someone drains your cell phone battery."

I look over at Carmine who's sending me an apologetic glance.

Dwayne turns back to me. "But then I met you at that ridiculous convention and I knew right away this could be a very advantageous trip. Nothing like teaching a witch a few tricks. You pagans are always good for a laugh. Too bad you didn't take me up on it."

Dwayne stands, reaches into his pocket, and throws his cell phone in my lap, not what I was expecting.

"What the hell am I supposed to do with this?"

He squats in front of me again and this time I crawfish backwards until I hit a tree. "Call Ricky. Tell him about Cora."

Is this man insane? "What? Why?"

Dwayne appears as if he's going to slap me again. "You know why. You know how she died and why she hasn't crossed over. Call him and tell him so she'll appear and we can get this over with."

I remember the article Jacob showed me, the one with a man who looked like Dwayne in the background. Then there's the secretive fellow in the parlor who owned the same height as Dwayne.

"You killed her, didn't you?"

Dwayne places a hand upon his chest and acts like he's insulted, although that sly smile returns. "*Moi?* How could I have possibly killed a woman almost two hundred years ago?"

I glance at Carmine and see his shoulders fall. Nabbing souls helps one become immortal, I surmise, something else my dear friend failed to mention.

"You steal their light when they cross over," I tell Dwayne. "You steal their souls and somehow that gives you strength, extends your life."

"You could have had what I have, stupid girl. You could have evolved and be talking to your daughter right now instead of sitting in the Devil's Punchbowl watching your friend die."

I look at Carmine who's now lowering his head in defeat. I

get the feeling he knew death was coming but I sure didn't. And the last thing he wanted was for me to watch it happen.

"You're insane," I repeat to Dwayne.

"Better than being ignorant, you stupid witch." He leans in close. "You don't even know what powers you possess. You're almost as bad as that dumbass husband of yours who can only help crippled girls out of cars."

This really pisses me off. No one insults my husband. I attempt to rise and say, "Don't you dare talk about..." but Dwayne pushes me back on my rear, grabs the top of my shirt and tugs so tight it cuts off my air.

"I'm losing patience, SCANC girl. Call Ricky. End this. Or I kill Carmine right now."

Even though I can't breathe, I shake my head. He's going to kill us anyway, so stalling would at least buy us time in case someone's out looking for us. Please, God, let there be someone out looking for us. Sure enough, the other cheek burns with impact. This time, his slap really cuts up my lip so I take the opportunity to spit the blood right in his face. Dwayne says nothing, quietly removes a handkerchief, and wipes the blood away.

"Fine," he says, standing. "We'll do this another way."

He grabs a rope he had laying on the ground by Carmine's feet and walks behind him, throws the rope over Carmine's head and pulls tight. The rope immediately cuts off Carmine's air and his eyes enlarge. I attempt to stand, to reach him and fight Dwayne off, but the blow to the head has given me vertigo and I feel like Jimmy Stewart in that Hitchcock film where the world tilts and spins like a vortex.

"Call Ricky," Dwayne demands.

Carmine shakes his head and I start to cry watching my friend in such pain.

Dwayne pulls the rope tighter.

"Call him."

Still crying, I pat the ground for the phone and plop down on my rear when I locate it.

"I don't know the number."

Dwayne jerks the rope one more time and Carmine utters this horrific, painful sound. "Stupid girl, I'll give it to you."

"Okay, okay," I shout like a babbling baby. "Leave him alone."

Dwayne releases Carmine and he falls forward, coughing. Dwayne shouts out the numbers and I dial them by knowledge and not by sight; I can't make out the cellphone's keyboard in the darkness. The wind whips around the trees, and my wet hair and the temperature change causes my teeth to chatter.

Ricky answers on the first ring.

"Ricky," I say, trying hard not to sound weird with my teeth rattling and my lips bleeding and swollen. "I have something to tell you about Cora."

"Viola?"

"Yes, it's me. I have something I need to tell you…."

"Where are you? Shelby called me and said you and Carmine have disappeared from the cemetery tour and the van's missing. They're worried about you."

I take a deep breath, try to clear my mind. "The cemetery tour was delightful, thanks."

He hesitates. "Are you okay?"

"Not really, no."

I hear Dwayne clearing his throat and look over. He still has the rope in his hands and it's back to being taut against Carmine's neck.

"I have to tell you about Cora," I repeat. "I found out something today that indicates she was murdered and didn't die inside an institution."

Again, Ricky hesitates. He's not sure what's going on and I don't know how to convey our danger. "It's okay Vi. Jacob showed me the documents earlier. I now know that she was the one who helped those slaves to freedom."

I close my eyes. At least one good thing happened today.

"But what's going on? Something happened to you and Carmine?"

"Yes."

"What is it?"

I look at Dwayne still holding Carmine captive. I'm helpless on how to make this right. If I say more, Cora will appear and cross over and I will cause her soul to disappear as well. If I explain where we are, Dwayne will undoubtedly kill Carmine, if not us both, and take off in the van.

Tears pool in my eyes but I can still see Dwayne gripping that rope and Carmine shaking his head.

"Forgive me, Cora," I whisper, then say to Ricky, "Cora was hit on the head by someone Wendell sent to murder her. She died in the pond."

Instantly, Cora appears, a wisp of a vision surrounded by soft, white light. Dwayne relaxes his grip on Carmine and he once again leans forward coughing. Ricky's calling my name in the phone, sounded more and more urgent, but my focus is on Dwayne, who's standing and about to join Cora to steal her soul.

"Devil's Punchbowl," I whisper to Ricky and hang up.

Cora looks at me and it's as if my soul floats there with hers. I've been a part of her life — literally — even if it's only been in visions. As she gazes at me with a sweet smile, knowing that the truth has emerged and she will go to a better place, something else passes between us. I slip my hands inside my jacket pocket and know I'm right.

Dwayne walks between me and Carmine heading to Cora's side but before he can reach her, I pull out the kitchen knife and stab him soundly in the foot. My nemesis howls and falls to the ground while I crawl to Carmine's side. In the meantime, Cora's light fades and she disappears.

"Bitch," Dwayne yells at me.

I reach in the other pocket and pull out my St. John the Conqueror root and hold it before both of us for protection. Dwayne pulls the knife out of his foot and turns, his gaze two blue flames staring at us.

"That won't save you."

I hold the root higher and proclaim, "St. John protect us. Let your unbeatable spirit surround us with your white light of protection and fight off the evil visiting us this night."

Dwayne steps back, unstable on his feet. I don't know if it's the wound I inflicted on his foot or St. John coming to our aid but it gives me time to think. I close my eyes trying to remember something Aunt Mimi might have taught me, something that might help deliver us from this evil man. Instead, I hear Dwayne laughing. At first, it's a chuckle, then it turns into a roaring guffaw.

"Stupid witch, stupid descendant of Gabriel." He walks closer and knocks the root from my hand. "Did you really think a bunch of hoodoo is a match for me?"

He inches closer, dragging that bum foot behind him until he's inches from our face. I reach behind Carmine and take one of his bound hands. He squeezes back.

"No one will know how you died, SCANC girl," he says so close to my face I can feel the warmth of his breath on my aching cheek. "Not your stupid husband, that's for sure. So, your ghost hanging around this remote place hoping for a SCANC to come along is a waste of time. Just cross over after I kill you and we'll call it even, okay?"

He gives us both that sickening sly smile and pulls that kitchen knife up to my chin.

"How about you go first, SCANC girl. I'll make the throat cut nice and clean."

I close my eyes for the inevitable, brace myself for the impact, say a prayer that God or whoever is out there will save me and my soul.

Instead, two sounds jolt me awake. Stinky lets out a howl, claws extended and heading straight for Dwayne's face. My husband stands above us, his entire body glowing with a blue light so intense it burns my eyes, his hammer held high above him like Archangel Michael fighting the dragon, yelling, "Get your hands off my wife!"

Dwayne screams in pain as my blessed cat claws the crap out of his face. He stumbles backwards on to the ground while TB stands over him with one foot on his chest, that hammer still threatening, and the force of that light blinding

Dwayne into submission. I see our nemesis hold up his hands in surrender and I can't help wishing TB would kill the son-of-a-bitch. But he doesn't, for sirens and cars are pulling up behind us, Shelby's voice shouting out our names. TB instantly returns to my carpenter husband, the hammer lowering to his side, and that intense light dimming like a lightbulb switch. Dwayne's hands are about his face, blood pouring through his fingers, and I see Stinky off to the side, cleaning himself as if nothing unusual just occurred.

I couldn't make this up if I tried.

The others rush over, Winnie untying Carmine and the police accessing the scene. Dwayne points to me and TB and starts muttering how we attacked him. No one believes him, of course, so he turns to the three women he made love him during our trek down the Natchez Trace.

"Pepper, Kelly, you know she's dangerous. She left that horrid animal at your camp and tried to kill you, Kelly."

I look at the women in question and wonder if, as happens so many times in this case, they will stand by their man. Instead, Pepper places her hands on her hips and Kelly looks fit to kill. But it's our non-committal PR person who has the final say.

"This man has been trying to hurt us since we left Florence, Alabama," Shelby says. "Officers, you need to arrest this man for kidnapping, stealing my vehicle, attempted homicide, and animal mutilation."

The police grab Dwayne and pull him to his feet and he screams bloody murder. They haul him to their cars and someone calls an ambulance. When Carmine's hands are untied, he takes me into his arms and hugs me tight.

"I'm sorry," he says.

I look over his shoulder and see my heroic husband standing there looking as if he's just another guy while one of the cops asks him questions. I expect him to rush to my side as well but there's something in his gaze that unnerves me, something holding him back.

When Carmine releases me my friends have a million

questions. Suddenly all that adrenaline and blood retreats and the vertigo comes back full force. I fall ungracefully into the mud, face first, and black out.

CHAPTER SEVENTEEN

I wake in a hospital bed, my head bandaged and an IV needle in my arm. My eyes aren't sticky anymore and the pain has subsided. In fact, I feel pretty good.

TB notices and rushes over. "How are you feeling?"

I nod and suddenly realize the pain's still there.

"You have a concussion," he tells me. "The doctor said it was mild and you should be better fairly quickly but it's best to relax. He thinks you can go home this afternoon if all goes well."

I sit up and realize it's not as bad as I imagined. There's a bit of dizziness and pain but nothing like the night before.

The night before.

I close my eyes remembering the horror of Dwayne kidnapping us, Cora's crossover, and how I tried to fight him off until TB arrived.

"Is Carmine okay?"

TB takes my hand. "Carmine's fine. He has a slight concussion like you do. His partner's here and will drive him back to Dallas."

"Stinky?"

TB grimaces and I dread hearing that my cat's lost in the woods.

"He's fine. He's in my pickup although I haven't been out there lately and I'm worried he's cold and hungry."

I doubt that Tabby will let anything harm him, even weather, but I feel TB's pain. "You should go and check on him."

TB looks at our entwined hands. "I wanted to be here when you woke up."

I wish I could say there was love and affection in that statement, although I'm sure he didn't mean otherwise, but an uneasiness begins in my belly. Something's not right here.

"What is it?" I ask, although I'm dreading to hear the answer.

TB swallows. "Why were you there, Vi?"

He's worried I went with Dwayne willingly? Seriously?

"Sweetheart, I was at the cemetery tour. He grabbed Carmine, then he grabbed me, and drove us out to that god-forsaken place. He wanted me to cross over Cora so he could steal her soul. Then kill us and do the same. He evolves by tapping into the light, has lived since Cora's time as far as I know."

TB doesn't look up through this whole explanation, but I guess he knows about Dwayne's life extensions since he saw the man in the newspaper article.

"But you knew something was going down tonight."

True. I look toward the windows. The wind has died down but no doubt it's cold outside since the front came through. The sun manages to filter through the blinds and feels warm on my bruised cheeks and I wonder how bad I look. I finally exhale the breath I'm holding.

"Carmine didn't want you to know about Dwayne, thought you'd be safer if you weren't involved."

TB laughs and shakes his head but there's pain in his gaze. "Right, he makes sure I come on this trip to protect you but I'm not supposed to know anything, not supposed to help."

This surprises me. "You knew about him arranging for you to be on the trip?"

TB stands, stuffs his hands into his jeans pockets, and heads to the window, staring outside. "Y'all think I'm an idiot, don't you?"

I use my elbows to rise to a better sitting position but the IV grows taut. "What? No."

"That I wouldn't know a descendant when I see one."

This shocks me, too, for Carmine insisted TB didn't know who he was. But then, after last night and TB's angelic rescue, not to mention that enormous bright light he possesses, I'm thinking my husband knows a lot more than he's letting on.

He turns and looks at me as if he reads my mind.

"Of course, I know. Both my parents are descendants, you think they wouldn't have told me what I was growing up?"

I shake my head since this is all new ground to me. "Carmine said...."

"Carmine's wrong." His voice rises and he appears like he did last night, a warrior with a hammer. Then TB looks away, that simple, sweet man returning. With a sad smile, he adds, "You didn't think I read Dwayne's aura and knew who he was?"

"Why didn't you tell...?"

"Tell *you*?"

I feel bad because my husband's right, he should have known what we were up against, knew the complete history between Carmine and Dwayne. He must feel as helpless as I did when Carmine routinely refused to tell me anything. And if he's as powerful as I witnessed him to be, we could have avoided the whole scene with his assistance.

"I'm sorry," I whisper. And I truly am.

TB leans against the table, his hands snug in his jeans pockets. "The trouble is, Vi, you don't trust me."

I try to rise again, but the IV and the pain in my head causes me to fall back against the pillows. "Of course, I do."

"Always trying to contact Lillye when I've told you...."

He looks away and I see his eyes glaze over.

"I know, TB. It's just that...."

"I failed her, you know."

This stops me cold. "Who?"

He frowns and doesn't answer and I realize he's talking about our child. "I should have protected her. I have it in my power and I couldn't protect her. I couldn't save her."

Tears pour down his cheeks and I wish with all my heart and soul I could get out of this bed and touch him.

"There was nothing you could do, TB. No one can save a person from leukemia. Not even an angel."

He rubs the back of his neck and looks away and I know that nothing I say will ease this guilt he carries with him.

"I'm not an angel."

But he is. On so many levels. I want to tell him so but watching him suffer and thinking of my own guilt forces a lump in my throat and my own tears fall.

"I'm no witch," I manage, because thinking back I should have known of something that could have eased her pain, could have stopped Dwayne last night.

To my surprise, TB smiles. "Yes, you are. It's one of the things I love about you."

What does that mean, I wonder? But I don't have time to ask.

"I can't do this anymore," he says softly.

I look up and find TB taking my hand once again and it feels wonderful touching him but that uneasiness has returned. "What do you mean?"

"I can't watch you chase after ways of reaching Lillye. I can't go through this anymore."

I'm ready to admit my mistake and tell him he's right, vow to speak to Lillye in my heart and know she's listening, but I remember the kitchen knife. I pull my hand free and this time manage to sit up.

"TB, I have evolved."

He shakes his head, exasperated. "Oh God, Vi, not this again."

"Something happened this time around. I wasn't just watching like I used to. I actually participated in the visions."

TB stands again and walks back to the window.

"Cora showed me a knife in her skirt when I was in her point of view. Did you hear me, I was in *her point of view*. As in walking in her clothes, thinking her thoughts. I did the same thing with Jacob."

He says nothing, keeps staring out the window.

"I had Cora's knife in my possession when Dwayne kidnapped us. That's why he was limping. I stabbed him in the foot before you arrived. With Cora's knife."

TB's still not looking at me but I see him shaking his head.

"Did you hear me? Cora gave me a knife from the Other

World."

This time, TB turns. "I'm taking some time off. I'm going to Florida to see my folks."

"Did you hear what I said?

He grabs his coat that's lying over a chair.

"Shelby will bring you back to New Orleans with the rest of the group. They all insisted on staying here until you and Carmine are better."

A panic begins in my chest. "You're leaving me?"

He looks at me then, that sadness still lingering in his gaze. I feel like he doesn't want to do this but he must. "I have to, Vi. I can't stand the secrets...."

"Secrets?" Now, my defenses are at attention. "How about you being an angel and going back to LSU?"

This takes him back. "I'm not an angel."

"Gosh, I'm so sick of people telling me that. And what was that angelic light saving my butt?"

"Nephilim lumen de lumine."

"What?"

He changes the subject. "I didn't tell you about finishing my degree because you'd probably think it was stupid."

I shake my head. Who is this man? "I think it's awesome."

He shrugs. "It's just a general studies degree. Nothing meaningful."

Now, I'm getting mad. "What are you talking about? It's everything. I'm so proud of you."

He looks down at his feet and for the life of me I don't understand why he feels this way. Who's been feeding him this nonsense? It couldn't have been me. Could it?

"TB, I'm sorry if I ever made you feel this way. I never meant to...."

He sighs and smiles and I sense a maturity that was never there before. "I'll always be there for you, Vi, but I need to do this. And I need to do this alone. You of all people should understand that."

But I don't. "Do what?"

"I need to be away from you."

The tears come fast and furious because I don't want this man walking out the door and out of my life. Dwayne was right. I am a stupid witch.

"I love you," I whisper, hoping that it's enough.

But it's too late. TB smiles sadly, a lone tear falling on his own cheek, and walks out of the room. I hear him say to someone in the hall, "She's all yours," and it's not two seconds before Winnie waltzes in and catches me bawling like a baby.

"Are you in that much pain?" she asks.

If she only knew.

By late afternoon, after being grilled for two hours by the police, I'm dressed and bandaged and Shelby's guiding us all to another van, this one smaller, brightly painted, and one she drives herself. I get the impression she hopes it cheers us up but we all remain silent the three hours to New Orleans. Winnie keeps a sharp eye on me but she lets me be quiet, thinking my head pain is too unbearable to speak. If only she knew my broken heart hurts so much more.

Carmine had already been picked up by his partner, Dale, by the time we headed back. I spent another hour crying over that goodbye. Carmine didn't ask about TB, and refused to comment on his own head injury.

"It's nothing," Carmine said, waving off my concerns. "But we need to talk. After we get home."

I wanted to talk then, but now I know that some things must wait. There's so much to digest it makes my head pound all over again. Why had TB never revealed who he was to me? Why had I not known who I was? All those herbal lessons from Aunt Mimi and she couldn't tell me once that I was a witch, descended from a long line of healers? My St. John root could have worked, I know it, but I failed to use it properly. How do I learn these things now?

And then, there's Dwayne. Police admitted him to the hospital for his foot and head wounds and kept an armed guard at his door. By morning, he had disappeared. Vanished. Poof. So, had the guard. What does that mean for Carmine and me? Will we be looking over our shoulders for the rest of our lives?

More importantly, how will I get my personal nephilim back? I feel like Scarlet O'Hara in *Gone With the Wind*. I must get him back but I can't think about it today.

Shelby pulls up to TB's house in New Orleans, the place where I left my car. It's really our house, but where once I didn't wish to remain in this home, now he doesn't want me here. I give my fellow travel writers hugs and assure Shelby that I'm fine, that I won't be suing anyone. She still gives me her lawyer's card and insists that I contact her. Winnie is last in the hugs, holds me tight, and tells me she will call every night to ensure that I'm okay. I tell her I'm fine but I'm anything but.

After more farewells, the van pulls away and heads to the airport. I watch it drive the few blocks and turn, disappearing into the city traffic. I stand in the middle of the street with my polka dot suitcase feeling lost until a driver pulls up behind and honks. I dig my keys from my purse and head to my Toyota and dump everything inside, then head for the house, using my old house key to retrieve Stinky. He's sitting by the front door waiting for me, but when I call his name he doesn't move. I call again and reach for him, but Stinky backs up, crawls underneath the coffee table and makes himself comfortable.

I get the message and that hurts almost as much as everything else that's happened in the last twenty-four hours. And yet, it's as if Lillye's here, petting my cat, and pointing the way. They're smiling at me, regardless of my broken heart, because they have given me the knowledge of where to head next.

I think of my husband and his insistence that Lillye is always with us. And there's my crazy cat who's probably not a cat at all, considering all the supernatural things I've learned in the last week. I thank them both and leave the house where TB, Lillye, and I spent many years, and get into my Toyota. Instead of heading west to Lafayette and my beloved potting shed, I turn east on Interstate 10. I'm heading to Alabama, the home of Aunt Mimi and Grandmother Willow, once the most famous soothsayer in the region. Time for some answers.

I'll find me a hill somewhere overlooking the sunset and, like Scarlet, will somehow find a way to get him back.

AUTHOR'S NOTES

When I'm not penning stories about ghost hunting travel writers from Louisiana, I'm working as a travel writer from Louisiana. Over the past few years I've had the pleasure of visiting Florence and Muscle Shoals, Alabama, as well as traveling down the beautiful, historic Natchez Trace, pausing at Tupelo, Mississippi, where I was entertained by a host of singing Elvi, or Elvis tribute artists.

The legend of Florence's singing river is true, as is the Swampers Bar and the 360 Grille within the Marriott Shoals Hotel, the chocolate gravy poured over biscuits at the River Road Café, and the dozens and dozens of famous musicians who have walked through the doors of FAME studios and 3614 Jackson Highway. I met Swampers Jimmy Johnson and David Hood with a host of journalists, Johnson pulling out a giant list of hits that had been recorded at their studio. It'll blow you away at the talent that has passed through that town.

Meeting Tom Hendrix, who sadly passed away in 2017, remains a highlight of my life, and I was fortunate enough to visit Tom's Wall twice, each time a remarkable spiritual journey. Like Viola, I sat in Tom's prayer circle and felt two hands on my shoulders, instinctively knowing they were my grandmothers'. On one occasion, Hendrix gifted me with an ancient arrowhead, which I cherish and keep on my writing desk.

You can view photos from my visits to the studios and Tom's Wall on my Viola Valentine Pinterest board and on my website blog posts.

The idea of ghosts haunting photos is also based on personal experiences, starting with the time I found young Gladys and Emily Whittington dressed as boys in the early twentieth century and standing on the steps of their cabin in Lithia Springs, Georgia. I had to know who these charming young girls were and that research started me collecting old photographs from antique and thrift stores, digging through Ancestry.com and other genealogy websites — much like TB does in the story — and posting them online so that family members may find them. I've been told that objects and photographs may have spirits attached but so far, no ghosts have followed me home. At least that I know of.

The gris-gris bags Viola and Pepper carry with them derive from New Orleans and Southern African American traditions. These bags made up of herbs, stones, and other talismans have always fascinated me, and fellow author Jude Bradley and I studied the tradition of protective bags over many nationalities and wrote a book titled *Magic's in the Bag: Creating Spellbinding Gris Gris Bags and Sachets.* The paperback is no longer in print but ebooks are still available through online stores.

All the places I mentioned located on the Natchez Trace exist, but I did fabricate why there are grass circles at Witch Dance. Briarwood — or Richfield — does *not* exist but I used a recent visit to the elegant Brandon Hall Plantation for inspiration. The gorgeous and massive old home only a few miles from Natchez is a must visit if you're fortunate enough to travel the Trace or visit south Mississippi.

I've been to the charming city of Natchez numerous times and, on each visit, discover something new. My last trip happened over early November and imagine my surprise to discover the Angels on the Bluff cemetery tour while writing this book! Life can be so incredible synchronistic sometimes. The cemetery event, and the nearby Devil's Punchbowl, screamed to be included in the story.

And yes, there are ghosts in King's Tavern.

If you'd like to learn more on Florence/Muscle Shoals, the Natchez Trace, and Natchez, you can read about my travel experiences at www.CherieClaire.net or view photos and stories I've written on my Viola Valentine Pinterest board.

ACKNOWLEDGEMENTS

Many thanks to those who helped bring this book to light, either knowingly or unknowingly. The incredibly talented artist, Joshua Coen, continues to create dreamy, mysterious covers for me, and does so with help from his equally creative finance Abraham Rodriguez. My biggest fans — Roxanne Moskal, LilyB Moskal and Danon Dastugue, as well as my husband Bruce Coen and son Taylor Coen — help clean up my manuscript and give me invaluable feedback.

Those who have assisted me in my travels include Georgia Carter Turner and Verna Gates in Alabama, Jennie Bradford Curlee in Tupelo, and Daylyn Weppner and Carlyn Topkin for Natchez. Thank you for showing me your delightful corners of the world.

BOOKS BY CHERIE CLAIRE

Viola Valentine Mystery Series
A Ghost of a Chance
Ghost Town
Trace of a Ghost

The Cajun Embassy
Ticket to Paradise
Damn Yankees
Gone Pecan

The Cajun Series
Emilie
Rose
Gabrielle
Delphine
A Cajun Dream
The Letter

Carnival Confessions: A Mardi Gras Novella

ABOUT THE AUTHOR

Cherie Claire is a native of New Orleans who, like so many other Gulf Coast residents, was heartbroken after Hurricane Katrina. She works as a travel and food writer and extensively covers the Deep South, including its colorful ghost stories. To learn more about her novels and her non-fiction books, upcoming events and to sign up for her newsletter, visit her web site www.CherieClaire.net. Write to Cherie at CajunRomances@Yahoo.com.